"THIS WAS GILLIAM NESS'S FIRST STEP INTO THE LITERARY WORLD, AND IT WAS A DOOZY."

"THE ACTION WAS NON-STOP, THE CHARACTERS WERE WELL DEVELOPED, AND THE PLOT LINE WAS FASCINATING TO SAY THE LEAST. I WOULD CERTAINLY READ THE AUTHOR'S NEXT WORK WITHOUT HESITATION."

"THIS TRILOGY KEEPS YOU ON THE EDGE OF YOUR SEAT RIGHT FROM THE START AND WHEN YOU THINK IT CAN'T GET MORE EXCITING IT JUST KEEPS ON GIVING."

"MR. NESS TAKES US ON QUITE THE ADVENTURE, CREATING A PAGE TURNER THAT IS DIFFICULT TO PUT DOWN!"

"THIS BOOK CAUGHT ME FROM THE 1ST PAGE AND DIDN'T LET GO!!"

GILLIAM NESS IS AWESOME! HIS WAY OF DESCRIBING WHAT HAPPENS, KEEPING THE STORY MOVING, AND JUST PLAIN STORYTELLING IS AMAZING, ESPECIALLY FOR HIS FIRST BOOK."

"DON'T MAKE PLANS FOR THE WEEKEND."

"A SPIRITUAL SCI-FI TECHNOTHRILLER THAT LEAVES YOU WHITE KNUCKLED AND HOLDING YOUR BREATH!"

"DISTURBING, DARK AND GUT WRENCHING AT TIMES. STRAP IN AND ENJOY THE RIDE!"

"I ENJOYED THIS BOOK FROM THE FIRST PAGE."

"THIS SERIES IS DEFINITELY ONE THAT I WILL BE READING MORE THAN ONCE."

"FAST PACED, LOTS OF ACTION, AND IDEAS THAT MAKE YOU KEEP THINKING ABOUT THE BOOK EVEN AFTER YOU'VE PUT IT DOWN FOR THE NIGHT."

THE LAST ARTIFACT

A TRILOGY BY GILLIAM NESS

Published by POLYMATH PUBLISHING
Toronto, Canada.

POLYMATH PUBLISHING and the portrayal of the letter "P"
within the box are trademarks of Polymath Publishing.

ISBN 978-0-9917265-8-5

January 2016

BOOK ONE
THE DARK RIFT

...And then the final days arrived,
When all the wild imaginings of men came to pass.
When the myths, theories, and legends were made manifest,
And the prophecies and suspicions were fulfilled.

In those final days they trembled and cried:
"How came we to conceive of such monstrous inventions?"
For the gods and demons they had imagined were all realized.
And a great shadow spread across the world.

-The Great Fall of the Angels
(From the Compostela Manuscripts, circa 865CE)

PROLOGUE
The Cantabrian Mountains – 2243 B.C.

A heavy mantle of fog clung to the surface of the small mountain lake, its dark waters emitting a profound stillness. Amid the gurgle of a slow-moving paddle a primitive dugout made its way out into the gloom, its two occupants dwarfed by the looming peaks that encased it on all sides. There was not a soul in sight.

The boy with the paddle completed another stroke, the boat sliding effortlessly forward. Their destination lay just ahead; a tiny island enshrouded in mist.

"It's certainly strange here," said the girl in the boat, chewing her lip, "but it doesn't seem as dangerous as they say."

There was something otherworldly about the place. It was sending waves of excitement through her. Like the boy, she too had turned twelve that day, and to celebrate their birthdays they had decided to investigate the mysterious island, knowing full well that they were forbidden to do so. She studied its dense tangle of trees.

"I want to go ashore."

The boy frowned.

"That wasn't the plan," he said. "We only came to look."

"We don't have to go into the shrine. We can just find it and see what it looks like."

The boy shot a suspicious glance at the island and then made up his mind.

"All right," he said, passing a hand through his shaggy hair. "Let's go."

They circled the island until they found a place to land. Above them a veiled sun was already beginning to dip behind the mountains and the girl felt a sudden twinge of fear. The shadowy trees were dense and ominous.

"It's getting dark too fast," she said. "Maybe we should go back."

"We're here already," said the boy. "Let's have a quick look."

He jumped from the dugout and dragged it up onto the rocks, holding out his hand for the girl to take.

"Very well," she said. "But only for a moment."

The island was unkempt, and the vegetation quite dense. Lush ferns covered most of the ground, and many of the rocks were rounded over with moss. From where they stood, a path could be seen climbing into the foliage. It picked its way through the rocky terrain in a series of natural steps and landings and the two were soon finding it quite easy to navigate their way up.

"This was a mistake," said the girl, following behind.

"Why?"

She peered into the woods. She thought she had seen a shadow moving through the trees.

"What if the Druid Fathers are right?"

"The Druid Fathers are old fools," said the boy. "Nobody believes their stories anymore."

It was not long before they arrived at a small, circular clearing, not twenty feet in diameter. There was a large, flattened boulder directly at its centre, and as they made their way forward, they could see the ancient image of a maze carved into its surface. There was a crude figure of a man standing at its entrance. It was unsettling, but more disturbing still was what lay at the outer extremities of the clearing: A grouping of fourteen standing stones, each as tall as a man, and forming a perfect circle around them.

"What is this place?" asked the girl.

The boy shook his head and frowned.

"I don't know…"

The sound of a large bird taking flight startled them, and as the girl's eyes followed it up through the tangled boughs, she saw how dim the sky had become. There was a darkness growing in the woods.

"I'm scared," she said, clutching the boy. "Let's go. I don't like the way this island makes me feel."

"Just a little while longer," he said, taking her hand. "Come on. We've got to be close to the shrine by now."

She followed him reluctantly, deeper and deeper into the thick. It seemed to her that the island was swallowing them alive. After a five-minute hike the boy stopped suddenly, his heart pounding with excitement as he pulled her into another clearing.

"This must be the place," he said, refusing to acknowledge the fear he felt.

"Wait," he muttered, his eyes straining. "What is this?"

He could see the standing stones looming in a circle around them again. They had somehow returned to the same place, and something felt terribly wrong. It was too dark. At some point the overcast sky had transformed into a starless void, and only the muted light of a crescent moon leaked through the twisted branches above.

"We've been walking in circles…" he stammered.

A shrill pitch of the purest fear was ringing through his body now. He could not understand. The air had become frigidly cold.

"The Druid Fathers were right…" he whispered, shaking his head in horror. "By the gods, what have we done?"

A deep and inky void had appeared where the central monolith had been, and just then, something even more unsettling came into view.

Shadowy figures were materializing behind the standing stones. They were stumbling forward, their arms hanging limply at their sides, and their gazes vacant and cold. The boy's eyes opened wide. These people were dead. Their flesh was crawling with worms, yet somehow, they still lived.

"No!" he grunted, unable to move. "This is impossible..."

It was only then that it came. An invisible force of unimaginable potency. It moved over them with the momentum of an ocean tide, forcing them to the ground and driving the sight from their eyes.

CHAPTER 1

Istanbul, Turkey.

Professor Agardi Metrovich staggered out of the examination room and into the hall of the private Istanbul hospital. He was a large, bearded man in his late seventies, dressed in an old tweed sports jacket with frayed cuffs. The door closed behind him as he exited, shutting out the chanting priests as they continued with their archaic ritual.

Through the walls, the weary professor could still hear the spitting curses coming from his patient, a sensation of pure evil crawling over his skin. As he had expected, he was instantly approached by his patient's father. Isaac Rodchenko was an inpatient at the institution as well, and stricken with paranoid schizophrenia. Over the course of the evening, the unearthly cries of his son had driven the poor man into a state of despair.

"Professor Metrovich!" he whispered, his eyes straining with worry. "You must tell me what is happening to my son!"

Metrovich could only stare back at him, his own face pale and drawn with fear. After decades of medically overseeing exorcisms, the seasoned professor had yet to overcome the horror the rituals consistently provoked in him. He struggled with his emotions, finding comfort in the words of an ancient text he had long ago unearthed in his research.

Fear is an illusion, a ghost without substance. It is easily dispelled.

In many cases, suspected victims were merely suffering from severe psychotic dementia, but on rare occasions such as this, events could not be explained so readily. Demonic possession was an anomaly that defied all rational thought. It was something not of this earth.

"Please, sit down, Mr. Rodchenko," the professor managed to say, and following his own advice, he collapsed heavily into one of the waiting armchairs. "You must give me a moment to regain my strength."

Isaac Rodchenko sat down at once. He had a healthy complexion for his sixty odd years, along with thick salt and pepper hair and black eyebrows. He wore an elegant charcoal grey suit and had an air of humble confidence about him, despite his distress. For a long moment Isaac waited obediently but could contain himself no longer.

"My son has spent thirty-three years in a vegetative state," he said, rubbing his hands together nervously. "How is it possible that he should have awakened from it now, and in this condition? I know you are keeping something from me, Professor. Have pity on a suffering father. Tell me, please!"

Metrovich held Isaac's gaze for a moment, but then let his eyes fall.

How could I possibly tell this man what I suspect to be true?

"Sir!" insisted Isaac. "You must tell me at once!"

The old professor looked up, his tired eyes scanning the distressed face before him. He opened his mouth to speak but an unearthly scream split the silence. It was followed immediately by a call from one of the priests inside.

"Professor! Come quickly!"

In one clumsy motion Metrovich rose from his chair and passed into the examination room, a stench of rot and suffering engulfing him as he entered. There in the half light, he could see two priests hunched over the possessed patient, his obese body contorting in a series of slow and twisting seizures.

Having already been severely deformed since birth, the effects of the possession had transformed the victim into something utterly horrific. Metrovich looked to the priests. They stood there in quiet resignation, praying silently over the poor beast.

"We are losing him, Professor," whispered the ancient Father Franco.

The professor's eyes found the electrocardiogram and saw that the old priest was not mistaken. The patient had entered into cardiac arrest. In his weakened state, there would be no way of saving him.

His joints creaked woodenly as he lurched and twisted, his enormous body becoming still before moving into a violent death rattle. When it was over, the heart monitor gave off a flat, uninterrupted tone, and crossing himself, Father Franco muted the alarm.

With the death of the patient, a deep silence had fallen over the room, a residual feeling of the supernatural hanging in the air like a pall. In all his years of overseeing exorcisms, Metrovich had never witnessed a ghastlier case than this, and judging by the expressions on the two priests, he could see that they had not done so either.

Metrovich moved towards the corpse. He had been plagued with a gut feeling since early that evening. It warned of something so unlikely that it seemed ludicrous that he should even be considering it, but it could no longer be ignored.

He reached down to take hold of the urine-soaked gown that covered the patient's lower torso but froze instantly in the act. He thought he had felt a slight tremor running through the corpse, and in that instant a fresh wave of fear rippled through him again. He looked more closely. The cadaver was visibly trembling. His eyes darted to the ECG. It was still showing a flatline.

This is impossible. The body is dead...

Metrovich looked back in time to see the ghastly corpse jerk to life.

"Ahreimanius!" it hissed menacingly, its upper body lurching violently towards him.

All watched in horror as the restraining straps gave way, the thrashing corpse coming dangerously close to the professor before collapsing back onto the bed. A final quake ran through the body.

Struggling to keep himself composed, Metrovich reached forward to resume his task, drawing slowly aside the gown that covered the lower half of its torso. What he saw filled him with horror and disgust. Father Franco gagged and coughed.

Plainly visible before them, grotesque and utterly malformed, were a pair of lacerated genitals, disproportionately large and belonging to both the male and female sexes. It was at that moment that a shaft of light split the darkness and Isaac's swaying form appeared in the doorway. He stared blankly at the scene before him. The professor's eyes remained glued to the patient.

"You did not tell us that your son was a hermaphrodite, Mr. Rodchenko..."

Isaac seemed to wince at the statement.

"Is he dead?"

Professor Metrovich turned to face the grieving father but said nothing, his expression containing a mixture of compassion and confusion. With this latest development, twenty years of skepticism had been suddenly stripped from his mind. The evidence was now irrefutable, the coincidences far too numerous to discount.

Through the death of this unfortunate victim, an ancient and obscure prophecy had somehow been made manifest. The impossible had somehow transpired.

"I know this is difficult for you, Mr. Rodchenko," said Metrovich slowly. "Can you remember where your son was conceived?"

The professor's words struck Isaac like a dull blow. He was too drugged to sense any pain, but the question probed one of the primary causes of his mental illness. The mother of his child had died giving birth to their misshapen son, and he had never recovered from the loss of her. Over the years he had progressively lost his mind. He slumped to his knees, rocking himself to and fro.

"My wife and I were on a religious pilgrimage in the mountains of Northern Spain," he muttered, his eyes squinting ever so slightly as he remembered. "We were on a small lake. We had found a little island…"

Metrovich tore his gaze from Isaac and turned to face Father Franco. The old priest looked back at him, his eyes alight with foreboding.

"God help us all," he said solemnly.

Outside a rumbling chorus of thunder sounded. The storm that had long been approaching had finally arrived.

CHAPTER 2

Florence, Italy.

The thirty-two-year-old Dr. Natasha Rossi sat amid the clutter of her small restoration shop. Before her on a battered workbench lay the ninth century tabernacle she was working on. It was almost finished, and behind it a large monitor displayed a three-dimensional infrared scan of the piece. She was using it to spot tiny deposits that had been missed during the restoration process.

Playing in the background was one of her many self-help audiobooks.

...for this reason, traumas in our past relationships can be part of the reason why we keep attracting selfish men into our lives. We feel compelled to fix what went wrong the last time, and this can happen over and over again until we finally become aware of the cycle...

Natasha applied solvent to a tiny deposit of paraffin lodged in the tabernacle's base, nodding in agreement the whole while. She pondered the seven months she had just wasted on her ex-boyfriend, amazed by her ability to find the tiniest flaws in artifacts, yet be utterly blind to the most blatant flaws in men. Or maybe she was aware of their flaws, and simply thought their imperfections were something that could be removed if she was meticulous enough, like stripping dirt from an old artifact.

"He really was a jerk…" she whispered, blowing a lock of hair out of her eyes.

It was a dark chestnut colour and it fell thick and curly around her shoulders. Natasha's accent was Italian, but three years at Harvard had tempered it nicely. She ran through her positive affirmations, feeling another wave of depression coming on.

I'm strong and powerful. My thoughts and actions create my destiny.

Christmas was approaching and Natasha was dreading it. There would parties and church functions to attend, and she would be alone the entire time. It seemed to her that she was always alone, even if she happened to be dating someone.

She only ever felt happy when she was dancing, but even her love of the ballet had brought her disappointment of late. Her role in this years' production of *The Nutcracker Suite* had disappeared when poor ticket sales had forced the show's cancellation. Months of grueling practice had been lost in the blink of an eye.

Natasha gazed out her shopfront windows to see the little piazza outside. Its stalls were uncharacteristically quiet for a December's night, and she found herself thinking how magical Christmas in Florence normally was. The reason for the sad state of things was quite understandable.

Following a horrendous terrorist attack in Los Angeles, the United States economy had collapsed like a house of cards, leading the rest of the planet into a severe economic depression. In addition to the sweeping devastation it caused, the heinous attack had left the streets of Florence bereft of tourists and holiday shoppers alike.

Natasha chewed her lip as she returned her attention to the artifact, reminding herself how fortunate she was. Despite the global crisis, the Vatican had continued with its museum renovations, providing her little restoration shop with dozens of artifacts needing to be cataloged and cleaned. It was a tedious job, but one that was constantly reenergized by the small chance that something new might be revealed as the layers of dirt were stripped away.

It was this act of revealing, and her strong passion for it, that had inspired Natasha to work in artifact restoration to begin with. Having grown up surrounded by religious relics, it seemed a natural extension to the doctorate she held in theology.

Natasha laid down her tools and rose wearily from her chair, stretching as she did so. Across from her a sixteenth century mirror reminded her of how many hours she had been working.

"I look horrible," she whispered.

As always, she absently arranged her hair to cover a pale, dime-sized scar at the centre of her forehead. It had been there for as long as she could remember; the remnant of abuses she had suffered in an orphanage as an infant.

There were other burn marks on her body as well. Plastic surgery had made them almost imperceptible, but they still haunted her. They were ghosts of an evil that had touched her before her earliest memories. They made her feel malformed and inadequate, even though they were practically invisible.

Continuing with her stretching, Natasha approached the windows in time to see a mass of heavy clouds rolling in. They blanketed the starry sky within moments, and heavy drops of rain began to spatter the cobblestones outside. After a barrage of thunder and lightning, Natasha turned to find that her computer had shut down, along with all the lights in the room. Outside, the storm exploded into a deluge.

"I forgot to save that scan…" she said gloomily, and her eyes darted to the front door.

A gust of wind had just blown it open, letting in the torrential rain. Natasha wasted no time. Priceless artifacts were getting wet. She arrived at the breach in seconds, reaching up to take hold of the outer door and slamming it down with a crash. The workshop plunged into darkness, and it was only then that an irregular banging could be heard coming from the back room.

"What is that?" she whispered, and a wave of fear ran through her.

Natasha was not one to be easily frightened but she could not deny the eerie feeling that accompanied the banging sound. With a decisive effort she dispelled her fears and made her way into the darkness to find its source.

For almost a hundred years, the back area of the workshop had been used as a storeroom; a place that she rarely ventured into. It was cluttered with thousands of religious artifacts, and bric-a-brac of every kind, its few naked bulbs never providing enough light to dispel the fears she had always held for the place. Nevertheless, she found herself venturing into its depths, groping forward with nothing but a flashlight to illuminate her way.

"Is someone there?"

A crack of thunder sounded in response. She could feel the little hairs on her neck standing on end as she navigated the maze of cluttered shelves. It was as if something had invaded her workshop; something paranormal; something demonic. She knew this was a ludicrous thought, but she frowned in confusion nonetheless. Her instincts were telling her to flee, yet there was something drawing her forward as well.

It was not long before she found the source of the banging, and she breathed a sigh of relief. The same gust of wind that had blown open the front door had opened the back door as well. She could see it swinging in the dim light of a gas lamp outside, banging the old frame at irregular intervals. Its rusted latch had obviously given way under the jolt of wind.

Natasha looked down suddenly and swallowed hard. There was a street dog crouching in the shadows by the threshold, its eyes glowing cold in the reflected light. It stood as if ready to pounce and Natasha felt her body go limp with fear. It was only then that she realized it was not growling at her, but rather at something else; something *behind* her.

She jerked around, the dog lunging as she did so, but there was nothing there. Turning again, Natasha saw the animal pacing nervously, the hair on its back still on end. She knew that animals could see things humans could not, but what had it seen?

Her mobile phone rang suddenly just then, and the shrill tone of it startled the dog. With a loud bark it bolted off, rushing through the door and vanishing into the storm.

"Pronto?" she said, bringing the phone to her ear.

She was hurrying to the door now, wanting nothing but to close it. Outside a sheet of lightning lit up the sky.

"Is this Natasha Rossi?" said a crackling voice.

It spoke in English but bore a heavy Spanish accent.

"Yes..."

"Miss Rossi, this is Sergeant Alberto Martinez of the Spanish Civil Guard. I am afraid I have some very distressing news, señorita."

"Yes, I'm listening," said Natasha, a sick feeling growing in her stomach.

She closed the door and locked it shut. Darkness engulfed her.

"I am so sorry, señorita. A private plane chartered yesterday by Professor Agardi Metrovich and Father Franco Rossi has crashed in the mountains southwest of Santander. All including the pilot have been killed. Father Franco was your legal guardian, no?"

"What have you done with him?"

"We managed to land a paramedic to see if there were any survivors, señorita, but there were none. Their plane is very high in the mountains, and it is in a very dangerous position to access due to the high winds. We have been unable to retrieve their bodies. This might not be possible for some months, señorita."

"I see," said Natasha, lost in a daze. "Thank you, Sergeant."

Natasha sank to the floor, the musty storeroom plunging into blackness as the light from her phone went out. Father Franco had cared for her since she was a little girl, and if those at the church orphanage had been her family, Father Franco had been her father. Now he was gone, and her heart burst with grief.

Natasha's thoughts went also to Father Franco's lifelong friend, Bishop Marcus Di Lauro. He lived close to the orphanage and had been like an uncle to her all her life. He and Father Franco had been inseparable since they were boys.

How can I tell him what's happened? He's too old. The shock will kill him...

Suddenly, from within the inky hollows that surrounded Natasha, the sinister presence she had felt only moments before returned. It flooded over her like fetid water.

"Please, God," she prayed. "Make it go away."

But the evil remained. In her sorrow, she almost welcomed it.

CHAPTER 3

Boston, Massachusetts.

Dr. Gabriel Parker tilted the bottle and watched as the golden liquid tumbled over the ice in his glass. It was shimmering in the halogen light of his bedside lamp, and he threw himself back onto the oversized pillows, bringing the glass to his lips and inhaling deeply before downing its contents.

He gazed up to see a beautiful young blonde working her way into a pair of tight jeans at the foot of his bed, and then watched expressionlessly as she slipped on a lacy bra. A second later she was back on the bed, straddling him and delivering a deep and sensual kiss.

"Yum," she said, savouring the whiskey on her lips. "You taste like a man."

Gabriel's hands explored her curves.

"I taste like whiskey," he said, giving her bottom a gentle slap.

The girl kissed him again and when she pulled away Gabriel noticed she was pouting.

"What's wrong now?" he asked, stretching over to refill his glass.

"What's wrong with *you*, Gabriel?" she said, her eyes downcast and sultry.

Her fingers were tracing over a dime-sized scar at the centre of his chest. It had always intrigued her. Gabriel took another gulp of scotch and then lifted her chin to have a look at her.

"Nothing's wrong," he said. "I'm just tired."

She raised an eyebrow.

"You've never been tired before…"

The girl ran her fingers through his shaggy hair and passed them over the stubble on his chin. He had a strong jaw, perfectly at home with his rugged features. On his throat she found another familiar scar, and pushing aside a lock of hair, she traced her thumb over yet another on his forehead.

"Are you getting tired of me?" she asked, concentrating on the mark.

Gabriel put down his glass and sat up.

"Listen, Mica—"

"Mica's my working name," said the girl with a frown. "You know that. I'm Mary."

"Mary—" began Gabriel, but she cut him off.

"You still haven't told me about these scars," she said, kissing the one on his forehead.

Gabriel felt the usual pang of discomfort at the mention of the blemishes, and it annoyed him as always. He was thirty-two years old. Should he not have got over this nonsense by now? A recurring scene played itself out in his mind.

"Hey, Ashtray!" cried one of the bullies who surrounded him. *"Has daddy been using you to butt out his smokes?"*

"Ashtray did it to himself!" said another. *"Faggets love pain!"*

The group of boys exploded into laughter.

"Ashtray's gay! Ashtray's gay!"

"Earth calling Gabriel…" said Mary, looking down at him intently. "The scars…?"

Gabriel drained his glass and pretended to be serious.

"Electrode torture marks from an Iraqi prison."

She slapped him playfully.

"You're never going to tell me, are you."

Gabriel reached over and poured out some more scotch. Time, and his general hairiness, had made the scars almost imperceptible, but it had not been like that when he was a boy. Back then they had stood out starkly, like bumpy red cigar burns.

Gabriel told himself the mysterious marks had made him strong, but the truth was they had only made him proud. As a boy, the constant taunting had turned his feigned apathy into arrogance, a defensive trait that still plagued him to this day.

"Tell me…" whispered the girl, nibbling at his ear. "You know how much I care about you."

Gabriel forced himself to be patient. He hated hearing this kind of thing. It was not necessary.

"You don't care about me, Mary," he said. "I'm just a regular customer who treats you well."

Mary smiled naughtily, her pretty hands finding his crotch.

"You treat me *very* well."

Gabriel gave her a playful shove that sent her tumbling to the other side of the bed with a squeal. He got up and pulled on a pair of baggy brown trousers and a sleeveless undershirt, securing his belt as he made his way to a nearby table. He had a flat stomach and a strong chest, his body shaped by a lifetime of deep-sea diving. He took hold of a battered leather duffel bag and opened it slowly, double checking what he had packed inside.

He was not having a great day, or a great month for that matter. Something in Gabriel ached with emptiness, and it was not just the recent death of his father that was responsible. He was feeling a general weariness with the world, as though everything were losing its meaning. He could not understand what was causing it because nothing had changed.

He had been happily living a full life for a decade now; lecturing at the university, researching and locating sunken ships, entertaining beautiful women, and getting together with friends and colleagues on a regular basis. Life was exciting, but even still, something was not right. He would be turning thirty-three soon and something was lacking, even if he could not say what it was.

"Where are you going this time, Gabriel Parker?" asked Mary, her voice sounding timid as she came up behind him. "Take me with you. I hate Boston."

Gabriel turned around and looked at her, forcing himself to smile. It was not difficult. The girl was riveting. He took her by a belt loop and pulled her close, giving her an assertive kiss. When he was done, he opened her hand and gave her a roll of banknotes, carefully closing her fingers around it.

"You don't have to pay me this time," she said quietly. "We haven't done anything."

He walked her to the front door, producing a buzzing phone as he did so. His electronic boarding pass had just arrived.

"I'm sorry to kick you out, Mary," he said, opening the door for her. "I've got a plane to catch."

CHAPTER 4

Rome, Italy.

To anyone else, the distant knocking would have been impossible to hear, but even in his eighty-third year of life, Fra Bartolomeo's hearing had remained as acute as it had been when he was a boy.

"A blessing and curse you have given to me, Father," he prayed aloud.

His accent was thickly Italian, but years spent in the service of a British-born bishop had made English his habitual tongue.

"Where is Suora when one needs her?"

The old Christian brother gave a sigh of resignation. He was in the kitchen's pantry, attempting to extricate a box of tea biscuits from the back of a cluttered shelf. The distant knocking was persistent, and he knew that it was coming from a rarely used service door located at the back of the rectory.

"Nobody ever knows which door to use..."

He made his way along ancient hallways belonging to what had once been a small monastery, centuries before. Located in the centre of Rome, it was now the private residence of the retired Bishop Marcus Di Lauro, a man who, despite his advanced age, was still very active in church matters, especially those pertaining to the paranormal.

Fra Bartolomeo accelerated his pace, arriving at the door as the knocking stopped. Opening it, he saw a delivery man walking away.

"Pronto!" he exclaimed, scratching the back of his head where a little bit of silver hair still grew. "Can I be of assistance?"

"I have a delivery for the bishop," said the courier, turning around.

Fra Bartolomeo gave a patient nod.

"I will take it to him, my son."

The old, white-bearded Bishop Marcus was at his desk when he heard the quiet knock on his door. He took one last look at the framed photograph he had been studying and then turned to place it back on the credenza behind him.

It was an image of himself standing before Mont St. Michel in the company of his two dearest friends: Father Franco Rossi, and Professor Agardi Metrovich; both recently deceased.

"I am an old man now," he whispered, producing a well-used handkerchief from his pocket. "I will see you both very soon, my friends."

He evacuated his nose in a series of short, staccato salvos and then cleared his throat.

"Come in," he said in a perfect British tenor.

Fra Bartolomeo appeared at the door. As always, he wore threadbare corduroy pants, a flannel shirt, and a tattered woolen cardigan, each article a different shade of the same muted grey. He held out a small parcel in both hands.

"A package has arrived for you, your Excellency."

"Thank you, Fra," said the bishop, smiling kindly. "Come in, come in. What say you to having our cognac a little early today?"

When their drinks were done, and the old brother was off on his business again, Bishop Marcus leaned forward and picked up the package.

"Father Franco," he said quietly. "What could you possibly have sent me?"

In the package the old bishop found the battered leatherbound journal he had so often seen the professor with. He picked up the accompanying letter and scrutinized it through a brass rimmed magnifying glass. It was from Father Franco, and written on the day of his death. He held it under his desk lamp and proceeded to read.

Istanbul, November 29.

My dear friend,

The exorcism was a failure, with our patient passing away several hours into the ritual. We were however, shocked to discover that he was intersexed; a hermaphrodite. Impossible as it seems, last night's possession reflects the professor's myth perfectly. He is now certain that the Cube of Compostela exists, and has deduced that it is residing in the archives of the Museum of Antiquities in Tangiers.

As I write, we are awaiting a chartered plane that will be taking us to the place of the hermaphrodite's conception, an island on a small lake in the mountains south of Santander. We fear that this is the same island mentioned in the prophecy. There is a deep dread in me.

The professor believes that the time has come to unite Gabriel and Natasha. He does insist, however, that the two of them be united before the Cube is recovered. He has asked that I send you his Cube diary so that you might study it with them. As you know, everything he has learned concerning the artifact is contained within it.

Enclosed you will find the name of the professor's contact at the Vatican Museum. He will assist you in obtaining the Cube from the Moroccan authorities.

Your faithful friend, F.R.

The old bishop laid the letter out on his desk and fell back into his chair, releasing a long, drawn-out sigh.

"I feel you are here with me, old friend."

He reached forward and took hold of the journal. On its tattered cover were the remains of what had once been a gold embossed stamp.

The Cube of Compostela
Reality or Myth?

Bishop Marcus hesitated a moment, and then taking a deep breath, proceeded to immerse himself in the mysterious lifetime obsession of his dear friend and colleague, the late Professor Agardi Metrovich.

CHAPTER 5

The Atlas Mountains, Morocco.

Gabriel grumbled under his breath. He was dragging himself through a copse of dry bushes that served as his only means of cover. He knew that the lack of a moon, coupled with the dark fatigues he was wearing, would make him invisible to the armed guards, and he was glad of the fact. They would, at that very moment, be scanning the castle's perimeter, including the place where he presently found himself.

Gabriel pulled down his cap. Invisibility was a good thing, and he thanked the dark night. If he were spotted, here in the shrubs, casing out the villa of one of the most powerful drug lords in North Africa, he would most certainly be skinned alive.

Completing the last leg of his approach, Gabriel arrived at his final position. He was high on a rocky perch now, hiding safely behind the cover of a dense grouping of shrubs. Below him, a panoramic vista of the Atlas Mountains spread out in all directions, lit from above by a star-studded sky that seemed to hover only inches above him.

Sandwiched as he was between that infinite glowing cosmos, and an earth that seemed to almost embrace him as he lay upon it, Gabriel felt a sense of safety that he had never before experienced. It seemed ludicrous. This was by far the most dangerous expedition of his career, yet instead of feeling anxious or worried, he was perfectly at peace. He whispered into his radio.

"I've reached the entry point."

"Well done, boss," came the muted reply.

It was his trusted assistant Amir who spoke, his Moroccan accent giving life to a peculiar fusion of British and American English. Amir was high in a tree, gazing at the castle through a pair of binoculars and chewing, as always, on a hot cinnamon toothpick. His build was agile and muscular, his groomed dreadlocks shoulder length and adorned with a few dark beads. He brought the radio to his mouth and whispered.

"They still haven't left the conference room."

"What's been going on in there?" asked Gabriel. "I thought I heard a gunshot."

"You did. Nasrallah shot one his guys in the stomach. The poor bloke's still there. They sat him right next to Nasrallah."

Gabriel shook his head in amazement.

"Let me know when they leave. As soon as that room's empty, I'm going in as planned. Over and out."

Gabriel settled in for what he knew could be a very long wait. Apart from illustrating Najiallah Nasrallah's cruelty, the shooting was an indisputable sign that trouble was afoot in the castle, and where there was trouble, routines would almost certainly be upset.

It could be hours before the smugglers vacated the conference room and settled into their nightly pastime. It was a ritual that would take place in what Gabriel had dubbed *The Opium Den;* a room filled with rugs and cushions where the men would lie nightly in drug-induced stupors. Across the gorge he could see the room's uninhabited window, a tiny black dot in a massive stone wall.

Almost two weeks had passed since Gabriel had left his home in Boston, and if anything, his feeling of world weariness was only getting worse. Adhering to his new habit, he locked away the painful emotions and focused on the many tasks at hand.

Over the past nine days he and Amir had photographed, filmed and recorded every event that took place in the castle, going to great lengths to gain every scrap of intel possible. At one point they had even entered onto the grounds in the guise of electrical repairmen, using the opportunity to map the areas of the castle pertinent to their mission.

Gabriel considered how the unexpected crisis in the castle might affect their plans, but he knew that ultimately it did not matter. It was too late to abandon the mission. Amir had laid explosive charges all over the castle grounds. Removing them would be impossible to do without being detected, and leaving them behind to be discovered at daybreak would make returning impossible. There was no turning back. All Gabriel could do was wait and hope for the best.

For more than ten years, Amir had been a close and trusted friend of Gabriel's. They had originally met in the port of Tangiers when Amir, then just a boy of fourteen, had approached Gabriel as his ferry had landed. Amir had been wearing a tie-dyed Bob Marley shirt, his messy head resembling a tangled brown mop. He had offered to be Gabriel's guide, and even though Gabriel had told him to go away over a dozen times, he had followed him all the way to the marketplace, singing *Everything's Gonna Be All right*.

"I will show to you the medina!" he had said as he jogged happily at his side. "I know best places to shop!"

To this day, Gabriel could not be sure if it was the long climb to the old Arab quarter that had finally broken his will, or if he had indeed taken a liking to the boy. In the end he had given in. It was the best thing he could have ever done.

"Very well," Gabriel had said, "but you won't get a dime out of me. You'll have plenty with all the kickbacks from everything I buy. Now where can I get a decent drink around here?"

"Kickbacks? No kickbacks!" the young Amir had said, a twinkle in his eye. "I work for free! I take you for drink! Very illegal. Best place!"

The medina's narrow streets had bustled around Gabriel in a dizzy tangle of crowded shops and bellowing merchants, and before long, Amir had led him into a secluded courtyard café. No sooner had Gabriel sat down than he was brought a forbidden bottle of Johnny Walker Black, coincidentally his favourite scotch. It had been the start of a great friendship.

Gabriel studied the castle through a pair of infrared binoculars, all the while thinking back on their long alliance. How many artifacts had they retrieved together? How many times had they narrowly escaped with their lives?

The reggae-loving Arab was truly fearless and had saved his life on more than one occasion, despite all the hashish he smoked. What was more, Amir had been a favourite of Gabriel's adoptive father, Professor Metrovich, and that was a very difficult standing for anyone to have achieved. The professor had been very selective with those he consorted with.

Gabriel put away the binoculars and reached sadly into his pack, unfolding a loose sheet of paper covered in his father's scribbled handwriting. He had found it stuffed into a notebook in the old man's desk; a letter to his colleague Father Franco that he had forgotten to mail.

Gabriel's mind went over the mysterious events for the hundredth time. The professor had been on an assignment in Turkey with the old priest. For some unknown reason they had chartered a plane to Santander. Two days later Gabriel had received a phone call from the Spanish Civil Guard informing him of their deaths. That was all there was. He was still reeling from the news.

It was thanks to his father that Gabriel had the unique career he had. Just as Professor Metrovich had been in his younger years, Gabriel too, was a treasure hunter, and a very good one at that. His father had taught him everything there was to know about locating and retrieving lost artifacts, especially those found in sunken ships.

Being on the board of directors for the Vatican Museum, the professor had also ensured that Gabriel's pieces would be purchased with no questions asked. In this way, Gabriel had become a very wealthy man. Even still, he would have given it all up if it had meant getting his father back again.

The professor had been everything to Gabriel. He had rescued him from an orphanage when he was an infant and had over the years taught him what it meant to be a man. Under his constant support and tutelage, Gabriel had grown up to become a noted archaeologist. As a child, he had practically lived on the Harvard campus where his father worked, spending his nights on the restored, turn-of-the-century schooner that was their home.

Since boyhood, Gabriel's life had revolved around sailing, diving, travelling, and above all else, studying. He had read more books than the most diligent of scholars, and had visited more countries than he could keep track of. To Gabriel, acquiring knowledge was an effortless pastime, like eating or drinking. Travelling, treasure hunting, diving, and sailing, were just the things he did in the time that was left over. It had always been that way.

Under the stealthy red light of a military flashlight, Gabriel scanned his father's letter until he found the part he was looking for. He had examined it countless times, but seeing it here, on the top of that ridge, high in the Atlas

Mountains, renewed his sense of purpose, and gave him the stamina he needed to go through with the task at hand.

On the paper before him, scribbled in the professor's barely legible hand, was a short paragraph concerning something that he was totally unfamiliar with. It spoke of a legendary artifact that Gabriel had never heard of before.

I've been turning over some rocks in Istanbul and have made an important discovery. The long-lost Compostela Cube might still exist. I have narrowed its location to one of three places. If it is found, the legend will be validated, and there will no longer remain any doubts concerning the mystery surrounding the births of Gabriel and Natasha, and their birthright to the inheritance of the Cube.

Below these notes, was a crude drawing of the cube that had been referred to. It appeared to be a medieval quadriform, measuring fifteen centimeters on each of its sides. In essence, it was a simple box. Jotted down next to it was a name.

Gutierrez de la Cruz
Priest / Cartographer
835 - 901 CE"

Below it three more lines had been written. Two had been scribbled over and were illegible but the last line was easily read.

The Museum of Antiquities, Tangiers, Morocco.

Gabriel folded the letter carefully and put it away. That was all there had been to go on, but given his passion for relics, and the knowledge that his father was not one to speculate on anything other than facts, it was enough to start him on a quest to find the Compostela Cube. Even still, there were so many questions left unanswered.

What was this cube? It appeared to be an important artifact, but if this were the case, in all his years of study, would he not have heard mention of it? And who was Natasha, and why was this artifact *their* birthright? Was it possible that he might have a sister? If only the professor were still alive.

All his life Gabriel had seen his father working in a battered old diary, but he had never been permitted to even look at it. His gut told him that the answers to any question he might have concerning the artifact would be found in that book, but where was it? Gabriel had turned the boat upside-down but had found nothing. He was perplexed, and his desire to learn more about the Cube had taken on an almost obsessive quality.

Within a few days of finding the scribbled letter in his father's desk, Gabriel had boarded a plane to Tangiers. At the Museum of Antiquities, he had learned that the Cube had been stored in the archives for as long as the museum had existed, but it had never been displayed to the public.

"It was a beautifully illuminated quadriform," the curator had told him, "but not particularly impressive when compared to other illuminated artifacts from the same period. For that reason, I was very surprised when the museum was broken into last year, and only that piece was stolen."

Not knowing where to begin his search, Gabriel's thoughts had naturally gone to his assistant. Amir had grown up in the streets of Tangiers. If anyone could find out who had stolen the artifact, it would be him.

It was not long before Amir and Gabriel were sitting in a busy café, sipping mint tea and talking to an informant that Amir had arranged to meet. He was a giant of a man, with a fleshy scar that bisected the entire left side of his face. His massive brown head was shaven clean, and a patchwork of scars and bumps covered it as though it were a piece of battered luggage. On his neck was the symbol of a moth; an artless image brought into relief by the crude branding of a primitive hand.

Gabriel had been impressed. Despite his rough appearance, there seemed to be a profound dignity to the ugly giant. There was a quiet wisdom in his eyes.

"Najiallah Nasrallah," he had said, his voice as deep as a diamond mine.

He spat in disgust.

"He is a dog, living in the palace of a king."

Gabriel could still remember the informant's face in every detail, and the way he had scowled when he had spoken that name. Amir had put a roll of banknotes into the enormous hand and exchanged a knowing look with the man. Moments later the dark giant had vanished into the milling crowds.

"Nasrallah's a powerful drug lord, boss," Amir had said, squinting up through his dreadlocks. "He's said to have a taste for archaeology. I should've known it was him. He employs a lot of people in this town, but everyone hates him."

"Where can we find him?"

Amir had slugged back the last of his tea and was holding out the glass, admiring the bright green leaves that filled it.

"He lives in a Moorish castle," he had said, sitting back in his chair. "It's high in the mountains, north of Tetouan. It's impenetrable, boss."

"Impenetrable," muttered Gabriel under his breath.

He was looking through his binoculars and had just seen the lights go on in the opium den.

"Impenetrable until the Moors decided to hook-up to the electrical grid..."

His radio vibrated.

"You're clear to go, boss. They all left the conference room. Be careful."

"All right, Amir," he said. "Here goes nothing."

Gabriel shifted into a low crouch and took a deep breath.

Everybody else gets lawyers to arrange their inheritance. Why does it always have to be so difficult for me?

Reaching up, he hooked an insulated zip-line trolley to the power line that hung above him. He could see it disappearing into the darkness, stretching across the gorge that separated him from the castle. Somewhere in the distance, the cable would end at a narrow sill where it connected to the castle's main power supply. He would have to drop ten feet to a rooftop below or be electrocuted instantly.

A flash of bright light spread out behind the castle just then, followed immediately by the buffeting sound of an explosion. Amir's distractions had been detonated, and for an instant the castle looked like it belonged in Disney Land. A huge starburst spread out behind one of the turrets, followed by another and yet another. The wheels were in motion. There was no going back now.

"I sure hope the brakes work on this thing," he said, leaping from the cliff face and sliding out into the starry night.

CHAPTER 6

Soho, New York City.

Christian Antov lay on the floor, curled into a semi-fetal ball at the foot of an enormous abstract painting. He was a middle-aged man, thin and pale, and as always, he wore a tailored grey suit with a white shirt and neutral coloured tie. Around him his art studio stretched out like a war zone, the lofty ceilings and exposed brick walls doing nothing to mask the sordidness of the scene.

It had been another night of debauchery, and the scattered debris of empty bottles and cigarette butts left no doubt that there had been a large gathering here the night before. Christian opened an eye to see the handful of guests who had spent the night. They littered the floor like scattered bodies after a lost battle, framed by a backdrop of the dark expressionist paintings that comprised the bulk of his work.

"Get the hell out," he said weakly. "Get the hell out of my house..."

He sat up with a groan and leaned back onto a fifteen-foot canvas.

"Get out you ungrateful pieces of shit!"

Christian's face contorted in pain from the effort of his cry, but he could soon hear groans and muttering, followed by shuffling sounds and the patter of footsteps. His guests were familiar with his unpredictable temper, and they made no delay in their exodus.

Seconds later, he heard the door slam shut and he cursed aloud, letting his head fall into his hands. His brain was still reeling from the drink, and his body trembled from the excessive cocaine. He swallowed hard, trying to control his loose bowels. At least he was alone now. All he needed was a cigarette and a drink.

He was bending to reach for an abandoned butt on the floor when he spotted two men at the door. They were wearing black suits.

"I told you to leave!" he screamed. "GET OUT!"

There was a long pause.

"That is no way to treat your guests," said one of them. "And it is certainly not the way you were raised to behave."

They were too far away for Christian to discern their faces, but he immediately recognized their Dutch accents. A feeling of hatred filled him as the last of his strength ebbed away.

"What do you want?" he said listlessly, falling back onto the canvas again.

He plucked the trampled cigarette and lit it, inhaling deeply.

"What the fuck do you want from me?"

He could see the men approaching. They were immaculately dressed, and they picked their way through the carnage of the party as though it were human waste.

"You will be grieved to know that your father is near death, Christian," said one of the men. "He has sent us to collect you."

Christian laughed coldly.

"He can die and rot for all I care."

"Get up, Christian," said the other man firmly. "The jet is waiting."

CHAPTER 7

The Atlas Mountains, Morocco.

"Amir!"

Gabriel's whisper sounded more like a scream. He was speaking into his radio, the sound of the fireworks outside still echoing through the castle.

"Can you hear me?"

"Where are you?"

"I'm still in the conference room. The Cube's not in the safe."

Amir threw down his toothpick.

"You gotta get out of there, boss. They're already starting to comb the place. You don't have much time."

"I'm not leaving without the Cube," said Gabriel, still searching through the safe. "Where are they concentrating their search?"

"Perimeters for now," said Amir, his normally smooth tenor beginning to roughen a little at the edges. "Guards are all over the grounds. They've even got dogs. It won't be long before they start searching the castle!"

"Where's Nasrallah?"

"I don't know!" he said, frustrated. "Inside somewhere. Boss. Truly. You gotta get out now. You're in a lot of danger. Your escape route could be cut off at any moment."

"I'm not leaving without the Cube."

Gabriel pocketed his radio and scanned the room. It was without a doubt the castle's most important chamber, its twenty-foot ceilings held aloft by four massive columns. On the room's northern wall ran a long arcade of elegant sandstone arches. They opened onto an expansive terrace. At some point the arcade had been glassed in, and it was through these windows that Amir had been spying on the meeting only moments before. In the centre of the room sat the large conference table where the criminals had gathered.

There was a pool of blood coagulating under one of the chairs there. It contents had been tracked all over the room, painting the stone floor as though it were an abstract canvas.

Gabriel stood before the empty safe he had only just blasted open. Its twisted door was laying on the floor at his feet. Next to it, he could see a set of footprints that stood apart from the other boot prints in the room. They were made by Nasrallah's dress shoes, and Gabriel followed them out of the room.

Whereas all the other traffic had gone in the direction of the opium den, Nasrallah had taken a different path. Gabriel could see traces of his prints leading down a long stone corridor and he followed them to a spiraling flight of descending steps.

Moving as silently as possible, he made his way down, arriving at a small antechamber containing a heavy wooden door. He could hear two guards calling out in Arabic somewhere above. He pressed himself against the wall and remained there motionless. Behind the door there was only silence. When the guards had passed, he tried the handle and found it was unlocked.

"Here goes nothing," he muttered, and then he slowly opened the door.

With nothing but the dim light from the stairwell to illuminate the room, it was difficult to see what lay within. Gabriel entered regardless, closing the door quietly behind him and making use of a large deadbolt to lock it shut. If the guards decided to come that way, they would have one more obstacle to get through before finding him.

With the door closed, the room plunged into darkness, but Gabriel had come prepared. In the green hue of his infrared goggles, he saw that he was in a storeroom of sorts. It was a narrow chamber, littered with cluttered tables and shelves, all laden with scales, cardboard boxes, and plastic bags.

"The packaging department," he muttered. "But no drugs anywhere. Weird."

There were three doors here. Two were shut and one was slightly ajar. From the open door came a cooler reading than the others, leading Gabriel to consider that the room might be a connecting chamber, and the one Nasrallah had taken. He approached it with stealth. In a chamber such as this, even the slightest shuffle would be amplified twenty times over. Gabriel eyed the door, listening intently for any sounds behind it.

"Let's see if you took door number three…"

He pushed the door open and switched off his night vision, turning on a black light scanner. Immediately he was able to see the glowing residue of blood from Nasrallah's shoes. It shone brightly back at him, leaving a track of irregular marks heading off into the chamber.

Gabriel entered silently and reactivated his night vision. He was in what looked to be the castle's original kitchen, the giant hearth before him still blackened by the soot of ancient fires. To his left, beneath a row of crudely hewn sinks, he noticed a drainage trough emptying into a narrow pit.

Gabriel cocked an eyebrow and pushed back his messy hair. A faint glow was radiating from an open doorway just ahead of him. He removed his goggles and approached it cautiously, pressing himself against the wall and peeking in.

Within was a medium-sized room, its worktables cluttered with computers and an assortment of scientific apparatus. What had once been a pantry had been converted into a laboratory of sorts, its tiled floors and walls providing the perfect hermetic environment.

He stepped forward silently. A particular table had caught his attention. It sat apart from the others and was the only one not covered in clutter. Above it hung a single halogen fixture, its dimmed light illuminating a very out of context piece of equipment.

What would a drug lord be wanting with a portable X-ray machine?

Gabriel made his way to the table and was almost disappointed by what he found. There, resting on a tray of lead, was the treasure he had been seeking, but it was by no means what he had been expecting. Under the halogen light he saw it for what it was: A typical quadriform cube, measuring some fifteen centimeters in width, and constructed from what appeared to be vellum or wood.

My God, is this what all the fuss is about?

Gabriel had seen countless treasures in his career; priceless works of art boasting outstanding materials and craftsmanship. Disappointingly, the piece before him seemed unremarkable, a mediocre artifact at best.

Typical of such quadriforms, each of its six sides were decorated with illuminations, but in this case, the illustrations consisted of six crudely rendered apples, their peels removed, but curiously left coiled around them. Gabriel was perplexed.

What kind of medieval subject matter is a peeled apple?

He bent closer to the relic, noticing only then the elegance of the framework that encased it. Constructed in time-blackened silver, it comprised an exoskeleton of intertwining branches, each section encrusted with what appeared to be heavily soiled rubies and emeralds.

It was not until Gabriel had carefully picked up the artifact that he was at last made aware of its uniqueness. Whereas most of the quadriforms he had encountered had been hollow and used for decorative purposes, this artifact was surprisingly heavy for its size.

Now I can see why he was trying to x-ray it. There's got to be something inside.

The artifact was not what Gabriel had been expecting to take hold of. In it he felt an inexplicable quality, something that defied any kind of rational description. As he turned it over in his hands, he would have easily lost track of time were it not for the vibration of his radio calling him back to reality.

"I found it," whispered Gabriel, snapping out of his trance. "Amir. I've got the Cube."

"Boss. You gotta listen very carefully."

It was the first time Gabriel had ever sensed fear in Amir's voice. By its varying volume, he guessed that Amir was running as he spoke.

"I had to give up my lookout point. There are guards everywhere. I just saw Nasrallah. He came out screaming. They know you're inside!"

Gabriel heard a violent pounding. The guards had arrived at the door he had bolted shut. He looked up, startled.

"Shit."

He could hear Amir's urgent whisper through the radio.

"Get to the escape route right away! You might still be able to make it there in time. Call me the minute you get through and I'll set off the charges. I'll meet you at the river rendezvous point."

"Amir," said Gabriel, his voice calm and steady. "I'll never make it out that way now. I'm deep in the castle. I want you to blow the escape route right away. With any luck it'll confuse them and give me time to get out of here."

"What? Are you crazy? That's the only way out. You know that! You gotta run!"

"Amir!" said Gabriel, a little too loudly. "There's no time to argue. Blow it NOW! That's an order. I'll meet you at the river. Just look out for me. I don't know where I'll be. Now do it!"

Gabriel turned off his radio. He could have no more distractions. He produced a plastic food container from his pack and put the Cube in it, sealing it tightly. He had got this far. He had retrieved the Cube; *his* Cube. He would get out of this place. He knew he could do it.

The pounding was getting louder. More guards had arrived at the door and Gabriel knew he had a minute at most. He sprinted back to the room he had just been in and approached the dark pit that the wash basins emptied into, producing a flashlight from his belt. The channel angled its way downward and looked to be unobstructed.

"The Moors were geniuses," he said to himself, trying to think straight. "Geniuses are practical people. Practical people always dump their shit into the closest body of water they can find."

He peered into the drain.

"If this goes anywhere, it goes to the river. It just has to."

Behind him, the banging had turned into a violent pounding. The soldiers had found something to ram the door with. They would be upon him in seconds. Gabriel tightened the straps of his pack. In the beam of his flashlight, he watched a six-inch millipede scurry into the pit. He passed a hand over his two-day beard and battled with his revulsion of the crawling insects.

Suddenly, the castle shook underfoot, jarring him to attention. Amir had just blown up his former escape route. Any other option he might have had for escape was gone now. Cursing under his breath, he lowered himself into the tight passage headfirst. At six-foot-two Gabriel was not a small man, but the channel was just big enough to wiggle through.

"Good thing I'm not claustrophobic," he muttered, lying.

CHAPTER 8

Los Picos De Europa, Northern Spain.

Only when the last throbbing beats of the rescue helicopter had faded away did Isaac Rodchenko regain consciousness. Before him, precariously perched on a cliff's edge, and set high amid a sweeping mountainscape, lay the wreckage of the chartered floatplane. Trapped in it were the bodies of Father Franco Rossi and Professor Agardi Metrovich (as well as the plane's pilot) all inaccessible to the Spanish Civil Guard's retrieval team due to the buffeting winds.

Only a single paramedic had been lowered on a cable to confirm there were no survivors. He had found the bodies of the dead but failed to locate Isaac Rodchenko. Having secretly stowed himself away on the plane, Isaac had not appeared on the manifest, and as he had been thrown clear of the impact zone, he had gone completely unnoticed. As it was, he lay pinned beneath a section of fuselage, with the corpse of his son emerging from a broken coffin at his feet.

Earlier that day, and much to the surprise of the professor and Father Franco, Isaac had listened attentively to their strange request and granted them permission to conduct a special burial ceremony for his son on the island where he had been conceived. Given his faltering mental health, it had been agreed that Isaac would not attend the ceremony, but unbeknownst to the professor and the priest, Isaac had secretly boarded the floatplane and hidden himself in the cargo area next to the casket.

The sun was low in the sky when Isaac began to slip once again into unconsciousness. His face was badly bruised, his dark grey suit torn in places but amazingly free of blood. Overhead a rushing mass of cloud sped past like a giant landmass, lulling him into a delirious half sleep.

Below the crash site, the jagged mountains of *Los Picos de Europa* stretched out like a mouthful of teeth, each peak a mountain unto itself. It was here in this wild place, far from the world of men, and surrounded by death on all sides, that Isaac witnessed something that defied all the laws of physical nature. To his utter horror, he could feel the corpse of his son jerking and twitching at his feet.

"Dear Father in heaven," he prayed, his eyes wide with fear. "Deliver me from this evil. Bring peace to the body of my child."

Isaac tried in vain to move his foot away from what he knew to be an abomination, all the while battling with his guilt for wanting to do so. This was his beloved son, his flesh and blood. But like a frozen stone, the malformed cadaver seemed to be drawing the life from him. Through the sole of his shoe, he could feel its malignance. This was no longer his poor and helpless son. It had transformed into something utterly evil.

Isaac looked down to see the body heaving and lashing about with great force. His son was dead. He had watched him die. What lay at his feet was no longer his progeny. It was a beast. A cold corpse that somehow still lived.

CHAPTER 9

Rome, Italy.

The rain was falling in torrents when Gabriel's cab pulled up to the old stone church. It was 6:30 a.m. and Rome was just waking up. In the distance he could hear the siren of an ambulance cutting through the humid air, the wet cobblestones at his feet reflecting the erratic flashes of headlights as a growing number of cars rumbled past.

"Grazie," Gabriel said, handing the driver a fifty euro note.

With a nod of thanks, the cabbie passed him his luggage. A single leather pack, travel worn and battered.

Navigating his way through an obstacle course of puddles, Gabriel made his way into the shelter of the monastery's arcade like a child playing hopscotch. Before him a towering wooden door barred his way. He shook the rain from his jacket and sounded a great iron knocker that hung at the centre of the portico.

Within moments a little door opened within the larger door and Gabriel had to duck low to get through. An old Christian brother was waiting on the other side, and he shut the postern behind him as he entered, the clank of its deadbolt echoing through the empty chapel.

"Good morning, my son," said Fra Bartolomeo, embracing him heartily. "The bishop is presently at his toilet. He will be meeting you for breakfast very soon."

Gabriel released him but kept hold of his shoulders.

"Thanks, Fra," he said warmly.

He was always amazed by the strength in the old man's body.

"It's good to see you."

"And it is always good to see you, my dear boy. I see you have not yet discarded that decaying pack of yours."

Gabriel held up the leather duffel bag. The old brother was right. If it were not for the meticulous repairs he had made to it, the thing would have fallen apart then and there. As it was, it was fully serviceable.

"It's hard to part with an old friend," said Gabriel, and he thought it funny that within such an old and battle-scarred pack could be one of the most important artifacts he had ever come across.

They made their way along the aisle of a dark chapel, passing a large bank of candles flickering in little red cups. Their wicks sent up plumes of vapor that mingled with the incense, and Gabriel breathed deeply. He loved the smell of the old church, and although an unbeliever himself, he had always basked in the profound sense of peace that radiated from the place.

Up in the rafters, the sound of the pounding rain could be heard on the chapel's roof. It echoed through the space, giving life to the marble statues that looked down at them from their niches above. It was a familiar feeling to Gabriel, being under their gaze; something that had always comforted him as a boy. His eyes scanned their stoic faces.

A manmade fantasy to explain the inexplicable.

He had never been able to understand how anyone could dedicate their entire life to a myth, but at the same time, he respected their faith. It was a testament to the power of the human mind, be it sane or delusional.

Fra Bartolomeo made a quick turn into a small alcove, and within moments they had passed through a concealed door that led into a narrow passageway. With the arched ceiling only inches above his head, Gabriel found himself having to duck at regular intervals to avoid the naked light bulbs that stretched out before him. He could see a long line of them ahead, emerging from a conduit that ran the entire length of the tunnel.

Where did this route come from? I thought I knew every inch of this monastery...

"Please pardon my detour," said the brother over his shoulder. "This way we can avoid getting wet from the rain in the cloisters. His Excellency's chambers are just up ahead."

Gabriel had to rush to keep up with the old man's pace.

"That's quite all right, Fra," he replied cheerfully. "I've only just been in much tighter quarters."

Gabriel shuddered at the memory of his harrowing escape. Not twenty-four hours had passed since he had made his way through the Moorish sewer. It had been a hell he would soon make every effort to forget. For over an hour he had squeezed his way through the entrails of the castle, caked in sewage, starved of oxygen, and beleaguered by rats and insects of every kind.

On two separate occasions he had been forced to cut through iron bars using the mini acetylene torch he had thankfully packed among his equipment. The choking fumes had nearly made him lose consciousness. With the stench of waste still trapped in his olfactory, Gabriel followed the old brother, reliving the final moments of his trying ordeal.

Deep under the Moorish castle, when he had at long last reached the end of the tunnel, he found that the passage plunged into a reservoir of sewage water. In his pack was a breathing apparatus containing just ten minutes of oxygen. It was meant to have been used to cover the short distance underwater that had been part of his original escape route.

On this occasion, he had no idea how long he would be required to stay submerged. With no other options available, Gabriel had donned the mask and proceeded.

"It won't be long now," said the brother, but Gabriel was too lost in thought to reply.

Nine minutes had already passed when he came upon a second set of iron bars. He knew he had less than a minute of air left and was unsure as to how much gas remained in the torch. He did not waste time finding out.

In the murky light of his flashlight, he could see that two of the three bars had already rotted in their mounts. He shook them and they fell away easily. The middle bar, however, was anchored quite firmly. In a moment his torch was blazing, cutting through the old iron. Even still, Gabriel wondered how much tunnel remained on the other side. His air had run out sometime ago now, and he had only been able to half fill his lungs. Suddenly the bar broke loose and he was through, feeling the surrounding water drop in temperature almost immediately.

With burning lungs Gabriel pushed his way upward, moving freely for the first time in over an hour. After what seemed an eternity he reached the surface, sucking in the night air hungrily. Somehow he had done it. He was out, and he was still alive.

"Boss. Is that you?" came the whispered call.

A large inflatable river raft appeared suddenly, and a strong hand grasped Gabriel's shoulder strap and hauled him aboard.

"Amir," said Gabriel, when they had landed on the river's edge at last. "If you'd shaved this morning, I'd probably be kissing you right now."

"Not smelling like that you wouldn't," said his faithful assistant, pushing aside his dreadlocks to get a better look at him.

He stuffed the raft under some bushes and covered it with twigs and dried leaves.

"Where the hell have you been anyway?"

Gabriel smiled and shook his head in disbelief.

"That was far too close…" he muttered under his breath.

"I actually thought it was quite out of the way," replied the brother, and Gabriel remembered how sharp the old man's hearing had always been.

Arriving at the end of the secret tunnel they approached a small wooden door that swung out effortlessly. Ducking low, Gabriel emerged into a large stone room. It was warm, and the furniture was plush and velvety.

"Wait here, Gabriel," said Fra. "The bishop will come down soon."

Gabriel made his way into the waiting room as Fra disappeared back into the tunnel. He had always loved this room, but he had never entered it as he had just now.

"Who would have thought," he muttered, looking back at the section of bookshelf as it swung closed. "A secret passage I didn't know about."

Gabriel walked into the carpeted room. Above him the vaulted ceiling rose solidly, with four gothic arches curving up to meet at a circular stone bearing the cross of St. George. Around him hung an assortment of detailed tapestries depicting great historical scenes. He approached his favourite one. It was a large work depicting the famous *Burning of Savonarola* in the Piazza della Signoria of Florence.

In the centre of the composition the puritanical priest could be seen chained to a great iron cross, with two of his supporters crucified to his left and right. At their feet, great flames licked upward. Savonarola had been a priest vehemently opposed to the Renaissance movement, and was infamous for his rampant destruction of what he considered to be immoral works of art. Below the scene, on the tapestry's ornate border, was an inscription quoting the executioner who had supposedly lit the pyre.

The one who wanted to burn me is now himself put to the flames.

"I see you are reliving one of the greatest victories of the Florentine artist," came a familiar voice from behind.

"Marcus!" said Gabriel turning. "Have I got something to show you!"

"Well," said the old man smiling. "I certainly hope it can wait until after breakfast."

The two embraced as they always did. A great love existed between them, and although the retired bishop had no blood relation to Gabriel, he had been a lifelong friend of his father, and as a result, had always been like an uncle to him.

Throughout his life, Gabriel had spent so much time in the old monastery that it was like a second home to him. He was familiar with the entire grounds. The bedroom he had always stayed in as a boy opened directly onto the main cloisters, and many a night he had sneaked out to explore the countless mysteries the old building had to offer.

Walking side by side, the two slowly made their way to the *breakfast room*, as the old bishop liked to call it. In truth it was a small overgrown greenhouse that opened into the monastery's private gardens. They arrived to find a little table set for two, complete with a linen tablecloth and full silverware. It sat amongst copious plants, and beside it a mossy fountain gurgled, silenced by the rain that pounded the panes of glass above. All around them finches chirped and fluttered.

"Your father and I breakfasted here quite often, as did you, my son," said the old bishop, sitting down slowly. "I can remember you as a boy, taking your sausages into the ferns, and feeding your crumpets to the birds on the sly."

Gabriel remembered too, and for a moment, a deep sadness took him. He missed his father dearly.

"Marcus, I've got something I want to show you."

"Tut-tut!" interrupted the bishop. "I know, my son. We have much to speak of, but first, we old men must have our nourishment. You forget the hour at which you come. I would normally still be sleeping."

"I'm sorry. I came here straight from the airport. I didn't think."

"Not to worry," said the old bishop with a reassuring smile, and just then, Fra Bartolomeo arrived carrying a large tray of food.

"Ah yes!" said the bishop, rubbing his old hands together. "God bless you, my friend, and thanks be to God. We have been graced with one more meal. Let us enjoy it. It could very well be my last!"

"If you continue to say such things, I will take this away and bring you lent rations," scolded the brother lovingly.

"God forbid such cruelty!" came the immediate reply.

Even perfect strangers felt a warm affection for the venerable bishop. It would have been impossible not to, and Gabriel smiled, knowing the old man's encompassing love for the gastronomical delights.

Looking down at his plate, Gabriel welcomed the hot food. As always, it had been lovingly prepared by Suora Angelica, a very competent Italian nun whom Gabriel had also known since childhood. It was the regular breakfast fare. Poached eggs, bacon, sausages, potatoes, fried fish, baked beans, fresh croissants, and coffee in a French bodum. The perfect continental breakfast, and the eighty-five-year-old bishop showed that he still had quite an appetite.

Gabriel was dizzy with sleepiness by the time he had finished the meal.

"Let us now retire to the library," said Bishop Marcus, noting Gabriel's fatigue. "There we can discuss your Compostela Cube."

"But how did you know?" said Gabriel, rubbing his eyes sleepily.

"I'm not as dumb as I look!" said the old bishop with a wink.

He scrubbed at his beard with a napkin, loosing a fragment of egg that had clung there the whole while.

"That is to say, I am much smarter than I appear!"

When they arrived at the library, Gabriel could barely keep his eyes open. The food was settling into his stomach, and his body was beginning to respond.

"Take off your shoes and lie yourself down on that sofa, my boy," said the bishop from the threshold. "I'll be right back. We've got a lot to talk about, you and I."

Finding himself alone in the room, Gabriel decided to take the bishop up on his suggestion. Wearily he kicked off his shoes and stretched himself out on the soft leather sofa. Beside him, thin orange flames flickered lazily behind the glass doors of a cast iron stove, and the familiarity of the room instilled a feeling of peace and security in him. As his eyes wandered around the paneled library, roaming dizzily from bookshelf to bookshelf, Gabriel began to feel a deep slumber take him.

"I'll just close my eyes for a second until he gets back..."

CHAPTER 10

Amsterdam, The Netherlands.

It was night when the private jet landed in Amsterdam. Christian had slept the entire way. He emerged from the executive cabin to find his two escorts standing on either side of the door, their arms crossed over their chests officially.

"I trust you had a good flight, Christian?" asked one of the men.

Christian walked past them as if they did not exist. He was a prisoner, and he always had been. Bending to look out the window he felt a distinct pang of hatred surface as he gazed downward. This was his hometown, and he did not know what he hated more, the city or his father. The mere thought of the man filled Christian with bitterness and scorn.

When the plane came to a stop beside a waiting limousine, Christian, familiar with the mechanism, opened the hatch in time to see a motorized staircase pull into place. He stepped onto it before it had come to a stop and made his way off the plane and into the car before his two escorts had time to follow.

"Take me to my family residence," he ordered, closing the door as the two guards approached.

"Now!" he barked.

The car sped off instantly, leaving the two men on the tarmac. Christian lowered his window, feeling a flow of cool, Dutch air wash over him. It was a familiar smell that he deeply despised. It was too fresh, too clean, and it smacked of the forward-moving mentality characteristic of the Netherlands. He lit a cigarette and passed a hand through his dishevelled hair.

The Antov family estate was located in the outskirts of Amsterdam, its manicured grounds, majestic stone walls and shining copper rooftops sending an instant message of power and affluence. How long these buildings had housed his ancestors Christian did not know, but if he was sure of one thing, it was that his family was much older than the stately Napoleonic residence: much older indeed.

"Take me to the west entrance," he ordered, "and call ahead to have a bath prepared for me. I want a bottle of red wine and Eggs Florentine waiting for me when I'm done."

"Very good, sir."

The car rolled down the long drive that led into the grounds, its wheels rumbling over the cobblestones. Christian lit another cigarette.

Maybe I'll get lucky, and he'll be dead already.

* * * * * *

"Your father has only just awoken," said the desiccated old butler. "Your timing could not be better, Master Christian. Please follow me."

Christian passed through the large oak doors to find his father lying on a great bed in his darkened chambers, a pair of nurses flanking him. A bearded doctor was there too, his patient's limp wrist in his hands. He looked up to see Christian enter the room and shook his head gravely. A feeling of relief sparked in Christian's heart.

Is he dead?

His hopes were soon dashed when he saw a brittle arm dart upward, its bony hand clenching the doctor's shirt and pulling him in with uncanny strength. Christian watched the doctor's face as his ear drew close to the patient's mouth, noting the change in his demeanor as the inaudible words were uttered.

"Everyone out," he whispered, coming to his feet. "The Baron wants a word with his son."

Christian remained motionless at the threshold, a knot tightening in the centre of his chest. In a matter of seconds, the medical entourage had flowed past, closing the doors behind them and leaving him alone with the man he most hated in the entire world. An instant later a deep fear was welling up in Christian, conjuring up specters of childhood abuse, and reminding him of his despicable and worthless status.

The room was dimly lit now, most of the light having vanished when the doors had closed. It was a massive chamber, with the distant walls and towering ceilings dissolving into the gloom. Only the oversized four-post bed was fully visible. It was a dais-like structure encased in hanging textiles and ornate cushions the colour of dried blood.

Christian stood there silently, frozen with a fear that had been nurtured in him since he was a boy. He could hear the scratching hiss of his father's breath and his knees felt on the verge of giving out.

It was all Christian could do to remain on his feet. Real or imagined, his father's customary psychic assault was working its way into his brain, and it was doing so with unprecedented intensity.

All power is based in fear. Fear must be maintained at all costs.

These were his father's words; words that had been drilled into Christian for as long as he could remember. They filled his head with the power of a swelling ocean. He had always felt his father's repugnant presence within him, but never with such clarity. What had always been vague and hidden was suddenly plain to see. It caught him off balance.

"Come," came the hiss, and like a lamb being led to slaughter Christian obeyed, his hatred giving way to a silent plea for mercy.

"Father," he whispered, arriving at the bedside.

The sight he witnessed was ghastly, and he fought back an urge to flee. It had been more than three years since he had last seen the man, and the transformation that had taken place in that time was nothing short of demonic.

There before him, lying amidst the finest silks in the world, was the grey and wasted form of what could only be described as a dying lizard.

"You need not fear me any longer, son," hissed the beast, craning his corpselike head closer. "Now that you have learned fear, it is *you* who shall be feared. You will know power the likes of which no other man has ever known."

The implications of such a promise made Christian's head spin, and it was only after a few seconds that a full comprehension of his new situation struck him. He was the sole heir. His father's entire empire would be passed onto him alone.

Christian swayed on his feet. Along with the intoxicating realization of his approaching inheritance had come the unobstructed awareness of his father's presence within him. It was a feeling similar to that of being violated, and the clarity of it made him seethe with repulsion.

Since early childhood, his father had infested him body and mind. The problem had been that he had never known any other way of being, and as such, the defilement had always gone undetected.

A tsunami of rage suddenly flooded into Christian, erupting with murderous intent. He heard the words leave his mouth like a curse. It was as if someone else was speaking them.

"Get out of me *you piece of shit...*"

Never before would Christian have dared to utter such a thing to his father, but his words flowed freely. With unrestrained contempt he spat on the old man, and to his utter surprise he watched as the reptilian face broke into a dry smile.

"Nautonnier!" cried his father suddenly, and then his head fell back onto his pillows, only to continue speaking in a whisper.

Christian bent closer despite himself, a look of disgust contorting his features as he strained to listen.

"It is done, Nautonnier," whispered his father weakly. "The boy is ready..."

With these last words he released a long, rattling breath, and just then Christian spotted the brittle figure of a man emerging from the shadows. His head was hooded, but hints of an ancient face could be seen in the lamplight. He approached the bedside and removed a serpentine ring from his father's finger.

"Behold," he hissed, proffering Christian the band. "Your father is dead. You are master now. Use your power wisely."

CHAPTER 11

Rome, Italy.

Gabriel awoke suddenly. The only light in the room was coming from a wood-burning stove that glowed warmly in the corner. The same person who had covered him in a blanket had also turned out the lights.

"What time is it?" he groaned, looking down at his watch.

The dial glowed blue in the darkness. 11:23pm. He sat up stiffly and made the calculations in his head. It took him a while. He was still half asleep.

"Let's see. I got here at around six-thirty... Finished breakfast by eight..."

He stopped short.

"Crap. I've been asleep for fifteen hours..."

Gabriel found his way to the end table and switched on a lamp. There was a note there. It was written in the calligraphic script of the bishop, a little shaky but still assertive.

I hope this note finds you well rested, my son. You have been through quite an ordeal. Please feel free to make yourself comfortable in the visitor's room. I will see you for breakfast at eight-thirty sharp.
M.D.L.

Gabriel put the note down sleepily. Had he read it more carefully, he would have understood that it was not his habitual room that he was being told to use, but rather a guest room next to the chapel.

He had no sooner started off than he was taken by a strong urge to urinate. With a bursting bladder he rushed along the dimly lit corridor until he arrived at the door of his usual room. There he would find a toilet, and with no time to spare.

Not wanting to wake the sharp-eared Fra Bartolomeo in his chambers next door, he moved the latch slowly. After that there was no time to even reach for the light switch. He knew that just to the right, past the armoire, was the door to the bathroom. He entered without hesitation and the relief that fell over him was encompassing. He sighed deeply, reveling with satisfaction at the deep rumbling sound of his stream.

"Seventeen hours without a leak…" he muttered, shaking his head in disbelief.

Feeling invigorated, Gabriel moved to the sink and rinsed his hands. It was there he noticed something was not quite right. Reflected on the tiles he could see light where there should have been no light at all. It was coming from the bedroom outside, a fact that puzzled him greatly considering there had been no lights on when he had entered. A feeling of dread washed over him.

"Shit," he muttered, the last of his grogginess vanishing.

He recalled the bishop's note.

The Visitor's Room. Shit!

Turning slowly, Gabriel made his way to the bathroom door. It was still ajar. Through it he saw that a lamp in the room had indeed been lit. Whoever was outside was clearly awake. He stood there without moving. Listening.

"Hello?" he said at last. "I think I might have just used your restroom."

A young woman's voice replied.

"Yes, I believe you did."

Her voice was timid, her accent Italian but schooled in American English.

Gabriel was at a loss.

This is not good. There's a girl out there and I just barged into her room and pissed in her toilet. Marcus is going to kill me.

He tried to think of what to do next, but no solution came. She was clearly in her bed, so he could not just walk out, but he could not remain where he was either. His mind seemed to stall. There was an awkward silence.

"Will you be staying long?" she asked.

It took a moment for Gabriel to respond.

"No. I'm quite done."

There was another pause.

"You can come through," she said. "It's all right."

Gabriel stepped into the bedroom and froze. Wrapped in the blankets of the bed he had always slept in was the most stunning woman he had ever laid eyes on. The soft light of the bedside lamp made her look almost angelic, and her startled eyes were large and childlike. Thick chestnut hair fell over her slender shoulders in heavy ringlets. Gabriel swallowed hard.

"I'm Natasha," she said carefully.

Gabriel was silent for a moment.

"I'm Gabriel."

Her stern expression made him want to smile, but something told him to be careful. His eyes twinkled despite his best efforts.

"My apologies," he said as sincerely as he could. "It's just that I normally stay in this room. Bishop Marcus is like an uncle to me. I was half asleep."

"I didn't know that Uncle Marcus had a nephew," she said, sitting up and eyeing him distrustfully. "And you would think I would know, considering that he is like an uncle to *me.*"

Gabriel was too unpolished for Natasha's tastes. He had a messy, travelworn look about him that made her want to throw him in a bath. She sat up a little more.

"And for your information," she added, "this is the room where *I* normally stay."

Gabriel's mouth hung open. He was about to speak when a soft knock sounded at the door. A second later Fra Bartolomeo poked his head into the room.

"Natasha," he whispered. "What is going on here? I thought I heard the voice of a man."

He looked around.

"Gabriel!" he cried. "What are you doing in this young lady's room? Have you lost your senses? This is completely unacceptable!"

"No, Fra. It was a mis—"

Gabriel's words were cut short as the old brother burst into the room and took hold of his collar, escorting him out with practiced agility. Fra Bartolomeo had long been a schoolmaster before his retirement.

"Fra!" pleaded Gabriel as he was removed. "I thought this was *my* room…"

CHAPTER 12

The Atlas Mountains, Morocco.

"You have betrayed me, and now you are lying to me. Tell me who stole the relic!"

It was Najiallah Nasrallah who spoke, his voice as greasy as his shoulder length hair. His accent was impossible to trace, and he wore a silky black suit under a blood-spattered apron. A shirtless, muscle-bound hulk was strapped to a barber's chair before him, slumped under a flickering fluorescent bulb in a windowless chamber.

"No, Master," muttered the giant of a man. "I would never betray you..."

His voice was deep and broken, but still dignified. He eyed the cattle prod in his captor's hand.

"There was talk in the streets," he continued, swallowing the blood that welled in his mouth. "An American was asking about your relic. His name was Gabriel Parker. There were leaks after the robbery. The informer could have been anyone."

"Do not lie to me!" snapped Nasrallah, pressing the instrument into the man's ribs.

The ensuing scream was deep and resounding, and much to Nasrallah's annoyance, the prisoner slipped into unconsciousness. Nasrallah jerked around to face a middle-aged doctor standing nearby. His lab coat was bloodstained too, his face pale from exhaustion.

"Why didn't the drugs keep him awake?" hissed Nasrallah.

The doctor pressed a finger to the prisoner's neck to check his pulse.

"I gave him a massive dose, sir, but he is still only a man. If you continue like this he will die."

With the prisoner's head tilting to the side, it was easy to see the large scar that bisected his face. In charge of two hashish production operations in Tangiers, and a smuggling ring in Algeria, he was Nasrallah's top captain; the only man left alive who had been involved in the Cube's robbery from the Museum of Antiquities.

Nasrallah scowled down at the unconscious brute, his upper lip tightening into a snarl.

"You're a slithering worm, Bahadur. You will pay dearly for your betrayal."

Within hours of Gabriel's escape, Nasrallah had ordered his helicopter to collect the giant and bring him to the castle. His family had also been taken, and they were currently locked in a cell within earshot of his screams.

Nasrallah stripped off his apron and turned to leave.

"He had a hand in this," he muttered under his breath. "I should have killed him along with the others."

Nasrallah's phone vibrated just then, and he stopped at the door to look down at it. His expression changed when he identified the caller.

"Father Vanderwerken," he said amiably. "How can I help you?"

His expression turned to shock and disbelief.

"But how can this be?"

He listened again.

"No sir, I do not doubt you. If you say the Cube is in Rome, then it must be. Yes, sir. Kindly relay your data and I will send a team out immediately. Yes, sir. At your service."

Nasrallah pocketed the phone and turned to face the doctor, his jaw tightening.

"Clean up Bahadur and make him well enough to work again!"

CHAPTER 13

Rome, Italy.

Gabriel sat in a plush leather armchair, scanning the guestroom he had just been escorted to. He was completely awake now, and he looked around with a refreshed alertness that was more in keeping with early morning than the time on his watch. His eyes fell on his leather duffel bag. He could see it resting on a rosewood table at the foot of his bed.

"Couldn't hurt to have a look," he muttered, rising from his seat. "Anything to take my mind off that girl..."

Even before Natasha had introduced herself, Gabriel had suspected that she was the woman named in his father's notes. According to the professor, the Cube was as much hers as it was his.

She said Marcus was like an uncle to her...

He rubbed the stubble on his face. It made no sense. Surely somebody would have mentioned her. What bothered him most was the way she had made him stop in his tracks. He shook his head and opened his duffel bag.

"She's got high maintenance written all over her. Another prissy little princess."

Gabriel shook off his misgivings and produced the container that housed the mysterious Cube. As he had noted before, it was surprisingly heavy, having a density that reminded him of an uncooked roast. A noise outside caught his attention just then and he turned to face the window. It had sounded like a dull thud. He remained motionless for a while, listening.

Most likely a tree bough downed by the storm.

The rain had yet to let up. Roman winters tended to be rainy, but this season had been particularly cold and wet. Outside, the downpour was pummelling the wooden shutters, and Gabriel was glad of the fire that burned low in the hearth. It was a foul night, and the room was quite comfortable. He moved to the desk and placed the artifact down carefully.

It was such an odd thing, this Cube, quite unlike anything he had ever seen before. When closely scrutinized it was easy to see that it was more than it appeared to be. Its density was of course the first give away, but surpassing this was the lack of attention that had been given to the illuminations that adorned it.

Compared to the detailed work that had gone into the carving of its external framework, the illustrations seemed overly crude. Each side contained the same image of an apple with its peel removed and arranged around it in a coil.

It was only then that Gabriel noticed something peculiar. Having studied similar quadriforms of the same epoch, he knew that their frameworks were always attached last, thus preventing any of the vellum from peeling off the artifact's surface over time. In this case, that precaution had not been observed. The edges of the vellum were peeling up, even if ever so slightly.

"Wait a minute..." he muttered, passing his finger over an upturned edge. "Is it possible there could be something behind these illustrations?"

Gabriel groaned as it dawned on him. These were not just pictures of peeled apples. They were instructions. He tested a loose edge with his pocketknife to find that the old vellum offered little resistance to being peeled back. He stopped himself immediately.

What the hell am I doing? I'm about to mutilate a twelve-hundred-year-old artifact...

Nevertheless, something drove Gabriel onward, and he was soon uncovering a golden sub-layer, one that was so well-preserved that in his excitement he forgot to breathe. He carefully pulled away the outer layers one side at a time, revealing a shining artifact beneath.

Adorned in intricately worked parchments of deep ruby reds and glowing emerald greens, it was a gold encrusted work of medieval art the likes of which he had never seen. Reminiscent not only of the Islamic and Christian works found in the cathedral of St. Sophia Hagia, the piece also reflected an uncanny similarity to the mystical arts of India, as well as the sublime elegance of those masterful works originating from the Far East.

"This is unbelievable..." he whispered, turning it slowly under the light.

The truth of the matter was that he had never laid eyes on such a masterpiece. It was beyond a doubt the finest example of medieval craftsmanship in existence, its authenticity unquestionable. It was only upon arriving at this conclusion that Gabriel noticed something that dumbfounded him.

"Wait a minute," he said aloud. "This can't be right..."

Reaching for his pack, he retrieved an examination kit and produced a large magnifying glass. After a moment's inspection there could be no mistake. On each of the six sides were miniature texts belonging to six distinct world religions.

"Buddhism," whispered Gabriel, turning the Cube under the magnifying glass, "Judaism, Islamism, Taoism," his eyes were wide with amazement, "Hinduism, Christianity. This is impossible..."

The likelihood of there existing a ninth century artifact that housed texts belonging to the six major world religions was unheard of. In this artifact was evidence of a cultural contact that, according to the history books, would not occur for another four hundred years.

Gabriel placed the Cube back on the desk and reclined in his chair, trying to digest what the existence of such a piece could signify. Who had made it? Why had they made it? Who in the ninth century would have had knowledge of the six major belief systems, not to mention knowledge of their languages? And what would have inspired them to want to unify them in such a manner?

"What the hell's going on here?" he muttered, taking his eyes from the Cube to look around the room. "Why is all this happening? Why did my father say the Cube was my birthright?"

All the while that Gabriel studied the Cube, and hours passed without him knowing, there resided in his heart a strange and disturbing familiarity for the object, one that he could not begin to explain. It was as though he had dreamed of the Cube, or perhaps seen it as a child. An elusive recollection of the artifact seemed to be hovering just out of reach, like a word on the tip of his tongue. Perhaps he had simply slept too much.

Sensing that he had had enough, Gabriel packed away the relic and headed for the bathroom.

It's almost two-thirty in the morning. I could use a shower and a shave.

CHAPTER 14

Natasha jerked herself into a seated position. A scuffling sound had just awoken her. It was coming from outside.

What is that? Is it the rain?

The noise sounded again. Natasha frowned and left her bed silently, approaching the louvered set of doors that led to the cloisters outside. What she saw there made her rub her eyes in disbelief. Through the downpour she could see a dog sitting patiently in the shadows, its wet fur glimmering in the lamplight. He pawed at the door again and Natasha gasped aloud, her intuition peaking.

"You again? But how's that even possible?"

Natasha's rational mind was sounding its objections. Florence was almost three hundred kilometres away from Rome. There was no way the dog could have found her here. Nevertheless, she was certain of it. The animal outside was the same one she had seen in her storeroom. She took a deep breath and opened the door.

CHAPTER 15

"Gabriel!" came the distressed call. "Get out of there and get dressed immediately. There is no time to waste!"

Gabriel shut off the water and poked his head out of the shower. Through the steam he could see Fra Bartolomeo standing at the door of the bathroom. In one hand he held a two-way radio, in the other, the battered old duffel bag that he had left lying on the bed.

"What's going on?"

The old brother held out a hand to silence him, bringing the radio to his mouth.

"It is true, your Excellency. There are men outside."

The bishop's voice sounded on the other end.

"Are the telephones still down?"

"Yes, and there is no mobile coverage either."

"Collect Gabriel, Natasha, and Suora Angelica. Meet me in my quarters immediately. I want all of you prepared to move. Bring warm clothes and any food supplies you can muster. Make haste!"

"What's going on?" asked Gabriel, donning a bathrobe.

"There is no time to explain," said the old brother, turning to leave. "I will wake Suora and get some supplies. Meet us at the bishop's study!"

The old brother handed Gabriel his pack.

"*E per tutti i santi*, Gabriel," he said. "Do not take your eyes off this. It is the Cube they have come for!"

Gabriel stayed looking at the door after Fra had gone.

What the hell's going on?

It did not take him long to get dressed. Begrudgingly he packed away his razor, rubbing at the three-day growth on his face.

"I'll get that shave if it kills me."

Making his way through the old familiar corridors, Gabriel found it difficult to believe there was an enemy outside. It was just the storm. It had to be. Even still, he was glad that Fra had left all the lights off. If there truly were men waiting for the right time to invade the monastery, it would be best to keep them thinking that everyone was asleep.

"Nasrallah could never have got on to me so fast," he muttered to himself. "It's impossible."

He made his way briskly towards the bishop's apartments, a thought occurring to him.

"Amir," he gasped aloud, his brow furrowing.

Had they captured him? Was that how they were able to locate him here in Rome? Could they at this very moment be torturing his friend? Gabriel stopped abruptly despite his urgency, an anger alighting in him.

If they've got him...

He shook it off and started walking again. He was just being paranoid. He had seen Amir installed in his Gibraltar flat not thirty-six hours before, safely out of Morocco and in one of the securest ports in the Mediterranean.

He brought his thoughts back to the matter at hand and just then arrived at the bishop's quarters. He burst into the room, forgetting to knock.

Gabriel found Natasha sitting on the corner of the bishop's desk, and he felt his heart skip a beat despite himself. She was dressed in blue jeans and a cream-coloured blouse, with a dark jacket that had an eclectic, military edge to it. Her black boots were soft-soled and low-healed, matching her little backpack perfectly. It sat next to her on the desk with a lit-up iPad sitting atop it. Oddly enough, there was a chocolate-brown hunting dog at Natasha's feet. Behind the desk sat the bishop, smiling as though there were no danger at hand.

"Well, well," he said in his British tenor. "It would appear that the long-awaited reunion has at last come to pass. I would introduce you if I had not already been informed of your accidental meeting earlier this evening."

The bishop shot Gabriel a stern look.

"You could have read the note a little more carefully, my son."

Gabriel gave a guilty shrug and then glanced over at Natasha apologetically. The bishop stood up and walked around the desk towards him.

"Do you have the Cube?" he asked in earnest, his untrimmed eyebrows gathering into a silvery mass.

Gabriel nodded.

"Would you like to see it?"

"No, no. Now is not the time. I must pack a few things."

With that the old bishop turned, instantly shaking off his seriousness. His eyes were alight with an almost youthful glow. In all the excitement, his eighty-five years of life seemed to have dissolved away. Even the old man's posture had changed, and as he walked across the room his gait seemed like that of a man twenty years younger.

He arrived at an antique armoire and removed a small pack from one of its shelves, whistling quietly as he filled it with some things. Gabriel glanced over at Natasha only to find that she was already looking at him, her eyes suspicious.

"I didn't see him in your room," he said, motioning to the dog.

"That's because he wasn't there."

She slid off the desk gracefully and kneeled beside the animal, scratching its proud neck affectionately.

"It's a very strange story," she said to the dog. "We met in my workshop in Florence about two weeks ago. I was sure he was going to attack me. Instead, he ran away, and I thought I'd never see him again. A few hours ago, he came to my door. I still can't believe it."

Gabriel frowned and then moved around the desk to sit in the bishop's chair. His body still ached from his ordeal in the sewage tunnel.

Why does her accent have to be so damn sexy?

He closed his eyes, opening them a minute later to find that she had taken up her place on the bishop's desk again. Gabriel frowned. She was looking directly at him; scrutinizing him again. He tilted the chair onto its back legs and closed his eyes.

"Shackleton's the reason why we're all up in the middle of the night," he heard her say.

Gabriel kept his eyes shut.

"Shackleton?"

"That's what I've named him," said Natasha. "He's quite the traveller."

"So it would seem."

Natasha examined Gabriel from head to toe.

"He led me to a little window in the bathroom."

She nudged his balanced chair with her foot.

"Maybe you know the one I'm talking about?"

Gabriel opened an eye and then closed it again. He had apologised enough times already.

"He got up on his hind legs and looked through the panes," she continued, chewing on her lip as she remembered. "He was grumbling. When I went to see what he was looking at, I saw two dark figures squatting by the fountain. Some of them were armed with rifles, so I woke up Fra. He says they're surrounding the monastery."

Gabriel opened his eyes and leaned forward.

"You're joking right?"

Natasha shook her head and Gabriel could finally see fear in her eyes. He rose to his feet, and just then Fra Bartolomeo entered the room. He was accompanied by a tiny old nun dressed in a pale blue skirt with a matching blouse and cardigan. She appeared to be laughing and crying simultaneously.

"Suora!" exclaimed Natasha, rushing to her and falling into her arms. "Don't be frightened. Bishop Marcus knows what to do."

Gabriel smiled despite his confusion. It felt odd that Natasha should be so familiar with Suora, and he felt a kind of childish jealousy seeing the two embrace.

"Ciao, Bellissima," he said, giving the little nun a hug. "Don't cry. Everything's going to be fine."

"Ah, my child," she said quietly, her Italian accent as thick as Fra's. "I am an old woman awaiting death. What could I be frightened of? I am not crying for fear. I am crying because I am happier now than I have ever been. I never thought I would live to see the two of you united. It seemed to me it would never happen. Thanks be to our blessed Virgin Mary!"

Gabriel and Natasha looked at each other suspiciously. They were standing on either side of the nun, each of them holding on to one of her hands. Suora Angelica had been like a mother to them both; the only mother they had ever known. Crying with delight, the old nun brought Gabriel and Natasha's hands together, intertwining their fingers as she spoke.

"The bond between you will see no bounds," she said.

Natasha exchanged an uncomfortable glance with Gabriel before pulling her hand away. In the meantime, the bishop had finished packing, and was in the process of throwing a dark cloak over his vestments.

"The time has come, my dear family," he said, slinging a pack over his bony shoulder. "We must flee this place at once. Follow me!"

CHAPTER 16

By the time the bishop had led them to the church's sacristy, Nasrallah's men were already making their move. With great stealth they entered the monastery and fanned out in every direction, their dark forms moving without a sound. Their orders were simple. Retrieve the Cube and kill everyone in the building. There could be no survivors; no one to relate what they had seen. For this reason, every square inch of the building would have to be searched.

* * * * * *

In the shadows of the sacristy the bishop used an old iron key to open a gate that stood before them, revealing a narrow flight of steps leading down into the darkness.

"We will be taking a secret underground passage that leads to what was once a convent, a very long time ago," he said in a barely audible whisper. "The tunnel travels for approximately one kilometre but I do not know if it is still passable. It is our only chance of escaping this place undetected. If nothing else, it will offer us a place to hide."

Natasha looked perplexed. A tunnel connecting a monastery to a nunnery defeated the purpose of each institution entirely. She looked over at Gabriel to find him digging through his duffel bag.

"We'll be needing these," he whispered, handing both her and the bishop a flashlight.

He produced a compass and yet another flashlight which he kept for himself. Fra approached suddenly, gathering the group together with his arms. His whisper was urgent.

"They are inside the building!"

All heads scanned the surrounding shadows. Even Shackleton was looking.

"Follow me," mouthed the old bishop, leading them into a chamber beneath the sacristy.

Gabriel locked the gate behind him, working the key as silently as possible. He was the last to arrive below and saw them standing in a small circular room. Its shallow domed ceiling was so low that he was forced to bend over as he descended into it. Gabriel knew that this was a burial place; a grotto containing the tombs of Christian martyrs from the second century.

The old bishop approached a round marble altar in the middle of the chamber. Around them, within evenly spaced niches, lay seven sarcophagi. The bishop embraced the dais and strained against it.

"We must slide this aside," he whispered. "The entrance to the tunnel lies beneath it."

Gabriel and Natasha jumped to his aid, and within moments the stone altar began to move. Fra Bartolomeo crossed himself, thanking God that the ancient hinges had somehow remained silent. Only a damp gust of wind escaped from the tunnel mouth, the thick air smelling of musty earth. It seemed terribly cold.

Suddenly from above, filtering down the marble steps, came the muffled padding of dozens of feet. All looked up. Nasrallah's men were just outside.

"We have no time to lose," mouthed the bishop. "I will go first."

One by one they climbed down a short ladder into the tunnel, including Shackleton, who surprised everyone by descending as adeptly as a circus animal.

The tunnel's walls were of raw earth, with the only support coming from crude timbers erected at odd intervals. Gabriel worked the altar's mechanism, delighted to find it swing closed with a quiet thump. Its mechanism had clearly been built for stealth.

* * * * * *

Bahadur stood dizzily beside the marble sacristy, his battered face pale and bloodstained. His scar looked gruesome in the sharp light of his flashlight, and the tattooed moth on his throat seemed almost alive, changing in shape every time he swallowed the blood that oozed from his broken sinuses.

The battered giant had been given no rest before being dispatched on his assignment, and his hulking body still trembled from its wounds. He watched silently as his men searched the small church. They had spread out into four lines and were combing the space, methodically checking every pew, every niche.

"My family will soon be safe," he muttered deeply, his elocution at odds with his brutish appearance. "We shall do this quickly. There is no other way."

Bahadur jerked his massive head around. He thought he had heard, or perhaps felt, something below, but he could not be sure. Moving with all the stealth he could muster, he made his way around the sacristy, his pistol at the ready. It was not long before he found the gate and saw a narrow passage leading down into the darkness. Finding it to be locked, he hissed at one of his men, motioning him to come.

"Open this," he mouthed, and within moments the soldier had picked the lock with an expert hand.

The circular chamber was empty, and Bahadur, weary with fatigue, approached the central dais and leaned on it heavily. He thought he had heard something, but he was no longer certain. Taking a final look around he pushed himself off the altar.

"There is nothing here," he said to his men. "Help the others. Search the rectory."

* * * * * *

Gabriel stood frozen atop the ladder; his left hand outstretched to the others in a plea for absolute silence. Above him he could hear the guards speaking amongst themselves. They seemed to be moving off.

"They've gone," he whispered back, wedging a spare battery into the hinge mechanism to prevent it from being opened from above. "We're safe for now. Let's get moving."

They proceeded into the tunnel, walking silently for some time. It was Natasha who broke the silence.

"Why was this tunnel made, Uncle Marcus?" she asked. "I thought that monasteries and nunneries were built to *separate* men from women."

"Right you are, my child," said the bishop, smiling. "But even under the most severe barriers, Mother Nature has a way of bringing together what was meant to be together."

"A tunnel of love," said Gabriel from behind.

The bishop's smile vanished when he shone his flashlight on the earthen walls.

"Yes, a tunnel of love," he said, "but also one of tragedy."

Under the roaming beam of light, all were able to see that the tunnel walls were lined with burial niches, or *loculi*, filled with the skeletal remains of infants.

"Behold the products of their love," said the bishop sadly. "The pregnancy of a nun could well be hidden under her habit, but once born, the child would be brought here and left to die."

Natasha cringed in horror. In the distance she could see the tunnel looming in the darkness, with row upon row of open graves in full view.

"But why didn't they cover them?" she asked.

"Penitence loves guilt," said Gabriel. "The corpses must have been a great way to remind them of their sins."

"Come," said the bishop. "Let us not linger here."

The group moved forward into the gloom, with Shackleton leading the way. Apart from the burial niches and wooden support structures, the tunnel offered very little to see. It worked its way forward, crudely veering around or beneath boulders, but always keeping to its general heading.

Gabriel followed with his compass, imagining what it must have been like for those who had dug the passage, and the decades of repressed sexual urges that had driven them to do it.

Ten minutes into their journey they approached their first major obstacle and both the bishop and Suora took the opportunity to rest. They sat down on some large rocks that had caved in from above. Fra was soon to follow. Their flight had been exhausting, and in the limited light offered by their flashlights, the obstacle looked impassable.

Gabriel lit a flare and the tunnel burst to life. Within their shadowy loculi, the sepia coloured remains of the infants glowed ominously, the flickering shadows bringing the skeletons to life. Whereas the addition of light would have normally made any place seem less oppressive, it was having the opposite effect here.

Behind them, at the fringe of the flare's reach, a curtain of impenetrable blackness loomed. Natasha concentrated on the obstacle before her, trying to forget the fact that they were in an expansive tomb filled with dead babies.

"We might be able to dig a way through up there," she said, pointing to an area below a collapsed support.

Gabriel shook his head.

"The dirt's too loose. It'll cave in on us."

"So what do we do?"

Gabriel looked into Natasha's eyes, lost in thought. She held his gaze for a moment and then looked away, recalling what Suora had said about the bond between them. She struggled to understand but drew a blank.

It was only then that she saw motion at the bottom of the caved-in section. In all the time that they had been looking for a way over the obstacle, Shackleton had found a way under it. Natasha's face lit up with delight.

"You're really pulling your weight this morning, Shackleton…"

The dog came out of the shadows and nudged her leg, spinning with wagging tail only to disappear back where he had come from. Natasha followed, shining her flashlight into the gap.

"It seems to go right through," she said, looking back at the others.

"Now who would have thought that I would be having such an adventure at my age!" said Suora, shaking her head in disbelief.

The old nun was on her hands and knees, halfway through the passage and laughing merrily. Gabriel watched Natasha as she helped Suora along with lighthearted words of encouragement. There was a sweetness about her that seemed sincere, and she was a lot like Suora too, able to laugh when anyone else would be scowling.

Gabriel felt a twinge of loneliness run through him, but he pushed it away swiftly. Deep down, he believed that women like Natasha were unattainable, at least to him. In so many ways Gabriel was self-assured and confident, but when it came to women, he was inherently crippled. There was something in him that prohibited any kind of fulfillment in a relationship, and as he was not one for *soppy introspection*, as he liked to call it, he clung instead to the same rationalization as always.

Wonderful girls only ever want assholes.

Of course, Gabriel had fallen for women like Natasha before, and every time he had been let down. He had long ago taken a more pragmatic road to companionship, and he believed that it was too late to go back now. All this being said, he felt emptier than ever.

It took the better part of twenty minutes for the party to traverse the obstacle, more than enough time for Gabriel to forget about his ruminations and get back to the task at hand. Being the last one through, he decided they should take a short rest, reasoning that they had all made quite an effort that morning, and that a break was well deserved.

"Fra Bartolomeo," said Bishop Marcus with a twinkle in his eye. "Might you have had a chance to bring along a few things to snack upon? Even your Lent rations would seem a feast in this place."

The brother's old face lit up at the suggestion.

"I did manage to put together a few items in our haste…"

He dug into his pack and arranged the contents on a nearby boulder. Around it a few large rocks had fallen, giving the elders a place to sit. Gabriel and Natasha found perches close by and soon all were resting.

"I see you found my pork roast," said Suora, shaking a finger at Fra.

The monk was carefully unwrapping the hunk of meat. He laid it down next to a crusty loaf of bread and then rubbed his hands together briskly, studying the thing as though it were a piece of sculpture.

"I know every one of your hiding spots, dear girl," he said, craning his neck to examine the thing. "And you'll not hide the crackling from me either!"

And then pulling out another wrapped parcel, he added, "Nor the gravy!"

Natasha clapped her hands in delight, her mouth watering.

"The pantry," proclaimed the brother proudly, "is the domain of the clergy!"

And with a magician's bow he produced a bowl of roasted potatoes.

"Dinner for breakfast!" he exclaimed, and all gave a cheer except Gabriel, who only rolled his eyes.

The old bishop pulled two bottles from his pack.

"And what is dinner, without water and wine?"

After a short prayer of thanks, the five of them dined happily under the light of a second flare. Shackleton laid himself down between Gabriel and Natasha and began working on the pork rind Fra had given him. Gabriel bent to speak into his ear, and oddly enough, the dog stopped chewing to listen.

"If faith is good for one thing, my canine friend," whispered Gabriel, "it's for the delusional sense of safety it offers. Anyone else would be trembling with fear, but these guys think they're on some kind of a holiday picnic."

Shackleton seemed to consider Gabriel's words before returning to his rind.

Their meal ended when the flare began to burn itself out. Fra and Suora busied themselves packing away the remaining food.

"That was exquisite!" said Marcus, rising to his feet and adjusting his vestments. "Excellent foresight, dear brother."

Fra bowed to the bishop and then passed Shackleton another chunk of roast before packing it away. The dog took it gently, looking up at him in thanks.

"You are certainly the most charming animal I have ever met," he said, patting Shackleton's back awkwardly.

Natasha gave the dog a potato and then bent down to kiss his head.

"Shackleton's saved us twice today," she said, ruffling his ears. "He's the best dog in town!"

The brown dog buried his muzzle in her lap and grumbled contentedly.

"All right guys," said Gabriel. "I hate to break it up but we really should get moving."

The tunnel continued on unchanged, and once the distressed areas had been left behind, it seemed no different to what they had already passed through. Inky blackness, eerie graves, and the unsettling skeletal remains of infants.

Gabriel calculated that they had already travelled more than a kilometre, and consulting his compass, saw that they were still headed in the same direction. Their pace was slow, but they were making headway. If they did not encounter any more obstacles, the chances were good that they would soon be arriving at the convent.

This being said, all hopes were soon dashed by yet another cave-in, only unlike the previous collapse, this one was most definitely impassable. Whereas the other had been comprised of boulders and loose rubble, the cave-in before them was formed entirely from earth and sand. There was simply no way through.

"It would appear that we have arrived at an impasse," said the bishop. "We will hide in the tunnel for as long as our food lasts, and then return to the rectory. Let us pray that the soldiers will have gone away by then."

"There's another option," said Gabriel, aiming his flashlight in the direction they had come.

Everyone turned to look.

"Not a hundred meters back I saw what looked like a tunnel leading off in another direction."

"Why didn't you tell us?" asked Natasha curtly.

Gabriel took note of her tone.

"Because I didn't think there was a need, Sergeant."

He looked over at the bishop.

"I thought we'd be arriving at the convent any moment."

"Well, my son," said the bishop, "it would seem there is a need now."

Gabriel gave a nod.

"Let's go back and take a look."

The opening was small, low, and crudely cut into the tunnel wall, almost as though the excavators had encountered it by accident. From within came a draft of slightly warmer air. Gabriel crouched and entered.

"I'll just take a quick look," he said over his shoulder. "Be right back."

The others stood by while Natasha squatted before the opening, gazing in. She watched as Gabriel disappeared past a curve in the passage, the light of his flashlight fading away soon after. All waited expectantly, but Natasha was the most impatient of all. As the minutes passed, she seemed to grow more and more anxious.

"What if he gets lost, Uncle?" she said, chewing her lip. "It's already been ten minutes and there's no sign of him."

"Have faith, Natasha," he said reassuringly. "Gabriel will be fine."

"Why do you say that?" she asked sharply. "I don't care what happens him. I'm only thinking of the three of you."

She rose to her feet and stepped away from the opening. Something was drawing her to Gabriel despite her distrust of him. In the end her concern proved impossible to resist and she made her way back to the opening.

"I'm going to take a quick look," she said, entering. "I'll be back in a moment."

No sooner had she gone in however than Gabriel appeared. There was not much room in the tight passage and his face was only inches from hers.

"Miss me?" he said with a smile.

Natasha looked daggers at him.

"What took you so long?"

"I wanted to make sure it was what I thought it was."

"Well? Was it?"

"I think it is."

The seniors watched them emerge from the passage.

"All right," said Gabriel. "There's a good chance we can get out this way, but it might take a while."

"Where does it lead?" asked Fra.

"To the catacombs," said Gabriel, glancing over at Natasha. "While those monks were digging their tunnel of love, they bumped into one of the largest necropolises in Europe."

"Good heavens!" exclaimed the old bishop, his eyes alight with excitement. "*The Catacombs of San Callisto!*"

CHAPTER 17

Amsterdam, The Netherlands.

Christian Antov walked briskly through the lobby of an opulent, five-star hotel. Around him were some of the most powerful people in the world, each of them members of a private organization that would soon be holding its yearly weekend conference.

He stopped at the reception desk, only to be immediately greeted by his new personal assistant. She was the youngest daughter of one of his father's associates, and she made no attempt to mask her innocent worship of him.

"Hello, Mr. Antov," she said flirtatiously. "Can I help you with anything?"

Christian did not return her smile, but instead looked down at the generous cleavage she seemed to be proffering. Cynthia had been a little girl when he had last seen her three years before, but she had since blossomed into a beautiful young woman.

"How old are you, Cynthia?"

"Seventeen and a half."

Christian paused, looking straight into her eyes.

"Email me a list of the guests who will be arriving today."

Christian moved off before the girl could respond, the hint of a cold smile on his lips. He would revisit her invitation in six months. For now, he would use her for other purposes.

All things considered; Christian was quite proud of how rapidly he was adapting to his new environment. It was a drastic departure from his decadent life as a New York City artist, but he was enjoying the power tremendously. It had only been two days since he had taken over his father's position as Chief Head of the Vanderhoff Group Steering Committee, but oddly enough, he felt completely at home with his new responsibilities, as though he had been born for the position.

Making his way through the lobby, he thought back on the previous day, still trying to digest all that he had learned from his uncle, Prince Vladimir Rodchenko. They had met outside the Vanderhoff Group Headquarters earlier that afternoon. It was a palatial residence in the centre of Amsterdam. The old prince had escorted Christian into the building, leading him through an opulent hall and up a sweeping staircase to his new offices. On the way Christian had been greeted by many staff members, each one offering their respectful condolences with regards to his father.

"Today I will be telling you many things you do not know, Christian," his uncle had said. "Things that will help you understand who you are, and why you were raised as you were."

Vladimir Rodchenko was the brother of Christian's late mother; a woman whom Christian could only vaguely remember. He was a brittle and impervious man, with a temper that could suddenly lash out like a whip, and then vanish just as quickly. Being the only relative that he had ever been permitted to meet, Christian was not sure who he hated more, the prince, or his father.

"This is your new office," the prince had said flatly, leading Christian into a luxurious apartment. "Everything here was your father's. It now belongs to you. All of its contents, along with the position your father held, are a part of your inheritance. It might seem strange to you, Christian, but you have been training for this job all your life."

When the prince had gone, Christian had settled into the leather armchair behind his father's desk. In the simple act of leafing through an appointment book, he had learned more about the man than he had done in the entirety of his life. Until that day, Christian would have been at a loss to explain exactly what it was that his father did for a living. His father had never told him. Nobody had.

Christian made his way into the hotel lounge and sat down at his private table, lighting another cigarette.

"Orange juice and champagne," he said as a waiter approached.

He checked his phone and saw that the guest list had arrived.

"Very prompt, Cynthia," he muttered, scanning the email.

He was soon lost in thought, smiling bitterly at what had always been kept from him. A scene played out from his childhood. He was in his bedroom, its minimal furnishings cold and sterile. With all forms of amusement strictly forbidden to him, not a single toy was in sight.

"Your father is a businessman."

It was his nanny speaking. She was laying out his clothing.

"That is all you need to know," she said dryly. "The rest is none of your business. You will not be disrespectful."

Having lost his mother as a child, the Austrian nanny had become Christian's only means of connection to his mysterious father, and indeed to the entirety of his family. She had been a cold and militant woman, following explicit orders to under no circumstances reveal anything to the boy concerning his relatives.

On one occasion, Christian had been told that his father worked with his uncles, but he had never been permitted to meet any of them. Prince Vladimir had been the only one; no grandparents, no aunts, no cousins. As a child, Christian had always been kept apart.

A barely audible alarm sounded from Christian's phone, bringing him back into the present and reminding him of the Steering Committee meeting he had to attend. He cleared his mind and made ready to be the new chairman. How they expected him to do this he did not know, but he would play along. As the prince had told him earlier that day, the machine was built and functioning. All that was needed was a steady hand at the wheel.

"All power is based in fear," muttered Christian, rising from the table. "Fear must be maintained at all costs."

The words were of course his father's, but Christian had long ago adopted them as his own, absently hearing them echo in his head more often than not.

Christian found himself thinking of his new position as he traversed the hotel's atrium, and all the responsibilities it would entail. There would be no person above him, and it seemed natural that it should be so. His father, it turned out, had been a leader of leaders, and all his life, Christian had been groomed to be the same. In his possession were the controlling shares of the Vanderhoff Group, arguably the most powerful organization in the world.

Smiling with self-satisfaction, Christian strode arrogantly to his first official meeting as the Chief Head of the Steering Committee. The Vanderhoff Group, he had learned, was named after the hotel where its first meetings had originally been held. What had initially started out as a handful of American, British and German businessmen working to smooth trade relations, had since grown into a collective of more than one hundred members, each of which dominated arenas in global business, media, and politics.

The group itself was an unofficial organization, regularly hosting annual conferences in five-star resorts in Europe and

North America. This year, the conference would be held here, in the same hotel where it had all begun; a hotel that had long ago been purchased by the founding member of the Vanderhoff Group, Christian's very own grandfather.

Officially speaking, Christian's new responsibilities did not extend beyond the role of host and organizer. Unofficially, however, he was the chief administrator of a deeply enmeshed geopolitical agenda, one whose nefarious roots dated back centuries.

Plainly put, his father's Vanderhoff Group was a secret society, one whose primary objective was to centralize economic and political power with the sole aim of forming a single world government, corporately run by their own offices under a false mask of democracy.

Leaving the lobby, Christian made his way along carpeted hallways until he had arrived at his private boardroom. He entered to find it populated by men, who in their own individual positions of power and social standing, comprised the steering committee. There were twelve of them in total, each one a blood relation, and they sat around a large wooden table engaged in a variety of isolated conversations.

Noticing that he had not yet been seen, Christian took the opportunity to scan the faces of the twelve old men who filled the room, amazed at how each bore the same bitter and hardened expression. He entered and walked to his place at the head of the table.

"Good morning, gentleman," he announced confidently. "I believe we will be discussing items relevant to a new North American currency in this meeting."

CHAPTER 18

Los Picos de Europa, Northern Spain.

The section of wing that trapped Isaac Rodchenko was merciful. By collecting the splashing droplets of a nearby spring, it was channeling a meager stream of water close enough to his face to hold death at bay. For many days now Isaac lay trapped in the airplane wreckage. He was high atop a frigid mountain in the wildest regions of Spain, battling a new and invisible enemy.

From the corpse of his son had come an unspeakable blight. The same demons that had possessed his child, were now accosting him. Wave upon wave their relentless attacks came, and in his weakened state he feared that it was only a matter of time before they entered into him.

Even in his struggle with mental illness, Isaac Rodchenko had remained a staunch Roman Catholic, and he now clung to its doctrine like a drowning man to a piece of flotsam.

"Dear Father in heaven," he prayed fervently, "I accept this punishment. I know it is my past sins that have caused you to unleash these demons upon me. Had I not abandoned Christian and Alina, none of this would have happened. What I did was unforgivable."

Isaac went over the events of his life. At the age of twelve, his father had sent him to live at Vatican City for a year. Following the council of a venerable priest there, Isaac had chosen to remain in the city-state, taking his mother's surname and disinheriting himself entirely from his wicked father. The priest's name was Father Adrianus

Vanderwerken, and he had consistently encouraged Isaac to forget his past and start anew.

"God has wonderful plans for you, my son," he had often said when sadness haunted young Isaac. "Have faith in His merciful will."

In not returning home, Isaac knew that he had abandoned his little brother Christian and his baby sister Alina to a hell at the hands of their abusive father. It was the guilt and regret stemming from this decision that had over the years become the root of Isaac's mental illness.

Despite Father Adrianus' smooth-tongued assurances that he had done nothing wrong, a dark specter of remorse had remained buried in Isaac's heart; one that would soon be growing in intensity as the numbing effects of his medications began to wear off.

Exposed to the elements and slowly dying, Isaac Rodchenko continued his hopeless battle against the demonic forces that accosted him. Unspeakable things had been happening of late. The corpse of his son was somehow reviving, its occasional twitches escalating into prolonged seizures that filled Isaac with horror.

Even now as it lay there motionless, Isaac could hear its icy whispers. The corpse was urging him to surrender; to let the demons take control.

CHAPTER 19

Rome, Italy.

"The most venerable and most renowned of all Rome!" exclaimed Bishop Marcus as he led the way through the dark tunnels.

He was quoting what Pope John XXIII had said of the catacombs of San Callisto in the early nineteen-sixties.

"When we were boys, Father Franco and I would sneak into the restricted areas of these catacombs!" he said brightly. "They might very well have been what inspired me to become a priest."

Natasha was amazed. That dark and tangled passages could be a source of religious inspiration dumfounded her. Even still, she had never seen her uncle so enthusiastic about anything before. It was as if the spark that had been rekindled in the old man earlier that morning had now blossomed into a beautiful flame.

"These Catacombs are a resting place for almost half a million Christians," he added. "As well as sixteen popes and many, many martyrs. The necropolis covers almost ninety acres!"

"That's quite daunting, Uncle," said Natasha. "Will we be able to find a way out?"

She was walking beside him now, trying her best to see the beauty he saw in the arched and crumbling passages.

"A way out? Oh, most definitely, my child!" he chimed. "We are presently on the lowest of five levels; an area off limits to the general public, but one that I explored at great length with my schoolmates."

Gabriel fell to the back of the group. Entertaining as the bishop's discourse was, he had become concerned about Suora. She was walking in front of him now, slightly behind Fra, and she seemed to be hunched over more than usual.

Her breathing had become laboured since they had entered the catacombs, and Gabriel could see she was having trouble keeping up with the group's already slow pace. Even Shackleton seemed to sense something. Instead of his normal place at the head of the group, he was lingering at the back, keeping near to the old nun and looking up at her every now and again with his gentle amber eyes.

"How's about a break, Suora?" asked Gabriel, trying to make it sound offhand.

"I am fine, my son," she said, giving her short little nods. "I was just listening to his Excellency. How incredible."

"There's no reason why we can't all have a rest."

"If I am not mistaken," said the old bishop, having overheard Gabriel, "we should soon be arriving at a wonderful little chapel. It would be a perfect place to take some refreshment."

Gabriel frowned. It seemed to him that his comment had made things worse for the old nun, reminding her of her fatigue. What was more, Fra had now brought his attention to her as well, and in the half light, Gabriel could see the concern on the old man's face. There was a great love between two.

As if in answer to the brother's prayers, the chamber the bishop had spoken of appeared suddenly to the right. Two heavy columns rose up on either side of the dark opening, with a crooked lintel holding them fast. The crumbling portal looked impressive. It was carved with what appeared to be Egyptian hieroglyphs, their strange shapes shifting under the roaming beams of their flashlights. A dark chamber lurked behind the pillars, radiating the scent of pungent mildew.

"How many flares do you have left, Gabriel?" asked Bishop Marcus over his shoulder.

"Just one."

"We had better save it then," he said, rubbing his chin. "If memory serves me correctly, this chapel has a hearth in it."

The crooked portico gave way to an open space that appeared palatial in contrast to the tunnels. Under a shallow domed ceiling they could see an altar adorned with peeling frescos. It sat between another two columns, with a life-sized wooden carving of a crucified Christ hanging at its centre. To the right and left of the altar, intricate freezes were carved into the stone walls. Natasha ran the beam of her flashlight over them, her background in historical artifacts piquing her interest.

"These carvings are obviously Christian," she said, "but they're Egyptian in style..."

Gabriel came up beside her as she passed a hand over one of the freezes. He could see she was not mistaken, and he was surprised by her knowledge.

Who is this girl?

"Christ is being portrayed as the Egyptian god Horus," she continued. "See the giant sun behind him? This is the traditional setting for a sun god."

Gabriel looked around, the beam of his flashlight finding a fresco depicting a scene of the Egyptian god being crucified.

"This chamber would have to have been built in the early fourth century," he said. "Most of these frescos would have been considered heretical any time after that."

Now it was Natasha's turn to be surprised, and she fought back an urge to look over at Gabriel. She had not imagined he could be interested in the early church.

"I can't believe I've never heard about this place," he continued, and Natasha noted the sense of awe in his voice. "It depicts clear parallels between Christianity and Egyptian mythology."

He looked over at the bishop.

"That's got to be why this level of the catacombs is off limits to the public," he continued. "The church has never been able to explain how the same stories in the bible were told in Egypt, thousands of years before they ever supposedly happened."

"That is a highly contested subject, my son," said the old bishop, his eyes wandering over the ancient paintings. "The fact of the matter remains that the early Egyptian Christians were of the most severely persecuted by the Romans. In all probability, this chapel was built as a shrine to them. If you look next to the altar, you will find a small doorway leading to a room that is filled with their bones."

It was not the first time that the old bishop had heard mention of the disputed pagan sources of Christianity, yet even though there existed a large body of archaeological evidence in support of this claim, he did not suspect it was a matter of simple plagiarism. He felt that there was a missing piece to the puzzle; a truth that would reconcile the chronological discrepancies, without destroying the essence of what Christianity stood for.

"Truly, though," he said, thinking of Suora. "All this is of no practical concern to us at the moment."

He turned away from the frescos and looked to the back of the chapel, shining his flashlight on something there.

"What *is* of practical concern," he continued, "is that the inspired gentleman who ordered this chapel built saw it fitting to equip it with a hearth. And as you can see, a long departed archaeological team has left us with plenty of material to burn in it!"

Gabriel and Natasha turned and focused their beams on the chapel's back wall. There, between two wooden scaffolds, was an enormous hearth under a full-sized statue of the god Horus. Its falcon's head was looking straight across the chamber to the crucified Christ that hung directly opposite. Scattered around the hearth were wooden chairs and a table. To the right of the scaffold was an old trunk filled with dust covered torches.

"Now there's a beautiful sight," said Gabriel, his beam focusing on the crate.

In no time the small party was huddling around a crackling fire, enjoying the first warmth they had felt in hours. Gabriel lit some torches and set them around the room. In the flickering light the chapel was brought to life, its mysterious purpose being revealed to them with utter clarity.

The chamber was clearly a sanctuary, but it also held a great secret, subtly revealing clues to a mystery that Natasha had always been fascinated by. The Egyptian roots of Christianity.

While Gabriel had been busy with the torches, Natasha had prepared a chair for Suora and placed it directly before the hearth, lovingly covering the old nun in a blanket the moment she sat down. Fra Bartolomeo, in all his foresight, had brought a small pot in which to heat the soup he had also stuffed into his pack. Only one portion could be prepared at a time, and against Suora's emphatic insistence to be left until last, the first bowl was given to her. The effects were nothing short of miraculous.

"Thank you, my dear ones," she said from beneath her blanket. "You are too kind to me. It was only these old bones and the dampness."

"Rest well, dear girl," said the old bishop gently.

He was lowering himself into a creaking chair before a worktable, an old leather-bound book in his hands.

"We will stay here for an hour or so," he said. "After that we will have a bit of walking to do. We are very deep, but I know my way. God willing, we'll be out of this place in time for supper."

Natasha was next to get her soup. She thanked Fra, and drew a chair up to the old worktable, sitting down close beside the bishop.

"What book is that, Uncle?" she asked, sipping her soup. It was warm and wholesome, and it drove away the last of her shivers.

"This is a book that belonged to Gabriel's father," he said, studying its worn cover. "I received it in the mail shortly after his death."

Gabriel was sharing some of the roast pork with Shackleton when he overheard the bishop's words.

"My father?" he repeated, his mouth full. "What book's that?"

"It is a book containing all of his findings concerning the Compostela Cube, my son. It is time that you both knew the knowledge it contains."

"The diary," said Gabriel. "I went crazy looking for that thing…"

"His life's work," nodded the bishop, pausing for a moment and then continuing slowly.

"Out of love, and an earnest desire to give you both an unburdened childhood and adolescence, much has been kept from you, but all will now be revealed. The time has come for you both to learn the truth about who you really are; a truth that we have long suspected, but one that has only recently been confirmed."

CHAPTER 20

Amsterdam, The Netherlands.

"Shall we get started, young man?" asked Prince Vladimir condescendingly.

He was seated directly to the left of where Christian stood, a sharp, hooked nose distinguishing him from the other old men in the room. He leaned over and stretched out a crooked finger, tapping a stack of papers on the table before Christian.

"It is all right there in front of you, boy," he said. "Right in the agenda."

Christian looked through the room's large windows and out onto the manicured gardens.

Boy? Go to hell you son of a bitch.

A group of men caught Christian's eye. At first, he thought they were gardeners, but as he looked more closely, he could see this was not the case. The figures were robed and hooded, and they appeared to be enveloped in a strange darkness, utterly out of context with the bright sunny day.

Christian frowned. Although they seemed to be standing still, the figures also appeared to be shifting from side to side. Their appearance was scratchy and difficult to discern, as though they were not entirely there.

A creeping fear was making its way up Christian's spine now, spreading through his body and making his eyes water. He tried desperately to control himself against the irrational emotion, but he found he was powerless against it, able only to maintain the outward appearance of calm.

"Well, Christian," said his uncle, humorlessly. "Shall we begin by discussing the first item on the agenda?"

Christian turned to face him. The prince's words had somehow broken the spell.

"Yes," he said. "Yes, of course."

Christian glanced back into the garden. The hooded figures had vanished, only to be replaced by a decrepit old man standing in the place where they had just been. He squinted at the figure, recognizing him immediately as the man who had been present at his father's deathbed; the same man who had given him his father's ring.

With unmistakable purpose the old man turned suddenly towards Christian, his cold reptilian eyes locking with his. A current of intense fear shot through Christian's body like high-voltage electricity. It nearly knocked him over.

"Pay no heed to the Nautonnier, boy," said the prince, his voice thick with disdain for the old man. "Father Adrianus Vanderwerken is a relic from the past. Look how his nurses come to change his diapers."

Christian watched as the old man was escorted from the lawns. His scalp was still itching from the cold sweat that had come over him when they had locked eyes. Why had he seen four figures where the Nautonnier had been?

He turned to face those in the room and gathered himself immediately. His mind was obviously playing tricks on him. He would give it no further thought. He had a meeting to direct. He would consult with his psychiatrist later. The dosages of his medications would have to be adjusted.

"Gentlemen," he said calmly. "I have been informed by the prince that the Federal Reserve will soon be replacing physical currencies around the world with a new digital currency. He also told me that the current economic collapse of the United States was engineered by the Vanderhoff Group as a means of ushering in this transition."

Christian moved closer to his chair.

"If I am to lead this committee, I need to know its motives, and its objectives. What kind of deal have we struck with the Fed to make us want to bring down the entire world economy?"

Christian sat down, glad of the opportunity to shake off the remnants of his disturbing hallucination. He heard an old man at the opposite end of the table clear his throat and make ready to speak.

"We have made no deals, Christian," he said condescendingly. "The Federal Reserve is not federal, but rather privately owned by us."

"What's that supposed to mean?"

"It means that every regional reserve bank is ours. They always have been."

Christian frowned.

"That means nothing. Those banks are all controlled by the Board of Governors, a *federal* agency."

The old man nodded patiently.

"Whose members are appointed by the President and confirmed by the Senate. In other words, by *us*."

Christian looked back at the man, remembering what the prince had told him about the multifaceted illusion that was called representational democracy. Centuries of finance, lobbying, and propaganda had given the Vanderhoff Group complete governmental control behind a façade of democracy, not just in the United States, but in every country that claimed to be egalitarian.

"It was the Vanderhoff Group that instituted the Federal Reserve system in 1913, Christian," added the old man. "Right after we engineered the banking crisis of 1907."

Christian was beginning to understand.

"So last month's terrorist attack in Los Angeles was our latest strategic crisis."

The old man clasped his hands over the table.

"A terrorist strike was needed to take down the U.S. economy and the greenback along with it," he said. "A standardized CBDC is the only global solution to the crisis now."

Christian smiled coldly. Fear and doubt had always been the two main weapons in the Vanderhoff arsenal. With them they had routinely manufactured crisis after crisis in order to implement their policies.

"And why a central bank digital currency?" asked Christian. "Are we not already in control of the existing currencies?"

"Our goal is to centralize power, Christian," said another man, his accent Texan. "A standardized CBDC will help us do that. The more we control monetary policy, the more we can shape other existing systems to suit our needs."

"This is what the United Nations is for, Christian," added another. "It provides us with a means to implement new infrastructures planetwide."

Christian could hardly believe what he was hearing.

"Are you saying the Vanderhoff Group created the UN?"

The Texan leaned forward in his chair.

"Our objective is a single world currency and a central world government, son. It'll be split up into four unions. The American Union, the Asian Union, the African Union, and the European Union,"

Christian shook his head in amazement.

"And we'll be the ones who appoint their *democratic* leaders."

A rumble of pompous laughter made its way around the table.

"Just like we've always done, Christian," said the Texan. "Just like we've always done."

CHAPTER 21

Gibraltar, Europe.

Amir stood on his balcony, looking out over the sunny rooftops of Gibraltar. He tilted his head to move aside his dreadlocks and then took a deep haul from his pipe. It was a ninth century chillum, the size and shape of a large carrot, and covered in ancient Vedic carvings. He had obtained the relic years ago while on an expedition in Thanjavur with Gabriel. It went everywhere with him.

Just as the wandering Hindu monks had done a thousand years prior, Amir had packed the pipe with a specially prepared mixture of hashish and kief. It was not for the novice smoker.

Amir glanced over his shoulder into the spacious flat behind him. His computer had just chimed an alert.

"Who could that be?"

Smoke lingered around his handsome features as he considered. Amir's skin was the colour of dark honey, and he had intelligent eyes that were bright and alert, despite his constant smoking.

He held in the vapours a little while longer and then released a billowing cloud of smoke, lazily watching it float out into the open air. When his computer chimed again, he groaned and turned to go inside. Someone was messaging him. He bent over the screen.

—*Amir. Something terrible has happened.*

It was Amir's cousin Abida who wrote. He sat down and began to type.

—Abida, you shouldn't be contacting me like this. It leaves traces. What happened?

Abida was the sister of Bahadur. She lived in Tangiers, and was constantly under the surveillance of Moroccan authorities, her family being directly connected to the smuggling cartel.

—Men came late last night and took Bahadur. They took the whole family along with him.

—Are you absolutely sure?

—I speak with them every day, you know that. When I didn't hear from them, I went to their house, but it was empty. The neighbour told me what had happened. She said that Nasrallah's men had taken them all away.

—Was anyone hurt?

—I don't think so. She said she saw them get loaded into a van. Even Jadda.

—Even Grandmother? Did she have her heart medicine?

—I don't know. If it was the government, we could ask about them, but it was Nasrallah. The neighbour's sure of it. What should we do?

—Abida, listen carefully. I'll take care of this. Don't speak of it to anyone. You'll do nothing. Do you understand?

—Yes, Amir. Thank you. I know you'll fix this.

—OK. Get some rest. Everything will be fine.

Amir rose from his chair and produced his phone. He paused a moment to think and then called Gabriel. It went directly to his voice mail.

"Boss," he said, stepping out onto the balcony. "There's trouble. Give me a call when you get this."

CHAPTER 22

Rome, Italy.

The firelight played on the old bishop as he sat before Gabriel and Natasha. Their eyes were glued to him as he spoke, his silvery beard and mustache picking up the hues of the fire that crackled behind them. Before him on the archaeologist's worktable lay the professor's tattered journal. On its leathery cover could still be seen the remains of a tattered, gold embossed stamp.

The Compostela Cube
Reality or Myth?

Fra and Suora had both fallen asleep by the hearth. They had brought their chairs together so they could share the same blanket, and now sat cuddled, the nun's head resting on the brother's shoulder. Bathed in the warmth of the firelight, the two old figures seemed to embody the objective of what the nunnery tunnel had attempted to accomplish so long ago: to unite what had always been meant to be together.

Shackleton was laying in front of them, his proud head held high as he gazed almost pensively into the flames. There was a consciousness in his eyes that seemed at odds with his species; a quiet wisdom that appeared almost divine. Within Shackleton's soul there was none of the conflict so common to the human condition, only a pristine desire to serve humbly and to protect.

He turned his noble head and looked at the three who sat there at the table, focusing his amber eyes on the speaking bishop. Entirely unconcerned with what was being said, Shackleton's satisfaction lay in seeing that everyone was safe, and getting the rest they so much needed.

"You see," said the old bishop, "if it were not for a legend, it is very unlikely that we would ever have found you."

"I don't understand, Uncle," said Natasha, snuggling into the dark wool of her jacket. "What does a legend have to do with it? I was very sick when I was a baby. Father Franco told me that he had arranged for the church to adopt me when they couldn't care for me at the orphanage anymore."

"That's more or less what the professor told me," said Gabriel, looking at Natasha and then back to the bishop. "After that he ended up taking a liking to me and decided to keep me."

"These stories are not lies, my children," said the old bishop, "but they also leave out much truth. Before I proceed, I must repeat that it was our intention to keep all the details surrounding your early months from you until we were certain of the facts.

"You must try to understand things from our perspective. We had recently taken on the responsibility of raising two beautiful children, and we wanted to ensure that the life we gave them was as rich and nurturing as possible. Of what good could it be to fill your heads with uncertain stories?"

"What stories?" asked Natasha.

Her face was earnest in the firelight, her eyes almost childlike.

"You mentioned a legend. Uncle Marcus, please."

The bishop smiled.

"I apologize," he said. "Be patient with me. There is much to convey, and I will start at the beginning. All I ask is that both of you never lose sight of who you are now, at this very moment. The things that happened in your past do not define you. They only explain how you came to be."

The bishop looked at each of them in turn and proceeded only after he was convinced they were ready.

"As you both know," he began, "I have, for many years now, held an office pertaining to church investigations of events that are often labeled paranormal. For me this term seems a contradiction to the truth, because things such as apparitions, demonic possessions, and other spiritual manifestations are indeed very normal, in that they have always existed, as opposed to the above-and-beyond meaning that the prefix *para* implies."

"Uncle Marcus!" cried Natasha, stamping her feet.

Gabriel was temporarily fixated despite himself. Natasha's display of impatience had displaced a lock of her hair. He watched it play around her lips for a moment before she tucked it away behind an ear.

"Yes, very well, my child," continued the old bishop. "I will get to the point. Thirty-three years ago, I received a phone call. I was at my desk, and as it so happened, Gabriel, your father was there with me. The call came from a deacon who was assisting me at the time.

I have received two separate calls relating to suspected cases of demonic possession,' he had said. *'A girl in Argentina, and a boy in Taiwan.'*

"Now while it was not uncommon to receive calls such as this from time to time, the remarkable thing was that in both cases, the children were newly born; something that I had never heard tell of before."

"Possessed babies?" coughed Gabriel.

A twisted scene of a demon-infested infant was playing out in his mind.

"That's pretty damn creepy, Marcus."

Natasha's eyes were wide with a mixture of fear and concern.

"It was the first case I had ever encountered," continued the bishop, clearing his throat with a barely detectable wince. "An abomination of Satan. The two children had spent their first month in a coma, only to regain consciousness in severely agitated states."

The bishop paused, taking hold of the professor's journal as if to open it, but refraining from doing so.

"Now if this were not already strange enough," he said, folding his hands over the weathered cover, "I would soon learn from the deacon that the babies had not only been born on the same day, but also at precisely the same hour."

The bishop sat back in his chair.

"Now although I thought it a great coincidence, I would most likely have left it at that, were it not for the fact that Professor Metrovich had overheard our conversation.

"'*Where exactly were they born?*' he asked, and I saw him take up a globe that was sitting on my desk.

"'*The boy, on an American military base in Taiwan,*' I repeated aloud, as I was given the information. '*The girl, in the village of La Quiaca, in Northern Argentina.*'

"The professor had then juggled the globe around until he had found Taiwan, and then proceeded to locate the village on the very opposite side of the globe.

"'*There could be more to this than mere coincidence,*' he said, and I will never forget the expression of concern that suddenly came upon him. I told the deacon I would speak with him shortly and hung up the phone.

"'*The military base is directly on the Tropic of Cancer. Up here,*' the professor said, pointing to the place on the globe. '*La Quiaca, is directly on the Tropic of Capricorn. Down here. And what is more, if you can see, they are exactly on opposite sides of the planet.*'

"I took the globe and looked for myself. I was amazed, for it was just as he said. The professor clearly knew something that I did not."

"And I was the little girl in Argentina," said Natasha timidly.

"Yes, my child, that was you," said the old bishop, smiling. "And the boy on the military base was you, Gabriel."

"I pretty much figured," said Gabriel, looking at Natasha and then back to the bishop. "So, what became of us?"

"Why we went out to get you!" said the bishop, smiling. "We brought both of you back to Rome, and Father Franco and I laboured for fourteen months exorcizing the demons that infested you."

"Demons?" asked Natasha, aghast. "There were more than one?"

"There were fourteen in total, my child," said the bishop rather plainly. "Seven in you, and seven in Gabriel. And as that particular ritual could only be conducted on the night of a full moon, it took us fourteen months to liberate the two of you. In the end we were successful, and miraculously, you only suffered minimal injuries."

"Injuries?" asked Natasha, leaning forward.

The old bishop nodded.

"Burn marks at the energy centres of your body," he explained. "These were the places where the demons were extracted."

Gabriel and Natasha turned to face each other in shock.

"Burn marks?" they exclaimed in unison.

Gabriel addressed the bishop with a frown.

"My father told me my scars came from someone who had abused me in the orphanage..."

Natasha was still looking at Gabriel.

"That's what they told me too..."

She reached over and pushed aside his hair. The scar on his forehead was in the exact same place as hers. Gabriel was confused until she moved aside her own bangs to show him. He had to bend close to see it in the firelight. The scar was barely recognizable, but it was nevertheless there.

"I've got them all over my body," he said, and then he turned back to the bishop, his frown deepening. "Why were we lied to?"

The bishop looked down at the table.

"I know that lying to you both was a sin but telling you the true story would have been extremely destructive. Knowing that you were mutilated as infants has been a cross you have both had to bear all your lives, my dear, dear children, but the truth..."

The old bishop's eyes became glassy with tears.

"We could not possibly have told you the truth."

Natasha fought back her tears as well.

"It's all right, Uncle," she said quietly. "You were right not to tell us. I always suspected that there was something more to the scars than I was told. When I was twelve, I learned about the seven Hindu chakra points, and I saw that all my scars aligned perfectly with them. It was not long after, that I found the one on the crown of my head."

"There's another one on our head?" asked Gabriel, searching through his messy hair with the tips of his fingers.

The bishop gave a single nod.

"That was from the last demon to be extracted," he said matter-of-factly. "He was by far the most tenacious."

"Lovely," said Gabriel. "Thanks so much for letting us know all these little details about our early childhood. Very nice."

The bishop only shrugged.

"Do not let it trouble you, my son," he said. "Let us continue with the tale."

Gabriel settled back into his chair, looking over at Natasha to find that she was already looking at him. She smiled and then turned to the bishop as he began to speak again.

"Is there something more that I should know about this coincidence?' I asked the professor. He had become very quiet since he had last spoken, as though he were lost in thought.

He continued to hold the globe between his two fingers, one upon each of the locations. At length he began to speak, and I was truly amazed by what he said.

"The professor told me of an obscure medieval artifact called the *Compostela Cube*. Unknown to but a handful of scholars, its story had grown to become a legend among certain monasteries in Northern Spain. The Cube was believed to be the true Holy Grail; a receptacle carrying the living blood of the Christ, which to the ancients was a metaphor for knowledge, or more specifically, *gnosis*."

"Gnosis?" asked Gabriel.

The bishop nodded.

"The secret alchemical knowledge of liberation and transmutation," he said. "A mystical, intuitive knowledge that can only be known when it is directly experienced, as opposed to the kind of knowledge that is gained through rational thought, or theoretical conjecture. It was said that within the Cube were stored the keys to the cosmos. There was also a prophecy, one that the professor found to be based on an ancient Egyptian creation myth."

"What myth is that?" asked Natasha.

"A rather obscure one, my child," replied the old bishop. "Originating from a pre-dynastic period. The myth tells the story of how the god Atum willingly sacrificed himself and let himself fall into the underworld so as to plant the *Seed Of Truth* for all mankind."

"Atum was the Egyptian god of completeness," said Natasha. "He was the embodiment of the Divine Androgyne, or the Alchemical Marriage; the merging of male and female forces. He was a hermaphrodite."

The bishop nodded.

"The myth goes on to say that from the seed that Atum planted sprung the Tree of Life. There are many such trees to be found in cultures around the world, but in our myth, the gods Osiris and Isis were said to have emerged from the tree in a state of earthly mortality."

"*Tep Zepi*," said Gabriel, remembering his Egyptology. "Also called *First Time*. The age of Osiris, when Egypt was believed to be ruled by gods in human form."

"Exactly," said the old bishop, gazing into the flames of the fire. "According to the myth, Osiris and Isis each represented one half of what had formerly been the god, Atum. In other words, his male and female aspects.

"They resided now in a dualistic world, where unity had been fractured into opposing states: Birth and death, high and low, light and darkness, good and evil, and so on."

"But what does the creation myth have to do with the Compostela Cube?" asked Gabriel. "And more importantly, with us?"

"Patience, my son," said the old bishop with a smile. "I will soon get to that. According to the myth, the Tree of Life also yielded a single piece of fruit, and this was symbolic of all the gnosis that had been lost after the fall of Atum; gnosis that Osiris and Isis would need to re-assimilate, if ever they were to resume their former state as the god Atum.

"Only then would the divided become whole again, and duality be transcended. After this, the underworld would slowly begin to be transformed into a heavenly place."

"Was the fruit an apple by any chance?" asked Gabriel, thinking of the images he had removed from the Cube.

"Indeed, it was," said the bishop. "The apple is present in many mythologies and cultures, and in almost every case, it symbolizes immortality, just as it does in this myth."

Natasha nodded and turned to Gabriel.

"Hercules travelled to the edge of the world to steal the apple of immortality," she said. "He took if from Hera, the Queen of Olympus. The apple's also identified with the Celtic god, Afallach, and his underworld home of Avalon. In folk tales and legends, the hero usually has to retrieve an apple to win the king's daughter and fulfill his destiny to be the one to save the world from evil. The apple's everywhere in mythology."

Gabriel feigned distrust.

"And how is it you know so much, anyway?"

Natasha was taken aback until she realized he was teasing her. She narrowed her eyes at him.

"Natasha is an accomplished theologian, my son," said the old bishop.

Gabriel was clearly impressed, but he continued with his playful scrutiny regardless.

"And from what Suora tells me, she's a professional ballerina as well. She's just full of surprises, isn't she."

Natasha rolled her eyes and looked away in a huff. Marcus sent Gabriel a playful wink.

"She could also inform you that in almost every story, discord soon arises with the appearance of the apple. Just like in the story of Adam and Eve."

Natasha smiled with satisfaction.

"Thank you, Uncle. Please go on."

The bishop looked at them for a moment before continuing.

"Similar to the Book of Genesis," he said, "our Egyptian myth sees the appearance of the devil. This is the god *Sutekh*, or *Set*, and in our myth, he comes in the form of a grotesque hermaphrodite beast; a desecration of Atum's divine androgynous state.

"Set was the embodiment of doubt and fear. He was both the creator and ruler of the underworld. He worked against Atum, filling Osiris and Isis with a fear of the knowledge that was housed in the apple. In short, Set drove the two further and further apart from each other, until they stood alone on opposite ends of the earth, lost in ignorance and misery."

The bishop paused for a moment to clear his throat.

"With each passing age, and to symbolize the cycle of birth and death, Osiris and Isis would emerge on precisely the same day, on opposite sides of the earth. Due to their longing for each other, they would be reunited, and made to traverse a great labyrinth. Within they would search for a stairway to the paradise they once knew, their only possession being a single apple to give them nourishment on their journey."

Natasha leaned forward, placing her hands on the table.

"And the professor believed that Gabriel and I are reincarnations of Osiris and Isis, and that the Compostela Cube is the equivalent of the apple spoken of in the myth."

The bishop looked over at her.

"To be incarnations of Isis and Osiris would be impossible, for they never existed. They are fictitious characters in a myth. The professor only saw an incredible similarity between your births, and the story told in the myth. The existence of a medieval prophecy surrounding the Compostela Cube only served to further his suspicions."

"Come on, Marcus. It's just a coincidence," said Gabriel, shaking his head. "How can we be expected to believe any of this nonsense? It's just a myth. It has no relevance to reality."

"A myth, Gabriel, is no small thing," said the bishop. "Housed within every myth is a wisdom incommunicable by any other means. Modern society has made the mistake of equating a myth with a lie, but nothing could be further from the truth. History, be it however well documented, will always be inaccurate, but the wisdom housed within myth will forever retain its meaning and purity."

The old bishop produced a crumpled handkerchief and proceeded to evacuate his nose in a series of brief, staccato rounds. He looked at Gabriel, considering his next words.

"Myths are not to be taken literally, my son," he said. "They are to be interpreted, so that the truth held within them can be understood and assimilated on a level much deeper than rational thought."

"Like the truth that's in the story of Narcissus," said Natasha, "and how he fell in love with his own reflection. Or of Icarus, flying too close to the sun because of his own hubris and pride. The fact that these events never actually happened doesn't change the fact that these traits can be found in every one of us."

"I suppose you've got a point," said Gabriel. "You could also go as far as to say that embodied in every mythical god, is a quality that can be found in the human psyche."

"Yes!" exclaimed the bishop. "And in its purest essence. Learn about any god, and you will only be learning about yourself, for the god is you. This was the great appeal of praying to a god whose qualities you desired. The patron saints of Christianity are no different."

"But what about the medieval prophecy you mentioned?" asked Natasha. "You've told us about the myth, but you haven't explained the prophecy."

"Right you are, my child," said the bishop with a wink. "The monks referred to it as *The Ascender's Prophecy*, and it stated that during the darkest hour, the Two would come again to release the gnosis that is locked in the Cube. In so doing, they would open a way for mankind to be awakened from its slumber of ignorance, and be initiated into the Cube's secrets."

Gabriel rolled his eyes and released a sigh of strained patience. The old bishop continued unfazed.

"Like Osiris and Isis, these two saviours would be born on the same day, on opposite sides of the world, and under the dominion of Lucifer. In other words, they would be demonically possessed when they were born."

"But that's an impossible coincidence," protested Gabriel.

"Yet an undeniable one!" replied the bishop firmly. "Even still, your father was not wholly convinced. It was not until he had witnessed the second half of the prophecy mirrored in reality that he finally accepted what he had always tried to explain as a freak concurrence of legend."

Natasha chewed her lip pensively.

"The hermaphrodite…"

The bishop nodded.

"The Ascender's Prophecy spoke of its coming too. It would be born on precisely the same day, and at the same hour of the coming of the Two. It would be a mockery of Atum and the sexual unity embodied in the divine androgyne. Unlike the Two, however, the beast would pass its entire life in a coma vigil, only to awaken and die on the first full moon before its thirty-third birthday. During this time, he would be possessed by the devil himself.

"The prophecy stated that once the body of the hermaphrodite had died, the Fourteen Emissaries of Lucifer would be released upon the world. They would come to command a mighty army and do everything in their power to prevent the Two from awakening humanity and unlocking the mysteries of the Cube."

Natasha leaned closer.

"These emissaries, Uncle. Are they the same fourteen demons that were removed from us when we were babies?"

"They were," said the bishop, shuddering at the memory of them.

"Fourteen," said Natasha, thinking. "There's something about that number. In another Egyptian myth, Set kills Osiris and divides his body into fourteen parts, spreading them throughout the lands."

Gabriel turned to the bishop.

"Who was it that made the Cube?"

"I can remember asking the very same question," replied the bishop. "*'What is this Compostela Cube?'* I asked, *'Why have I never heard mention of it before?'*

"'*Few have,*' the professor told me in response. *'It is believed to be a Christian relic, but I suspect that it is much older.*'

"He went on to tell me how he had first come to learn of the Cube, deep in the archives of a monastery in Toledo. Curiously enough, it was an Islamic text that he had found, a single Arabic manuscript dating back to the time of the Moorish occupation of Spain.

"The Cube of Knowledge, it explained, was the central subject of a treasure known to the Moors as *The Book of Khalifah,* a secret codex that had been passed from caliph to caliph over the centuries. Finding this book became an obsession for the professor, but in all his years of research, he was only able to gather a few scraps of information concerning it.

"From the manuscript he had found in Toledo, the professor learned that the Compostela Cube held mysterious runes, and that the Book of Khalifah contained the only record in existence of their translations. It was said that without these translations, the Cube's mysteries could never be unlocked. The manuscript stated that the Book and the Cube were linked, and that whoever possessed one, would be led to find the other."

"Who authored this book?" asked Natasha, fascinated.

The old bishop shook his head in bewilderment.

"It is in part an Arabic translation of an ancient Greek text that was long ago destroyed," he whispered. "One that related to an ancient Mesopotamian tablet. This tablet spoke of a *lost Cube,* said to contain a wisdom capable of emancipating man from the confines of mortality and matter."

The bishop looked at both of them in earnest.

"As well as giving detailed descriptions of the artifact," he continued, "the tablet also spoke of the Cube's possible location in the mountains of Northern Spain, and of its original resting place at the entrance of a mysterious labyrinth; a place where it would one day need to be returned in order that humanity might be made ready to receive its secret knowledge."

Gabriel was perplexed.

"Exactly how old is the Cube supposed to be?"

"The professor could not say with any certainty," said the bishop. "He suspected it to be pre-Egyptian, and perhaps even pre-Mesopotamian. The Book of Khalifah describes the

Cube as the most prized of all treasures and refers to it as the most ancient of artifacts.

"It was to the Moors, what the Holy Grail was to the Knights Templar, and the professor believed that the two were in fact one and the same thing. According to him, the Cube was the reason why the Moors invaded the Iberian Peninsula to begin with."

Gabriel pondered what the old bishop was telling him, nodding his head as he began to understand.

"Once the Moors had crossed over the Strait of Gibraltar, they made a beeline directly for the north coast of Spain. Historians have never been able to understand the need for their urgency. They cut their way through the Visigoths in less than a year."

"Theirs was a holy quest for knowledge," said the bishop, nodding. "Although it was not they, who in the end would recover the Cube."

"So who was it that found it?" asked Natasha.

"The manuscript states that a Catholic priest found it," said the bishop with a smile. "And that he found it while on the *Camino de Santiago de Compostela.*"

"And that's where the Cube gets its name," said Natasha. "I thought it might be named after the city."

"Can somebody please fill me in?" asked Gabriel. "What Camino?"

"The *Camino's* a Christian pilgrimage," explained Natasha. "It follows an ancient Celtic footpath that makes its way through the mountains of Northern Spain. It ends at a big cathedral in the city of Santiago de Compostela, the place where the remains of St. James are said to be kept."

"It begins in France," said Gabriel, nodding. "I've always heard it referred to as the *Chemin de St. Jacques.*"

Natasha nodded as well.

"There's an old legend that tells the story of how St. James' long-lost crypt was found on that trail. It says that a goat herder named Pelaio stumbled on it in the ninth century; that he heard angels singing while out in the mountains at night. He walked towards the music and saw thousands of stars raining down on the tomb. That's why they call it Compostela. It comes from the Latin *Campus Stellae,* or *Field of Stars.*"

"Exactly," said the old bishop. "But the Arabic manuscript told a tale far more intriguing than the popular legend."

The fire crackled in the hearth as the three of them huddled closer together at their table. Encased as they were, deep within that sprawling tomb, it seemed to them that the very walls were comprised of the dead. Even still, the wooden planks from the old scaffolds were thick and dry, and they burned well, shedding a much-welcomed heat, and reassuring them that they were very much alive and well.

Taking a sip from the cup before him, the old bishop straightened his black cassock and continued.

"In the year of our lord, eight hundred and sixty-five, almost fifty years after the tomb of St. James was claimed to have been discovered, the Arabic manuscript tells of a church expedition that went missing in the north of Spain.

"Its objective was to survey an ancient Celtic route that ran the entire length of the mountains, and to map any potential sites where strongholds might be built against the ever-advancing Moors. The leader of the expedition was an Asturian priest and cartographer by the name of Gutierrez de la Cruz.

"Hours before dawn, while deep in the mountain wilds, Gutierrez and his expedition were said to have been overtaken by a potent demonic force; one that came upon them at the bottom of a dark valley, on the shore of a fog enshrouded lake. The party, it is said, heard the tortured cries of two children coming from out on the lake, but the evil that accompanied these cries was such that all but Gutierrez fled into the night, never to be seen again.

"Gutierrez then mounted a raft and followed the cries until he had landed on a small island. There he was overcome by a deep slumber and witnessed the apparition of two angels in a dream. They had taken the form of a boy and a girl, and they appeared hovering over a gaping fissure at the centre of the island. From within this fissure there was said to have come great flames, and a chorus of wailing."

"A gateway to hell," said Gabriel, swallowing despite himself. "Nice dream."

The bishop looked down at the journal, passing his hands over its worn cover and remembering what he had read therein.

"The legend goes on to say that the angels then spoke to Gutierrez about the fissure, referring to it as *The Portal of Ahreimanius.*"

"Ahreimanius was a Zurvanite god," said Natasha, frowning. "A very evil one. He originated in the Sassanid Empire of Persia, around 400 BCE."

Gabriel locked eyes with Natasha and then turned to the bishop.

"But what about Gutierrez?" he asked. "How did he find the Cube?"

"The angels told him where it was," replied the old bishop with a shrug. "When Gutierrez awoke, he followed their directions, and arrived at a tomb. It was in this tomb that he found the legendary Cube, and it is here where the manuscript begins to take some unexpected turns. The tomb that Gutierrez supposedly found was said to have belonged to St. James the Just."

"The brother of Jesus Christ," said Natasha. "I can see the connection now. There were two St. James' in the bible. One was Jesus' famous apostle, but the other was James the Just. He was the biological brother of Jesus. The church has always tried to leave him in the shadows.

"Some historians believe that James the Just was the person Jesus chose to lead the church after his death. They claim that the Jewish high priests murdered him before he could take control."

"All right," said Gabriel. "I get how there were two St James', but so what? What does any of that have to do with the Cube? And why would the church make up a story that would put a lost tomb of St. James in the north of Spain to begin with? It's not like it was just around the corner from Jerusalem. It doesn't make sense."

"The church legend is a fabrication," said Natasha. "It states that after Herod beheaded St. James —the apostle, not the brother of Jesus— his body was put into an unmanned boat that made its way to the north of Spain under the guidance of angels. They say that a fisherman found the body at sea, and buried it in the mountains, where it stayed lost until Pelaio found it eight centuries later."

"It definitely sounds like they made it up," said Gabriel. "But what was the church's motive behind the fiction, and what's more, how could the Cube have been found with the body of James the Just? The Cube's medieval. I've got it right here in my pack. It's plain to see. A relic from the time of Christ could never have looked like that."

"Nevertheless," said the bishop, "the Cube is what Gutierrez is said to have found in the tomb of James the Just. The true motives behind the church's legend of St. James, and indeed the truth behind all of this, has yet to be revealed."

For a while, the three remained silent, with Gabriel and Natasha trying to digest everything they had learned thus far. There were so many questions, so many loose ends.

"Uncle Marcus," said Natasha at length. "You said the professor had been very concerned with the similarities between the Egyptian myth and the births of Gabriel and I.

Even if all this is true, and we're somehow connected to the artifact, why would the professor need to be so concerned?"

The bishop looked up at Natasha, his silvery brow furrowed.

"Because of what the Ascender's Prophecy relates, my child," he said slowly.

"What do you mean?" asked Gabriel, bending closer.

"It states that the coming of the Two will be marked by a great, world-altering cataclysm. One that will mark the end of an aeon and the beginning of a new epoch."

"A metaphorical cataclysm is what you mean to say, right?" said Gabriel. "A symbolic destruction of the earth."

"The professor believed that it would be very real, my son," said the bishop, "and that it would take place on the winter solstice of the very year that we now find ourselves in."

"But that whole doomsday thing belonged to the Mayan calendar," said Gabriel. "That winter solstice came and went, remember? Nothing happened."

The old bishop only shrugged.

"The myth tells of how Osiris and Isis attempted to escape from the Great Labyrinth during this cataclysm and save the world from destruction."

"But the winter solstice is less than two weeks away," said Natasha. "It's on the twenty-first of December."

"The day we both turn thirty-three," said Gabriel. "What exactly is going on here?"

"I have no idea," said Natasha, a fear coming over her, "but thirty-three seems to be an important age in this prophecy."

She turned to the bishop.

"The hermaphrodite was one full moon away from being thirty-three when he died."

"Indeed, he was," said the bishop slowly. "Jesus was also thirty-three when he was crucified."

Gabriel shook his head and frowned.

"Genetically speaking, thirty-three is also the age when the human body reaches its full development. After that, our DNA begins to develop errors during mitosis."

The old bishop looked down at the tattered journal, his face growing dark.

"The Ascender's Prophecy admonished that if the corpse of the hermaphrodite were taken to the portal before the day of its thirty-third birthday, and buried there in a special ceremony, the Fourteen Emissaries would not be able to enter onto the earth-sphere, and humanity's transition out of the fifth age would be made less catastrophic. This was what both of your fathers died trying to do. They failed."

Gabriel pushed back his messy hair and gazed into the flames of the hearth.

"So, what you're saying is their deaths were no accident."

"It would appear not," said the bishop. "Something caused their plane to crash, and I believe that it was a supernatural force that did it; a demonic force to be precise."

Natasha looked at Marcus, her big eyes filled with fear. She had felt that same demonic force in her workshop just the other day.

"What did the myth say would happen if Osiris and Isis failed to find their way out of the labyrinth?"

The old bishop cringed at her question, and just then the catacombs seemed to close in around them. A frigid draft had suddenly entered into the chamber. It sent chills through them.

"The myth spoke of perpetual night," he said solemnly. "It spoke of a *Great Dying*, and the loss of all hope."

It was at that moment that Shackleton rose from his place before the fire. He approached the door with stealth, his nose raised and sniffing, and the hair on his back on end. He turned and focused an intense look upon Natasha, just as Fra was opening an eye and cocking his head to listen.

"Someone is coming," he whispered. "I think they have found us."

CHAPTER 23

Amsterdam, The Netherlands.

Christian awoke with a start, his heart racing from the remnants of a nightmare. Following the steering committee meeting, he had retired to his room to drink a bottle of wine. He had fallen asleep soon after and dreamed of the four hooded figures. He could still hear his father's voice echoing in his mind.

"Heed the Zurvanites! Heed them! Heed them well!"

Christian ran his hands over his face. He was drenched in sweat. The telephone rang.

"Christian," came the prince's dry voice. "Proceed to the Vanderhoff suite immediately."

"Bloody Christ," groaned Christian. "I'm taking a nap."

Prince Vladimir coughed angrily.

"Go there at once!" he hissed. "The Nautonnier has summoned you!"

Christian heard the line go dead.

The Vanderhoff suite was located in the same wing as Christian's penthouse, and it was not long before he found himself stumbling there, a tumbler of wine in one hand, and a lit cigarette in the other. He recalled what his uncle had told him of the Nautonnier earlier that day.

"He is a figurehead," the prince had said, his voice tinged with hatred for the old man. "He is a remnant of old traditions and outdated superstitions. In all my life I have never seen him do anything of any importance. Your father feared him. Why, I do not know."

Christian thought back to the first time he had seen the Nautonnier. It had been at his father's deathbed, and a sinister power had radiated from the man, one that he could still feel. The Nautonnier's sudden appearance on the lawn earlier that day had only increased Christian's trepidation. The old man had been standing directly where the hooded figures had appeared, as though he and they were somehow connected.

Christian drained his glass and tossed it away. If his father had feared the Nautonnier, it must have been for a good reason. He made his way along the plush corridor, feeling the tyrannical presence of his father more poignantly than ever now. It settled around him like a cold fog, pressing down on him, suffocating him.

All power is based in fear. Fear must be maintained at all costs.

Christian arrived at a pair of towering doors, only to see them open of their own accord. He squinted into the darkness. The light from the hallway was doing nothing to illuminate the room within.

"Come in, Christian," said a brittle voice, and in that moment, Christian was filled with a deep and inexplicable dread.

Every instinct was telling him to flee but something held him fast.

"Fear me not, boy," came the voice again. "I am no stranger. Please be so kind as to close the door behind you. Your eyes will soon grow accustomed to the darkness."

Christian stepped forward and did as he was told, shutting the door and waiting for his eyes to adjust. It was not long before an ancient man materialized before him. He was seated at a small table, the light of a dim candle illuminating his strange and unsettling features. He sat regally, his brittle white hair as thin as cobwebs, and growing from a pasty grey head that appeared to be moulting.

With the exception of his long, hooked nose, the Nautonnier's bone structure was almost reptilian. He had no eyebrows or facial hair of any kind, and his tripe-coloured skin was like scar tissue, thin, and brittle as old parchment. He reminded Christian of a pagan oracle; powerful and merciless, and almost skeletal. The hard line that was the Nautonnier's mouth transformed into a slit when he opened it to speak.

"I have summoned you here so that you might fulfill the final part of your inheritance," said the Nautonnier. "In order to do this, you must be made aware of certain facts that have been kept from you. After this, you must make a special pledge."

"A pledge?" asked Christian, arriving at the table. "What are you talking about?"

"Sit down, boy."

Christian obeyed, lowering himself slowly into a chair.

"You are of an ancient linage, Christian," said the Nautonnier, his voice like dry leaves. "Your family has always held power over others. It is no coincidence that things have been this way. Many attempts have been made to usurp your family's control, but there has always been a force that has kept it intact."

"Yes," said Christian. "It's called ruthlessness."

The old man smiled slowly, and it seemed to Christian that his skin could be heard cracking as he did so.

"Yes," he replied. "And the driving impetus behind this ruthlessness has always been granted from below."

Christian cocked an eyebrow.

"What are you talking about?"

"I am speaking of Ahreimanius," said the Nautonnier. "The Dark Lord of Matter. The highest servant of Lucifer."

Christian stared into the Nautonnier's reptilian eyes and then began to rise from his chair.

"I'm leaving."

"Sit down!" came a sudden hiss, but it had not been the Nautonnier who had uttered it.

Christian felt something invisible push him back into his chair. His head swelled dizzily. His father was present. He denied it.

"You need not be fettered as you are, boy," continued the Nautonnier, more urgently now. "Forfeit your will to that of the master's and you will be more powerful than any man alive."

"You will assume your responsibilities!" hissed the voice.

Christian scanned the shadows. There was no denying it. The voice was clearly that of his father's. His mind reeled. His father was dead. They had buried him.

"What the hell's going on?"

The Nautonnier smiled dryly, holding up a wrinkled hand in a gesture of peace.

"I am a fair man, Christian," he said. "I will answer any questions you might have. When you are satisfied, you may proceed with the pledge, or you may choose to abstain from making it. Is this acceptable?"

Christian could feel the hold on him lessen in intensity and he took the opportunity to reposition himself in his chair. Whatever it was that was happening, he would have to play along. The man before him was obviously his superior. His father had feared him. He was beginning to understand why.

"What kind of a title is Nautonnier?" he asked. "What makes you so important?"

The old man nodded.

"Nautonnier is the title given to the leader of our ancient society. It means *The Great Navigator*. It is a lifetime position, and one that has been held by very important personages throughout the ages. It is a position that is held until it is taken away, for there can only be one Nautonnier."

"And who is Ahreimanius?"

The old man gazed into the flickering candle, his eyes betraying a deep fear.

"He is the greatest demon of the Luciferic Order. He is a son of Lucifer and was first called Ahreimanius by the followers of the ancient prophet Zoroaster. He is his father's arm and fist on the earth-sphere. Ahreimanius is merciless and terrible."

"And why can't Lucifer be terrible himself? Why does he need Ahreimanius?"

"Lucifer cannot access the earth-sphere in his bodily form. He can exist here only in spirit. For this reason, Lucifer bestows great power onto Ahreimanius, along with all the souls who are loyal to him. We are such souls, you and I."

Christian scanned the shadowy room. All the shutters and drapes had been drawn tight. Not a sliver of light could be seen anywhere.

"And what is there to gain by serving Ahreimanius?"

"By serving Ahreimanius, we serve ourselves," said the old man. "In exchange for our loyal acts we receive power over others, and great dominion over the matter that he is the master of. Everything that you have in this life, Christian, you owe to Ahreimanius."

Christian was not a spiritual person, yet he could distinctly feel a dark and sinister presence around him. He was certain he must be imagining things. The doses of his medications required altering. He would call his psychiatrist when he was done.

"Your soul is much older than you realize, Christian," continued the Nautonnier.

"What do you mean?" he asked, his fear and confusion mounting. "What are you talking about?"

"The soul of every being that inhabits this planet is ancient, to be sure, but whereas most of these souls are lowly, and of no importance, your soul has been in league with Lucifer since the time of the Great Fall. You are a prince among the fallen angels, Christian. It has always been so, and just as in each of your many previous life incarnations, the time has come when you must renew your pledge to the master once again."

Christian locked eyes with the Nautonnier. As irrational and superstitious as it seemed, he sensed that this was no trivial request.

"Have you any more questions?"

Christian remained silent in his confusion.

"Very well," said the Nautonnier slowly. "There will be other opportunities for you to learn more. As I promised, I shall now permit you to decide how you wish to proceed."

"I choose to sleep on it," muttered Christian, rising slowly from his chair. "I'll get back to you after the conference."

The Nautonnier gave a dry chuckle.

"Oh no, Christian," he said. "I made no mention of giving you time to deliberate. That is not an option. You will decide now. You are free to take any decision you choose but know this: Should you decide to abandon Ahreimanius, your special place at his table will naturally be taken from you. You are free to decide, but you must decide now and forever. Be sure not to err. Ahreimanius knows not the meaning of forgiveness."

Christian could feel the psychic tentacles of his father worming into him again.

All power is based in fear. Fear must be maintained at all costs.

"Follow your heart, Christian," whispered the Nautonnier. "What is it telling you to do? You are free to decide."

Hearing the old man speak had a great effect on Christian. He suddenly felt as though it were still not too late. A sense of urgency filled him. Around him the room had begun to warp and twist.

"What do you want me to do?" he whispered; his eyes wide.

"Merely to sign a contract," said the old man. "It is but a symbol of allegiance to Ahreimanius. A formality. It states that you align yourself with him and offer up to him all that you possess."

The Nautonnier placed a large book on the table and opened it. It was ancient and brittle, and Christian could see that it was a ledger of sorts; a record of all who had signed their souls into the service of Ahreimanius and Lucifer.

The Nautonnier took Christian's hand and pricked his thumb, filling the quill of a pen with the blood that emerged. He laid the pen next to the open book.

"You may sign it here," he said, his crooked finger pointing to a spot at the bottom of the page.

Christian took up the pen and watched his hand move the quill to the age-old parchment. A mark was made, and knowing that it was done, he quickly finished the stroke.

Christian felt a dizzying surge of dark power flood into him just then, and he shuddered unexpectedly. Something was awakening in him; something that should never have been disturbed. He looked up to see that the Nautonnier was watching him intently now, an expression of cold malice spreading across his repugnant features.

"It is done," he hissed, blowing out the candle.

"Wait a minute," said Christian, but the room plunged into darkness.

A sudden realization flooded into him.

"What have I done? What have you made me do?"

"The way to Ahreimanius has been opened," came his father's hiss. *"Behold the newborn son of Lucifer!"*

Christian staggered through the darkness, finding the door to the suite and jerking it open. The light from the hall filled the room, but the Nautonnier was nowhere to be seen.

"What's happening to me?" he gasped, squinting into the shadows, his eyes wide with panic.

In the corner of the room, he could see the shapes of four hooded figures, their bodies jerking violently from side to side, and coming in and out of existence.

"The Cube!" they hissed in unison. *"The Cube!"*

"No!" gasped Christian.

His fists were clenched, and his heart was racing.

"This is impossible!"

CHAPTER 24

Rome, Italy.

"We must move quickly!" whispered the bishop.

Gabriel tiptoed to the entrance and poked his head out into the cold, dark passage. He heard footsteps and then saw a light flash suddenly in the gloom. Within seconds, two figures had become visible. One of them was holding a lantern, but both were holding guns. They were clearly Nasrallah's men.

Gabriel darted back into the chapel. His intention was to wake up Fra and Suora, but he found them both on their feet. He motioned Natasha and the bishop to draw near.

"Nasrallah's men are just up the tunnel," he whispered. "I don't know how they got here. We should have seen them pass."

"They have come from above," said the bishop.

"But that's impossible. The only way they could have found us would be through the nunnery tunnel."

The bishop took hold of Gabriel's shoulder and passed him his father's journal. He had sealed it in an envelope. He drew Natasha nearer as well and spoke to them both.

"There are dark forces at work here," he whispered urgently. "Their knowledge of where the Cube is at any given moment is directly related to the amount of spiritual separation that exists between the two of you."

"What's that supposed to mean?" asked Gabriel, frowning.

"Listen carefully, my son," said the bishop. "When you retrieved the Cube without Natasha being present, it would appear that you inadvertently directed certain dark forces to her. These forces have been with her ever since, and according to the professor, they will continue to follow Natasha until you and she are able to fully merge."

"Merge?" whispered Gabriel urgently. "This is no time for superstitious nonsense, Marcus! The bad guys are just down the hall. What are you talking about?"

"The answers are in the book, my son. Until you resolve these problems, you will find that the enemy will always have a general idea of where you are."

Gabriel and Natasha looked at each other and then back to the bishop. He was gazing up at the scaffolding now. In the light of the fire it could be seen rising up the frescoed wall and ending at the ceiling. There was an old ladder strapped to its side.

"If memory serves me correctly, there is a trap door up there," he said, pointing. "I believe the scaffold is hiding it. It will lead to the next upper level. Go now. You must still find your way out of the catacombs. That will be no easy task."

"But, Uncle," said Natasha, her eyes welling. "The three of you could never make it up that scaffold..."

The old bishop noted her tears and reached into his vestments for his handkerchief.

"We will not be going with you, sweet girl," he said gently.

Familiar with the bishop's grubby napkins, Gabriel stuffed a clean tissue into Natasha's hand before the bishop could offer up his own. Being no stranger to her uncle's hankies, she shot Gabriel a teary-eyed look of thanks.

"What do you mean?" she sobbed.

The bishop pocketed his crumpled rag absently.

"The three of us will stay here and hide, my child."

Gabriel's frown deepened.

"They'll find you and kill you all."

"That is not certain, my son," smiled the bishop. "There are spirits of God here who are helping us. Have faith, and fear not for us."

"But Uncle—" pleaded Natasha.

"Go!" said Marcus, a rarely seen anger flaring up in his eyes. "There is more at stake here than you can possibly imagine, and there is no time!"

To everyone's surprise, Shackleton took to the ladder in a single leap, making his way to the top swiftly and without pause. From below the others watched him disappear onto the top platform, only to see him poke his head out and look down at them.

"Who would believe a dog could do that..." whispered Gabriel, shaking his head in amazement.

In a moment he had taken up both of their packs and was guiding Natasha to the scaffolding. She resisted at first, but Gabriel's touch seemed to reassure her.

The timbers were old but strong, and at the top they found the trapdoor the bishop had spoken of. It was barely big enough to squeeze through, but as Gabriel shined his light into it, he could see that it opened into a tunnel above. Shackleton had already passed into it. Gabriel could see him in the shadows, sniffing the air and looking around.

"I'll go first," he said, stuffing the packs up and hoisting himself through.

He held a hand down for Natasha to take.

"Come on," he whispered. "There's no time."

Natasha was looking over the edge of the scaffolding. She could see the bishop helping Suora into the tiny opening at the base of the altar. They would be hiding in the room that was filled with bones. Natasha saw him look up at her.

"Go!" he mouthed, motioning at her with his hands.

Natasha saw him smile reassuringly, and then disappear into the opening.

"I'll see you soon, Uncle," she whispered, and just then, Nasrallah's men burst into the chapel.

Natasha saw them make for the hearth. These were not the uniformed figures she had seen earlier in the courtyard. They were plainly dressed men and would have appeared to be tourists were it not for the guns in their hands.

Gabriel poked his head down and was going to say something, but Natasha silenced him. She gave him her hands and let him pull her up.

* * * * * *

"Radio Bahadur," said one of the mercenaries in Arabic. "Search every corner of this place. They were just here. They could not have gone far."

Bahadur arrived moments later to find most of his men in the chapel. They were all in plain clothes now, two of them emerging from behind the altar. They had found a backpack. They approached him with scowling faces.

"They were sleeping in that chamber, sir," said one of them, handing him the pack. "The room is full of bones, but there is a blanket spread out on the floor."

Bahadur took the pack from the mercenary and reached inside. He brought out a package, unwrapping it to find a large piece of cake dripping with honey. He smelled it and took a huge bite.

"Has this space been fully searched?" he said, chewing.

"Yes, sir," replied the soldier. "We have found nothing here but the traces they left behind. They must have been eating when they became alerted to our presence. There is still soup in the pot."

"Soup?" repeated Bahadur, raising an eyebrow in the direction of the hearth.

He had not received a morsel of food in more than twenty-four hours and his tortured body was in desperate need of nourishment.

"Continue with the search as planned," he said. "They are obviously not here. Go! The sooner this is over the better."

Within moments his men had vanished, leaving Bahadur alone before the crackling hearth. He sat himself down in one of the chairs, wincing in pain as he reached for the pot. It rested on an iron grating with hot embers still burning beneath it.

Beside the pot he found a slice of bread laden with what appeared to be slices of roasted pork. It had been Gabriel's, and only a single bite had been taken from it.

"Lentils," he said, blowing on a spoonful of soup. "And roasted swine…"

He paused for a moment, thinking.

"A sin to eat, but Allah will understand."

CHAPTER 25

By the time Gabriel had lifted Natasha through the trapdoor, Shackleton was nowhere to be seen. Gabriel shone his light down the passage in one direction and Natasha in the other. There was no sign of the dog anywhere.

"Shackleton!" whispered Natasha. "Shackleton!"

Gabriel turned to face her.

"He knows what he's doing," he said quietly. "We've got to keep moving. This place is crawling with Nasrallah's men."

"But which way do we go?"

Gabriel pulled out his compass.

"The main entrance is at the southern end of the necropolis."

"But we're still three levels beneath it," said Natasha.

"Good point. Let's just look for a way up then. Any preference in direction?"

Natasha pointed into the shadows.

"That way."

"West. OK. I'll always trust a woman's intuition. Let's go."

"I hope that Shackleton has the same intuition as me," said Natasha, but Gabriel had already moved off.

The tunnel they found themselves in was identical to the others. To their right and left were the countless loculi with their sepia-coloured bones. Unlike the tunnels of the lower level however, these wound and split, bringing them to many forks and junctures along the way. They stopped at every one, each time Gabriel asking Natasha for her first intuitive direction.

"Left," she would say after a moment's pause, or "Straight through," or "Left," "Right,".

They walked like this for what seemed hours, feeling themselves more and more entangled in the knotted passageways. With each step, Natasha felt her hopes fading. She no longer felt the pressing danger of those who pursued them. Everything had been overshadowed by a desperate need to escape this place; to simply get out.

Natasha felt as if the dead were calling to her, and with every step she feared more and more that they would never leave this place alive.

"Is it true that some people have entered these catacombs and never found their way out again?"

She could see Gabriel up ahead, his dark form silhouetted by his roaming flashlight. He stopped and turned to face her, suddenly aware of how frightened she was. He pushed a hand through his hair.

"Come on," he said gently. "You're lagging."

Natasha came closer and Gabriel took her hands into his. In the darkness he could feel them cold and trembling.

"Everything's going to be fine," he said.

Natasha forgot her misgivings and fell into his arms.

"I'm scared, Gabriel," she said amid shivers.

"Now listen to me," he replied softly. "I've been in much worse places than this. Really, I have. I'm not worried. Believe me. We're going to get out of here."

Natasha chewed her lip.

"But what about Uncle Marcus, and Suora and Fra?"

Her eyes were wide now, staring out into the darkness that loomed around them.

"And where's Shackleton?"

Gabriel said nothing. He could already feel her calming down as the warmth spread between them. He was feeling something he had never experienced before. With their bodies pressed together, the inner void that had plagued him felt suddenly full.

Gabriel pushed her gently away but kept hold of her arms. Women like her were incapable of accepting the kind of love he had to give. It was a lesson he had learned the hard way many times. The objective here was simply to cheer her up a little. That was all.

"Never lose sight of the facts," he said.

Her scent was intoxicating.

"Marcus knows these catacombs well, and he's been full of surprises up to now."

He moved a lock of hair out of her eyes.

"You might have all your woman's intuition," he added, frowning at an unexpected surge of affection in him, "but I've got my gut, and it's telling me we'll be seeing them again really soon."

Gabriel was having a considerable effect on Natasha. In the few minutes they had been together, almost all her fear and coldness had vanished. As surprising as it was, she could not recall having ever felt safer than she did right now, lost as they were in that dark and dreadful place. She swallowed slowly and collected herself, stepping back and wiping away her tears.

"You have a way with ladies, Gabriel Parker," she said, giving him a smile that was suspicious and timid all at the same time.

Gabriel was going to say something, but she reached up and put a hand over his mouth. She could see a flickering light in the darkness behind him, not fifty paces away.

"Somebody's coming," she whispered.

Gabriel took hold of her hand and pulled her back into the shadows.

"Don't even breathe," he whispered severely, poking his head out into the tunnel.

He could see the light clearly now but was surprised to learn that it did not come from a flashlight. It appeared to be the light of a lantern, or several lanterns. It was illuminating a large area of the tunnel. Within moments the patter of many feet was echoing around them. A voice spoke out in an Italian accent.

"Now, please, ladies and gentlemen. We will continue to follow him, but keep together. We do not want anyone else getting lost."

Gabriel turned to Natasha.

"Did you just hear that?"

Natasha had a smile from ear to ear.

"Let's stay here," said Gabriel. "We've got to be absolutely sure."

Gabriel poked his head out again to see a group of a few dozen tourists behind their guide. Directly before the man was a handsome brown hunting dog, urging them all to follow him.

"Shackleton!" shouted Gabriel, jumping into the passage. "Come here, boy!"

Natasha burst from her hiding place just in time to receive the dog into her arms. He had come bounding down the passage like a horse at play, slowing only just before arriving, and gently finding his way into Natasha's embrace.

"Oh, Shackleton!" she said. "What would we do without you?"

* * * * * *

The setting sun was blinding as they emerged from the necropolis, and a relief flooded into them that could only be described as euphoric.

"What a beautiful evening," said Natasha, taking in a deep breath of the fragrant air.

Around them Rome bustled in its familiar way, oblivious to the damp graves and catacombs that lay underfoot. Shackleton let sound a deep bark.

"What is it, Shackleton?" asked Natasha, bending down.

"He's trying to tell us something," said Gabriel, squatting next to Natasha. "What is it, boy?"

As if in response to Gabriel's question, Shackleton raised a paw and laid it on Natasha's bent knee, nuzzling his head into her lap.

"Shackleton!" she said laughing. "What are you trying to tell us?"

The dog answered her question with a happy bark and then bounded off suddenly.

"Shackleton!" cried Natasha. "Come back!"

They stood up to see him trot past a group of tourists and disappear into the crowds. Natasha looked at Gabriel in distress.

"Now don't start worrying about him again," he said, holding out his hands. "I've got a hunch that dog knows more about what's going on than we do."

"But where's he going?" she asked, pouting.

"I haven't a clue," said Gabriel. "But if I'm sure of one thing, it's that we'll be seeing him again, and probably when we need him the most."

CHAPTER 26

Amsterdam, The Netherlands.

"Ladies and Gentlemen, I would like to introduce the president and owner of AuraChip Industries, esteemed member of the Vanderhoff group since nineteen eighty-four, Dr. John B. Middleton."

It was early evening, and the conference was concluding its second day. The keynote speaker stepped onto a podium in the hotel's main banquet hall amid a full round of applause. Before him were the world's elite, more than a hundred and twenty strong. They sat at large round tables, arrayed with the finest china, and lit by the warm light of massive chandeliers.

"Thank you," he said, waiting for the applause to subside. "It seems like only yesterday I was up here boring you all with the tiring details about radio frequency identification microchips, and their many biometric potentials. I can recall we were just about to have dinner, and that's probably why none of you left the room."

Laughter spread through the hall.

"You'll be happy to know I'm going to skip past all the technical stuff this time and go straight into what we at AuraChip have accomplished over this last year. Although our outlook is quite extensive, it can all be summed up in two words: Human Implantation."

He was forced to pause until the applause died down.

"Out of the veritable cornucopia of cutting-edge biometric technology, human R.F.I.D. implantation promises to be the ultimate game changer. Over and above the many ways it will improve health, lifestyle, and security, perhaps the most powerful will be in social guidance, and its ability to rein in outlaws, terrorists, and anyone who refuses to adhere to societal norms."

Another round of applause sounded. Population control was one of the Vanderhoff Group's primary objectives, and the group was delighted with what they were hearing.

"The moment laws are not followed, AuraChips will simply be deactivated, leaving deviants trackable, and without resources. In a world where all your money is on your AuraChip, and cash does not exist, what will a deviant do if he's offline?"

"He'll clean up his act and get *in*line, God damn it!" exclaimed an old American man at a nearby table.

His comment was met with a healthy round of applause.

"Yes, I'm afraid he'll have no choice but to shape up and become the kind of good citizen he was always capable of being," said the speaker. "Unless of course he wants to live like a caveman."

The laughter continued.

Christian took the opportunity to rise from his table and leave the hall. Over his shoulder he could still hear the speaker.

"Now the world at large is still unaware of our plans for the AuraChip, and this leaves us with a tremendously exciting, and extremely lucrative opportunity to be the ones to implement this new technology across a full spectrum of applications. What I'd like to go over now is a detailed plan of action that—"

Christian closed the door behind him. Any interest he might have had in the conference had by now been replaced by a cold contempt for all those attending.

"Maggots and parasites," he muttered bitterly. "Putting on airs of helping humanity when all they want to do is subjugate it. If they openly admitted to what they were doing, I could respect them…"

Ever since the proceedings with the Nautonnier that afternoon, Christian had been consumed with anger and hatred. Although intoxicating, these nefarious emotions also frightened him. They seemed to come from a dark personality within him, a previously dormant shadow-self that had been awakened when he had signed the ledger.

Christian began to tremble with rage the more he thought of it. The Nautonnier had tricked him into taking that pledge. He would make the old man pay dearly for what he had done.

I'll murder that son of a whore with my own hands…

As he marched towards the main lobby, Christian could not help but flinch when he saw his reflection in a passing mirror. It jerked him back into reality, checking his wrath almost immediately. He had never been a saint, this was true, but in his eyes he had just seen a cold-blooded killer.

He stopped in his tracks and walked back to the mirror, looking at his reflection with deep concern. For a fraction of a second, he could have sworn that his eyes were not his own, but rather those of a reptile. He produced his phone on an impulse.

"This is Christian Antov," he said. "I need to speak with Doctor Bennington immediately."

There was a pause as he listened.

"It does not concern me that he's on holiday in Paris. He will drop whatever he is doing and call me at once!"

CHAPTER 27

Rome, Italy.

Gabriel could not help thinking he was in a photo shoot for Architectural Digest. The minimalist pomp of the five-star suite was completely at odds with his tastes. Despite having managed to amass a considerable fortune retrieving lost treasures over the years, Gabriel had never been taken by the luxuries such wealth offered. With the exception of his love for Italian motorcycles, German cars, and American gadgets, his tastes had remained simple and down to earth.

In almost every case, Gabriel preferred the clay goblet to the golden chalice, and if he had brought Natasha to this hotel, it was only because he wanted to be sure that she would be as comfortable as possible. She was currently showering in the adjoining suite, the door that linked their rooms kept open on her insistence.

"I hope you don't mind," she had said timidly, "but Uncle Marcus said that those men will always have a general idea of where we are. And then there are those dark forces that he said were following me... I'd feel safer knowing you're close by."

Gabriel peered into her room uncomfortably. Over the sound of the shower, he could hear her singing an Italian pop song. He shook his head incredulously.

How can a nation that spawned the likes of Puccini possibly produce a song that bad?

He called the bishop's phone again. When the voicemail sounded, he decided to leave a message.

"Marcus," he said. "I hope you get this. Natasha and I are out of the catacombs and checked into a hotel here in Rome."

He paced around the room as he spoke, not knowing what to do with himself.

"Something's come up. It turns out the informant who gave us the location of the Cube was Amir's first cousin, a guy named Bahadur. Nasrallah suspects he had something to do with the robbery and he's holding their family hostage."

Gabriel moved to the enormous bed, looking down at its oversized pillows and sterile coverings.

How's anyone supposed to get comfortable in a place like this?

He reached down and pulled away the silken cover.

"Before we do anything about the Cube, I've got to get Amir's family out of there. I'm responsible for all this. Natasha's insisted on coming with me. We'll be flying to Gibraltar tomorrow, and then heading to Morocco from there. Call me the minute you get this. We need to know you guys are safe."

Gabriel pocketed the phone and laid back onto the bed's many cushions, his arms behind his head. He could still feel the grit from the catacombs in his hair and felt far too dirty to be lying where he was. He got up almost immediately, looking around the suite and feeling a growing anxiety for the three dear seniors. The fact that he had intentionally left them behind was proving difficult to bear, especially given the luxurious surroundings.

"We had no choice," he muttered to himself. "They'll be fine. Everything will be fine."

Gabriel paced aimlessly. He had promised Natasha that he would wait until she finished showering before doing so himself. He moved to a little glass table by the window and pulled up a chair. His battered old duffel bag was on the settee beside him, and as he took hold of it he noticed that it had already soiled the cream coloured upholstery with rusty catacomb dirt.

"Oh, man," he sighed, moving it onto his lap. "So much for the damage deposit."

He reached into it, carefully removing the Cube. There was something about the artifact that drove him to hold it, something that made him feel as though it needed his attention. It was as though it were somehow alive.

Removing it from its container, Gabriel was instantly made aware of its strange characteristics, and once again found himself unable to pinpoint exactly what it was. He had seen countless artifacts over his career, but there was something different about this one. Gabriel looked up suddenly. The shower had stopped.

"I'm almost finished," chimed Natasha, and another surge of affection filled Gabriel's heart.

Don't go there, buddy. She's not for you.

It was at that moment that he noticed something very peculiar. A glimmer of light had caught his eye, one that appeared to have originated from the Cube. He glanced up to the ceiling, expecting to find a recessed light that might have reflected in its gold leaf, but there was nothing there. He looked around the room and found no lamp that could have produced such a reflection.

"Do you see how quickly I shower?" came Natasha's voice, pulling him from his thoughts as she appeared at the threshold. "I'm just like a man that way."

She was wrapped in a thick white towel and in the act of brushing her liquescent hair. Gabriel was captivated once again. It took him a few seconds to register that her happy expression had changed into one of wonder.

"So that's the artifact then…" she whispered, stepping into the room and pointing to the Cube in his hands. "What makes it glow like that?"

Gabriel looked down and was unable to believe his eyes. There was a shimmering blue light emerging from the relic's surface. He jumped to his feet, dropping the Cube onto a chair and instinctively moving away.

"What the hell is that?" he said, shielding Natasha as though it might explode. "Medieval artifacts aren't supposed to glow…"

As one, they inched closer to the relic, intrigued by the magical quality of its light. Gabriel was perplexed. He had examined the piece on several occasions and had been certain of its authenticity. In a split second all that had changed.

"This is clearly some kind of hoax…" he said, moving to squat before it.

Natasha kneeled next to him.

"The light seems to be leaking through cracks at the edges of the parchment," she said, picking up the artifact and coming up close to Gabriel so that he might study it too. "Do you see what I mean? Right here, where the vellum meets the framework."

"It looks like there's another layer…" he said, intoxicated by the smell of soap on her skin.

"Another layer?" she asked, turning to look at him. "What do you mean?"

Gabriel felt himself falling into the depths of her big brown eyes. He was suddenly oblivious of the artifact. It was taking all his will to stop himself from kissing her.

"It used to have a crudely painted outer shell…" he muttered dizzily. "I removed it back at the monastery. I kept the pieces if you'd like to see them…"

Natasha was as transfixed as he was. Her vision seemed veiled in mist as she gazed back at him. Her reply came in a soft whisper.

"Are you saying this artifact had an outer layer?"

Gabriel nodded slowly in response.

"Why didn't you tell me…?"

"I was going to…"

"You were…?"

Gabriel nodded again, his eyes drinking in her features.

"I must have forgotten…"

Natasha glanced down at his lips.

"Well, don't let it happen again."

Gabriel's gaze deepened still, and Natasha felt herself being drawn into a vortex of sorts.

"Because if the Cube had one layer…" she managed to say, "It could easily have another…"

"I think it does…"

"I think it does too…"

It was only then that Natasha began to break from the spell. She had dedicated her life to artifact restoration, and here was the most mysterious artifact she had ever encountered, potentially ready to reveal another layer of itself. The realization filled her with a flood of urgency, and in a split second her eyes were alight with excitement.

She sprang to her feet with the Cube in hand.

"This is incredible!" she cried. "Where are the pieces you removed?"

Gabriel blinked up at her and rose with a groan. He pointed a thumb at his tattered pack.

"Go crazy," he said, a little annoyed for having let himself get caught up in her like that. "But don't be too excited. My guess is you're going to find a couple of nine-volt batteries in that thing."

"We can't be certain until we've studied it," she said, rummaging through his bag.

She produced the parchments and glanced up in time to see him walking away.

"Where are you going?"

"To take a shower," said Gabriel, feeling almost relieved that the Cube had turned out to be a hoax. "You know that drug lord really had me going. Apart from the silly light trick, that artifact's a brilliant forgery."

CHAPTER 28

Bahadur mopped up the remaining soup with a crust of bread held between a massive thumb and forefinger. It had been the first thing he had eaten since Nasrallah had interrogated him, and although it had done him tremendous good, he was still not satisfied.

He hunched over and picked through Fra Bartolomeo's pack, wondering if he might have missed something. He found a bottle of water and a flashlight.

"This is very strange," he said to himself. "Perhaps they left their food and water behind in their haste… But how far could anyone go in this darkness without light?"

Bahadur tested the switch and saw that the batteries were still good.

"Something is not right," he muttered, and his voice seemed as deep as the catacombs.

Groaning in pain, he rose from his chair and made his way to the room where the guards had found the pack. In the roaming beam of his flashlight, he could make out the somber mounds of bones, finding at last the small blanket that lay spread out on the floor.

"Why sleep here when you could sleep by the fire?" he said slowly.

Grunting with effort, he bent low and squeezed himself through the tiny opening, unholstering his handgun as he went. He made his way to the blanket and pulled up the edge.

"Allah be praised…" he said in his deep basso.

There in the floor, directly beneath where the blanket had been, was a trap door made of old wooden planks. Holding his gun in one hand, he took hold of the door with the other and swung it open, his eyes opening wide at the sight before him.

There, lying trembling in the cold ground, he could see three figures looking up at him, their eyes wide with fright.

"What have we here?" he said, holstering his gun. "You all look quite old, but hardly ready for the grave."

Bending down, Bahadur took hold of Suora's arm, and, gentler than might have been expected, helped her out of the shallow pit.

"Sister," he said respectfully, his voice like a bass drum. "Please. Allow me."

He shook the blanket that had been lying on the floor and wrapped her shivering body in it.

"Why, thank you, my son," said Suora, more than a little surprised.

The enormous baldheaded man appeared to her to be a kind of monster. His scarred face was badly cut and bruised, and there was a gruesome image of a moth tattooed to his throat. He wore a black sweater and military trousers, his massive, horse-like muscles stretching the material taught. Strapped to his waist, on the opposite side of his handgun's holster, was a combat knife large enough to gut an elephant.

Even still, there was a keen intelligence and deep wisdom in his eyes, and the three seniors could see that this was no monster at all, but rather a tame and noble giant.

"Please," he said to the bishop and brother, reaching down to help them.

They each took hold of a massive hand and rose slowly to their feet. They had only lain there for ten minutes at most, but the ground was cold and damp, and their old bodies had not taken kindly to the accommodations.

Bahadur helped them out of the pit, looking back over his shoulder as he did so.

"You need not fear me," he said, his battered face at odds with his words. "I am not a murderer, and especially not of those in the holy service. I only ask that you assist me in my endeavor. Where is the Compostela Cube?"

"I am Bishop Marcus Di Lauro," said the old bishop, "and I thank you for your kindness and civility. I must say it is greatly appreciated. The Cube is not in our possession, although we were close to its keeper not so long ago."

"Gabriel Parker," said Bahadur, frowning. "Where is he?"

"That I do not know," said the bishop, "but I must confess that even if I did know, I would not tell you under any circumstances. You see, the Cube belongs to Gabriel by birth. It is his for the keeping and I will not betray him."

"Yes, of course, your Eminence," said Bahadur, nodding solemnly. "This I can understand, but you must also understand that if you will not cooperate with me, I will be forced to take you as my prisoners until the Cube is recovered. It is not I who decide it, but those to whom I am bound."

"You are a good man," said Suora suddenly. "In your heart you are true, my son. It is the wickedness of others that has led you astray."

Bahadur turned to face the little nun, his expression gentle.

"Thank you, Sister," he said deeply. "You are very kind and very observant, for ugly as I am, I try to be my best under the eyes of Allah. I have taken many lives, but never those of the innocent. You are safe while under my charge, but I cannot guarantee that my master will be so kind. Please now, you must come with me."

He led them out into the tunnel.

"I will give you a choice," he said, stopping and looking very serious. "I will be taking you to our headquarters. To do this we must first leave the catacombs. We can do this by going back to the monastery the way you have come, or we can take the much easier route up through the catacombs, and out the public entrance."

The bishop moved to say something, but Bahadur silenced him with a gesture.

"Were we to take the way through the catacombs, and enter into the general public, any one of you could easily scream out and draw attention to us. What kind of promise can you give me that you will not do this?"

"You have shown us mercy, my son," said the old bishop in earnest. "In exchange for your kindness, I give you my word that we will not cry out. We will go with you peaceably to your headquarters, or anywhere else you wish, and we shall trust in God, or Allah if you prefer, for He is the father of us all."

"And I will honour your promise, your Excellency," said Bahadur. "Please, come this way."

The sun had already set when they approached a black van parked on the roadside, meters from the catacomb entrance. Bahadur slid open the side door, much like a chauffeur might do, inviting the three to enter with a polite bow.

"Please," he said. "You will find the seats comfortable after your long flight."

"Thank you, my son," said Fra Bartolomeo, being the last to enter. "God bless you."

Bahadur closed the door and Fra watched him through the windows as he made his way around the van. He stopped just outside the driver's door and made a phone call. Fra listened in with his sharp ears.

"He must be talking to Nasrallah," he whispered to the bishop and nun. "Judging by his tone."

He listened intently.

"He is telling him that he has found us, and that his men are still searching for Gabriel and Natasha."

Fra looked at the bishop in surprise.

"He has been told that they are no longer in the Catacombs."

The bishop took hold of the brother's arm, a combination of joy and worry engulfing his features. The old brother held up a hand in a plea for silence.

"They do not know exactly where they are. Somewhere in the city centre. Bahadur is agreeing to regroup at headquarters."

Just then the driver's door opened, and Bahadur entered the van.

"Do you require food or drink?" he asked over his shoulder. "I am afraid I have eaten all of your provisions."

"A cup of tea would be very nice," said Suora. "If you might be so kind."

"It will be my pleasure, Sister," said Bahadur, "and a fair price for such fine lentil stew. The honey cake was also very good."

"Oh, I am so glad that you enjoyed it, my son!" said the old sister. "It is my specialty. The lentils, however, were Fra's humble invention."

She timidly pointed her thumb at the old brother and smiled ear to ear.

"I thank you," said Bahadur. "My employer had given me a sound thrashing and nothing to eat for more than a day."

"Oh, my goodness," said Suora, and just then the bishop's phone beeped.

"Excuse me, your Excellency," said Bahadur. "It would appear you have a message waiting. Perhaps you might put the phone onto its speaker mode, so that we all might hear it."

"Of course, Bahadur," said the bishop, fumbling with the phone. "I understand."

Gabriel's message played out and Bahadur turned in his seat to better hear it.

"-before we do anything about the Cube, I've got to get Amir's family out of there. I'm responsible for all this. Natasha's insisted on *coming with me. We'll be flying to Gibraltar tomorrow, and then heading to Morocco from there. Call me the minute you get this. We need to know you guys are safe."*

Bahadur nodded slowly when the recording had ended.

"If you will please excuse me for a moment."

With that he left the van and began pacing outside, bent in thought. He returned a few minutes later, speaking only after he had closed the door behind him.

"Amir is my cousin," he said deeply. "His family is my family, and it would appear that Nasrallah is an enemy to us all."

He rubbed the back of his thick neck and frowned as he thought.

"I can help Gabriel Parker," he continued. "But he will have to promise to help me in return. Nasrallah is a very dangerous man. If he learns of my betrayal, his vengeance on my family will be swift. He would have to be brought down quickly and decisively. Would Dr. Parker be willing to help me do this?"

Bishop Marcus, Fra, and Suora all nodded emphatically.

"I have known Gabriel all his life," said the old bishop in earnest. "He will most definitely help you, my son. Of this I am certain."

Bahadur gave a single nod. Amir had always spoken well of Gabriel Parker and had related more than a few tales of his bravery and loyalty.

"Then I will arrange a private flight to Gibraltar for us later tonight," said the giant. "While I do this, if your Excellency will please contact Dr. Parker and inform him that you are here with me, and that you are safe. Allah willing, we shall free my family, even if we must raise a small army to do so."

Suora squeezed her companion's hands excitedly, delighted with the new plan. Bahadur produced his phone and put it on speaker mode so that they all might hear. The connection went straight to Nasrallah's voicemail.

"Master," he said. "There has been a change in plans. I have extracted information from the hostages and killed them. A trap has been laid for Gabriel Parker at the Trevi Fountain tomorrow at twenty-three hundred hours. I have learned that he has hidden the Cube. For this reason, he must be taken alive and made to talk. I promise to have the artifact for you in thirty-six hours. Please call me if you have any questions. I am your humble servant."

Bahadur sent a text message and then made another call.

"Stop your search," he said sharply. "Regroup all the men. We will be laying a trap at the Trevi Fountain. I have sent you the details."

He was silent while the mercenary spoke.

"No!" barked Bahadur in his deep basso. "I have other business I must attend to. You are in command now."

Bahadur put away his phone.

"The game is afoot," he said, starting the van's engine and pulling out into traffic. "May Allah help us."

He accelerated up to speed.

"Now for more important matters," he added, tapping the navigation system. "British tea!"

CHAPTER 29

Los Picos De Europa, Northern Spain.

"To the Black Lake!" hissed a demonic voice.

The sun had already disappeared behind the mountainous peaks as Isaac battled his way down the rugged terrain. Around him the tangled branches of countless black trees encased him like threads in a spider's web. At his feet, a tarp covered sled fashioned from plane wreckage carried what was left of the rotting corpse of his son. The stench of it made him nauseous.

Dear Father, give me strength to endure this trial.

Isaac could do nothing to escape his fear. In the end the demons had won. They had taken possession of his faculties and left him with barely enough consciousness to know what it was they were making him do. He was in a waking nightmare, and while he had no control of his actions, he struggled desperately to keep control of his thoughts.

His memory told him that he had managed to free himself from the wreckage of the plane, and that he had been dragging the corpse for days now, crossing treacherous barriers, descending perilous rifts, and all the time being made victim to an icy voice that filled his mind like a swelling ocean.

"To the Black Lake!" it hissed over and over again. *"To the Portal of Ahreimanius!"*

It was his son who spoke, and if he knew this, it was only because he was of his own flesh and blood. Isaac had spent a lifetime at his side. Singing to him, caring for him, loving, as best he could, a child who had never once uttered a single word to him; a child who had caused the death of his beloved wife.

It had been a thirty-three-year-long vigil of parental duty, and even now in death, the child would still give him no peace. Isaac felt a deep hatred for his son rise up within him, and with it came an encompassing sense of guilt for feeling this way.

"To the Black Lake! To the Portal!"

It was a cyclical litany, minute after minute, day and night. It came as from a hungry infant; pleading, insistent, selfish, parasitic. On occasion the corpse would throw itself into violent tantrums, its stiffened bulk twisting and jerking beneath the battered tarpaulin like a great dying fish.

Isaac made his way downward into the woods. Below him he could see a tiny island, the place of his son's conception. He began to feel a great weight pressing down on him just then, and it drove the air from his lungs, and the sight from his eyes. He brought his hands to his face as a vivid memory flooded into him.

He could see his late wife Alina materializing out of the blackness. She was on the edge of a circle of standing stones, the tangled trunks of the little island's interior surrounding her. They had only just docked their boat. Alina had playfully run into the woods with a picnic basket and Isaac relived the intensity of his love for her. It ached in his heart and made any other pain he was experiencing seem insignificant by comparison.

Almost thirty-four years earlier, Alina had been introduced to him by Father Adrianus. She had been a beautiful girl, over a decade younger than himself, and deeply in need of love and support.

"It is time you took a wife, my son," the priest had told him one day. "You will take this young woman as your bride, and together you will raise a family."

As always Isaac had done as he was told. It was not long before he had found himself on his honeymoon, walking the pilgrimage of the *Camino de Santiago* with a young wife at his side.

Now, in his delirium, he was revisiting that time and place, and he saw that he and Alina were once again making love atop the great monolithic stone. A chilling fog had settled in and something seemed terribly wrong. He glanced down at Alina and found to his horror that the corpse of his son had taken her place.

Isaac broke from his twisted reverie, his eyes finding the cadaver at his feet. Through the tarpaulin he could make out its macabre form and a sudden desire to destroy the thing filled him to the quick.

CHAPTER **30**

Rome, Italy.

Gabriel emerged from the bathroom, cleanshaven and wrapped in a plush white bathrobe. He found Natasha sitting cross-legged on his bed. She was wearing a pair of hotel pajamas two sizes too big, and her chestnut hair was piled loosely on her head, accentuating her graceful, ballerina's neck. A tray laden with food sat at the foot of the oversized mattress, its contents covered with silver lids.

"I asked room service to put it here," she said casually, reading his thoughts. "I hope that's all right. I thought it would be more fun this way. Like a picnic."

She smiled shyly.

"It looks like you ordered every item on the menu," said Gabriel with a wink.

Natasha beamed and then moved away a pillow that had been in front of her. Gabriel gasped in surprise. His new friend had been busy. The Cube had undergone a complete transformation.

The artifact lay there amid six, cross-shaped sheets of parchment, and a completely dismantled jewel-encrusted framework. All that remained was a perfectly formed cube that looked to be made of semi-translucent stone. As before it was glowing, and the colour it took on was an incredibly beautiful iridescent blue.

"Happy to see me?" flirted Natasha.

"I am..." Gabriel said, coming closer.

His eyes were glued to the artifact.

"How did you know?"

"Because it got brighter when you saw me."

Gabriel sat on the bed; his attention fixed on the strange relic.

"What the hell is this thing? Is this some kind of a joke?"

Natasha crawled to the foot of the bed and began to pour out some coffee. Gabriel glanced up for a moment, his stomach rumbling, but his eyes returned to the artifact like iron to a magnet.

"It's no hoax, Gabriel," she said plainly. "I'm certain of it. Whatever this is, it's authentic. Look at those parchments and you'll see why."

Gabriel examined them each in turn. They were cross-shaped, comprised of six, equally sized, square-shaped sections. Their creases revealed how they had previously been wrapped around the Cube. The parchments were beautifully worked, each one written in tongues belonging to the six great faiths: Islamism, Hinduism, Buddhism, Judaism, Taoism, and Christianity.

Gabriel could not understand. Their level of detail was tremendous. It would have taken a forger years to complete a work of this magnitude. The parchments simply had to be authentic.

"Look on the back of the one that's written in Latin," said Natasha, pouring out the coffee. "It's signed by Gutierrez de la Cruz. Do you remember him?"

"He was the priest in Marcus' story," muttered Gabriel, picking up the parchment with great care. "The guy who found the Cube. He appears to be representing the Christian faith in these documents."

Gabriel turned his attention back to the Cube itself, laying down the parchment and picking up the strange, semi-translucent stone. He was amazed by what he saw. Covering its glowing surface were strange and ancient symbols.

"These must be the runes that Marcus was telling us about," he said, looking up at Natasha. "The ones that were deciphered in the Book of Khalifah."

He returned his attention to the artifact again.

"This Cube isn't Sumerian, Natasha. It's Neolithic. By the structure of these runes, I'd say it was proto-Basque."

"How old do you think it is?"

"It's difficult to say," he said. "The origins of the Basques have always been shrouded in mystery. Many theories point to them being the first Cro-Magnon people to populate Europe, some forty thousand years ago. By the looks of these proto writings, they might be right. If it's genuine, this Cube could easily be that old."

"Can you read the runes?"

He shook his head as he studied them.

"They're abstract symbols," he said. "Proto writings. The Sumerians were the first to come up with an actual alphabet. Before that, people just drew pictures to tell stories. Whoever deciphered them must have been privy to some very specific knowledge. These symbols could mean absolutely anything."

Gabriel looked up at her before returning his attention to the artifact.

"At least this explains how Gutierrez could have found this in the tomb with James the Just," he continued. "This artifact would have been ancient even by their standards. It must have been Gutierrez and his contemporaries who built the framework and covered it in the illuminations. There's only one problem. How the hell can a forty-thousand-year-old artifact be glowing?"

Gabriel shot a baffled glance at Natasha and then returned his attention to the Cube.

"To produce this kind of light, a power source of some kind would be required. It's too bright to simply be phosphorescent."

The more Gabriel turned it in his hands, the more confused he became. The material it was comprised of had a strange, organic quality to it. What was more, there was still the matter of its bizarre density. More than ever, it reminded him of firm flesh, similar in density to the flank of a strong horse but looking very much like translucent stone.

"I've never seen anything like it…"

Natasha handed him a steaming cup of coffee.

"Would you like to see something really amazing?"

"Sure," said Gabriel, taking a sip from his cup.

"Empty your mind of any thoughts," said Natasha. "Just think of your coffee."

"All right…"

No sooner had Gabriel done so than the Cube ceased to glow.

"What?" he said, looking up at Natasha, only to see it come to life again.

She clapped her hands in delight.

"It's magical, Gabriel!" she chimed. "It only glows when we're thinking of each other."

"How on earth did you figure that out?"

"Because you stopped thinking about me when you went into the bathroom."

Gabriel paused before answering.

"As a matter of fact, I did," he admitted. "I was feeling a little overwhelmed about everything. I decided to have a timeout."

"Interesting," said Natasha, rubbing her chin. "And how do you feel now?"

Gabriel returned his attention to the artifact, his brow furrowed.

"Overwhelmed."

Natasha leaned forward and kissed Gabriel's cheek.

"I like you very much, Gabriel Parker," she said, rolling off the bed before he could react. "And just for your information, I'll be returning to my room as soon as we've eaten. So don't get any ideas."

Gabriel gave her a curious glance, his eyes following her as she made her way to the suite's balcony. Her words had sounded more like an invitation to him than anything else.

Don't even go there, buddy...

"You seem so familiar to me, Gabriel," she continued, gazing out over the glittering lights of Rome.

Gabriel tore his eyes from her and brought his attention back to the Cube. She seemed incredibly familiar to him too, but he would not allow himself to be drawn into this conversation. There were more important issues at hand. Namely, a forty-thousand-year-old artifact that somehow glowed.

Gabriel emptied his mind of Natasha and watched the Cube grow dim as a result. After a few minutes Natasha returned to the bedside to see that Gabriel had completely put her out of his mind. The Cube was like a lifeless stone.

"Earth to Gabriel," she said with hands on hips.

When he looked up at her the Cube burst to life again.

"This thing really can read our thoughts..." he said, returning his attention to the artifact yet again.

Natasha watched it grow dim.

"That's what I said..." she muttered dejectedly.

She climbed onto the bed and busied herself with the food, glancing over at Gabriel as she prepared the plates. She was unsure when the change had taken place in her, but at some point her suspiciousness of Gabriel had turned into a kind of fascination.

She caught herself feeling oddly jealous of the artifact for holding his attention, and she tried to understand what it was that drew her to him. Gabriel seemed to reside in his own universe, and did not seem to need anything from anyone, least of all her. He was like a planet, and she like a reluctant moon caught in his gravitational field.

I should never have let him hold me in the catacombs...

Gabriel continued to study the glowing Cube, oblivious of Natasha's thoughts. He was not one to believe in magical trinkets. There was a scientific explanation for its light, and another to explain its obvious thought reading, neurofeedback capabilities. The Cube somehow knew when they were thinking of each other, but that hardly meant it was magical.

He passed a hand over his jaw, absently looking for any stubble he might have missed. He could remember reading about brain-computer-interfaces, but he had never heard of wireless versions before. He could devise no hypothesis that might explain why an object of such seemingly advanced technology would be inscribed with Neolithic proto-writings and wrapped in thousand-year-old manuscripts. It simply did not make sense.

Gabriel noticed the lights in the room dim just then and looked up to see Natasha standing by the light switch. The sight of her sent the enigmatic Cube into a brilliant blue glow again, and he felt as though he had been freed from one trance only to be trapped by another.

He watched her climb gracefully onto the bed, taking up the two plates she had prepared. The delicious aroma reminded him of how hungry he was.

They ate mostly in silence, each of them lost in thought. Gabriel was trying hard not to think about Natasha, but he was failing entirely now, and the glowing Cube betrayed his attempts at indifference. It amazed him that they could be so comfortable together, sitting alone in a hotel room without having to say a word. Despite his dislike of the minimalist suite, he could not recall having ever felt more at home than he did right now.

When they had finished eating, Natasha piled the dishes onto a tray and carried them back to the serving cart. When she returned Gabriel had leaned back against the headboard and closed his eyes. She stood there silently for a moment and then gave a forced yawn.

"Well, I guess it's bedtime, then…" she said.

He responded with a drowsy grunt and pushed himself back into his pillows. Natasha watched him drift off to sleep, her eyes scanning his features. Every man she had ever loved had broken her heart, and she wondered if Gabriel would do the same.

Go to bed, Natasha. You're thinking too much.

She moved to the bedside to turn off the lamp and reached down on an impulse to touch his face. At the last minute she desisted and smiled softly at her silliness. Seconds later she was back in her adjoining suite, leaving the door slightly ajar behind her.

CHAPTER 31

Amsterdam, The Netherlands.

Christian stood on the terrace of his penthouse suite, a lit cigarette in one hand and a brimming glass of red wine in the other. A full moon was beginning to rise over Amsterdam, and far below he could see the last of the conference attendees boarding their limousines at the hotel's front entrance. He drained his glass as if to toast their departure and ended the farewell with a grimace of disdain.

Turning back inside, Christian took up the wine bottle and drew heavily from his cigarette as he poured out the Bordeaux. He could still hear the insistent voice of his father in his mind. It echoed only two words, over and over again.

"The Cube!" it whispered urgently. *"The Cube!"*

Having no idea what this could mean, Christian was content to suppress the message, using the familiar tools of denial and alcohol to get the job done. There was no need to worry. His doctor would soon be providing him with medications that would silence the voices completely.

He fell onto the sofa and clicked on the television. It was eleven o'clock and one of the many Vanderhoff-owned news channels was filling the screen, its famous slogan being proclaimed against a background of flashing imagery and hypnotizing graphics.

"GNN. The planet's most trusted news network."

Christian smiled wryly.

"What a joke," he said bitterly. "The only reason they're the most trusted is because they don't stop saying it."

He watched the introduction finish with a flourish, and soon the anchorman was announcing the top story.

"Today, leaders from around the world sign the final legislative documents ushering in a new age for global economics. On the first of January, the World Bank's "CREDIT" will become the new currency of the global marketplace, completely phasing out all forms of cash across the majority of the planet by the end of the year. Coming up, a rebroadcast of this evening's Presidential address from the White House."

Christian turned off the television. It disgusted him. He had only wanted to see that all had gone as planned, and it had. The machine he had so recently been given control of was working perfectly.

He threw the remote onto the coffee table, and just then heard a knock at his door. Rising slowly, he made his way to answer it.

"Hello, Mr. Antov," said the beautiful young woman.

She had an innocent, seductive smile, her hair red and curly.

"Good evening, whore," he said quietly, not even attempting to mask his disdain. "I want you naked on the bed, and I don't want to hear another word coming out of that painted mouth of yours for the rest of the night. Is that clear?"

The smile vanished from the girl's face. She nodded in affirmation and entered silently.

Christian watched her undress and climb onto the oversized mattress. She was perfect in every way, but he saw no beauty in her. He was drowning in hatred and violence. He could feel it churning within him like an alien entity. An unexpected knock sounded just then and Christian shot a glance over his shoulder, his hatred transforming into fury. He reached the suite's door in a series of aggressive paces and jerked it open.

"What part of *Do Not Disturb* do you not understand?" he said, but instantly he fell silent.

Standing on the threshold was none other than the Nautonnier himself. Christian felt the room suddenly reeling around him. He hated this man more than he had ever hated anyone before, and an urgent desire to snuff out his repugnant life flooded into him again.

"Perhaps it is not what I understand that is important," said the Nautonnier in answer to his question, "but rather what your master *requires* of you."

With a dismissive shove, the old man used his bony forearm to push Christian aside and enter the suite. No sooner had he passed inside however, than he raised his long nose into the air, taking two quick sniffs.

"You have a lovely scent, sweet girl," he announced. "Now put on your things and leave us. We have important business that need not trouble your pretty little ears."

Christian was puzzled by the Nautonnier's remark. It had been his specific request that the girl wear no perfume. Within moments she emerged from the bedroom, her clothes donned haphazardly.

Her head was lowered in humility and fear as she made for the door, but the Nautonnier's ancient hand shot out as she passed, clamping onto her arm with uncanny strength. He pulled her close, running his grey lips over her delicate neck and inhaling her scent deeply.

"Ah," he said, sniffing her as a dog might do. "I can see he has not got to you yet..."

And then shooting a glance at Christian he added:

"See the pretty redhead saved from a ravishing! You might thank me, little one."

The girl twisted under his grip, smiling politely while trying to free herself from the stench of his breath.

"Thank you," she said meekly.

"You do not know the thrashing I have saved you from, my sweet," breathed the Nautonnier.

He glanced over at Christian.

"Neither does our esteemed Mr. Antov. Now go! And never whore yourself again! Go to church, girl! Ask Jesus for forgiveness!"

He released her and she hurried to the door, fumbling nervously with the latch before finally escaping. The Nautonnier made for the door as well.

"Get your things together, Christian," he said over his shoulder. "You will meet me in the Vanderhoff suite in fifteen minutes. Is that clear?"

"Get out of my room," came Christian's reply.

His hatred and fury were merging into a barely containable wrath.

"You can expect me within the hour. If you don't like it, you can go to hell."

The Nautonnier turned slowly to look at him, smiling darkly the whole while.

"I see you are feeling the power of the dark lord Ahreimanius," he said knowingly. "We will be waiting for you."

Christian followed him to the door only to witness something deeply disturbing. As the Nautonnier had made his exit, Christian had caught sight of four quivering shadows being cast onto the carpeted floor of the hallway outside. He could not bring himself to look for their source. A feeling of deep foreboding was churning in his stomach.

What is this? What the hell's going on?

He closed the door quickly, but the low chime of an arriving elevator came to his ears just as it shut. The sound seemed a kind of death knell to Christian, summoning that dark self within him, and sending a jolt of hair-raising fear through his entire body.

Christian retreated into his suite on faltering legs, a snakelike voice whispering its unending message into every corner of his psyche.

"The Cube," it hissed. *"The Cube!"*

CHAPTER 32

More than an hour had passed, by the time Christian arrived at the Vanderhoff suite. He had purposely lingered at the hotel bar, wanting to make it clear that he was not one to be ordered about. He prepared to knock, but just as they had done on his first visit, the doors opened before he could do so. The dark and somber room came into view.

"You may come in, Christian," said the brittle voice of the Nautonnier from the shadows.

The doors closed silently behind Christian as he entered, plunging the room into inky blackness. He could feel a strange presence very close to him now, almost brushing his face and body. A subtle yet unmistakable stench filled the room. It smelled of death and rot.

A terror began to take hold of Christian, and it was only a sudden rush of anger, brought on by that dark self within him, that prevented him from collapsing to the floor.

"This is bullshit!" he barked, his fear transforming. "I didn't come here for a spook show. Turn on a bloody light or I'm leaving, and you can go to hell!"

He heard a match being struck, and saw a candle come slowly to life. It sat in the corner of the suite, illuminating a round table, along with its five shadowy occupants. They wore dark, hooded robes.

"I didn't know this was a Halloween party," said Christian dryly.

He saw the Nautonnier rise to his feet and throw back his hood.

"You will have respect!" he hissed.

"Fuck you."

The Nautonnier sat down as Christian approached, and the others remained motionless in their seats. The air seemed to crackle with energy.

There was an empty chair at the table, and as Christian arrived, he stood by it, looking down at the robed figures. It was the first time he had seen them up close, and their rate of oscillation seemed to have slowed, so that they almost appeared to be solid. Christian fought back an urge to vomit. They were repulsive to him.

"Sit down!" came his father's icy hiss.

Christian did his best to ignore it.

"Show me your faces!" he demanded.

As one, the four reached up and pushed back their hoods. Christian stepped away in shock.

What is this? How can this be?

Fluctuating between grainy ghostliness and solidity, he could see four visages before him, so ancient that their appearance seemed to defy the laws of nature. They stank of rot and decay. That something could be so old seemed to Christian utterly impossible. He bent forward despite his disgust. Their features were clearly reptilian.

"What the hell is going on here?" he asked, looking over at the Nautonnier.

"Our brothers are ancient by all standards," he said. "They belong to a race of beings that dwelt on the earth long ago. We are of their bloodline, Christian. Please, sit down. I beg you."

Seeing that the Nautonnier was finally assuming a respectful disposition had a calming effect on Christian. He had had enough of the old man's impertinence. He sat down and lit a cigarette, blowing smoke into the Nautonnier's face.

"Start talking," he said, feeling his self-confidence fading. "I'm a busy man."

"You are nothing without the master!" hissed the four in unison, each of them rising to their feet.

In that instant, it seemed to Christian like a great weight were suddenly pressing down on him, as though he had been submerged in very deep water. The pressure made his head reel in pain, but he could not cry out. He watched the Nautonnier rise to his feet and disappear behind him. The pain was intensifying. He could do nothing but grasp the arms of his chair and writhe in agony.

"Can you now feel what you are up against, boy?" came the icy whisper.

Christian heard the voice as though it were filtering up from the floor. The stench of the Nautonnier's breath curled over his neck and into his nostrils.

"Fuck you," he managed to utter.

"You will learn respect!" cried the brittle voice, and suddenly Christian felt a piercing pain burning into his lower spine.

It shot up into his ears, silencing his scream and sending all the muscles in his body into spasm. The room went black.

When Christian regained consciousness he found that he was still seated in the same chair. He looked up to see that the table before him was ablaze with candles, each one placed at the outer points of a pentagram that had been drawn crudely on its surface. At its centre lay a dagger with a serpentine blade. Surrounding the table were the four ancient figures, and the Nautonnier. He could feel their wicked eyes on him.

"Who are you?" muttered Christian at last, looking to the four.

"We are the Zurvanites of Ahreimanius," came the frigid whisper. *"We are the keepers of the Eternal Temple of Set."*

Christian passed his hands over his face. His head was spinning.

"They are *The Four*," said the old sage, nodding. "Since ancient times they have served the Nautonnier and given him knowledge and power. They represent the four great forces of destruction and are the keepers of the four dimensions. They answer only to Lucifer."

"How can you expect me to believe any of this nonsense?" asked Christian weakly.

"You will believe when you witness the destruction they shall reap through you," said the Nautonnier. "You were always a disbelieving boy. It is time you opened yourself to the truth."

"How would you know what kind of boy I was?"

"Ah, but you forget, my child," whispered the Nautonnier. "We were great schoolmates."

In the depths of his heart, Christian felt a sudden pang of intense emotional pain. It seemed to come from a long way off; from another life, or from a nightmare. He squelched it immediately, denying it utterly.

"I see you choose to forget our special friendship," hinted the Nautonnier, a sly smile spreading over his face. "And after all the fun we had together..."

Christian battled with himself. Memories he had long ago buried were coming up from his dark childhood. His loveless father, his cruel nanny, the loneliness and isolation. They had sent him far away, to a horrible place. It was an institution. There had been teachers. *Brothers* they had been called. Catholic priests. Christian squirmed in his seat, feeling the cruel eyes of The Four on him.

"Oh," said the Nautonnier in a playful tone, "I think he is starting to remember those things we did together."

Christian squirmed. The Nautonnier's voice was like a scalpel.

"How could you have forgotten? You are breaking my heart!"

Christian looked directly at the wispy haired Nautonnier. The latter was staring back at him now, an exaggerated pout distorting his repugnant features. In his cold, cruel eyes Christian could see something vaguely familiar, and in an instant, long drowned memories came flooding back to him, as though a dark gate had been lifted, or a tired dike thrown down.

"Father Adrianus…" breathed Christian in horror, moving his head from side to side. "No… It can't be you…"

A darkness was enveloping Christian now. It came in from his periphery, engulfing everything in an inky blackness. Out of the shadows a scene materialized. He was remembering. He was a child. He was in a study room in the school's library.

"You've been a very dirty little boy, Christian," whispered a voice, and Christian knew at once that it belonged to the Nautonnier.

"What you have done to me is very wrong, and very dirty."

"No!" cried Christian in tears. "You made me do it! You made me!"

"Dirty boy!" scolded the voice. "Now you will do it to me again, or I will tell everyone what you have done!"

Christian jerked into the present. He focused his eyes on the Nautonnier, remembering fully what he had been made to do.

"You!" he said, trembling with fury.

A deep shame was making its way through Christian now, as though he were drowning in it. The seething hatred and anger that came in its wake threatened to consume him.

"I will kill you for what you did to me!"

"He remembers!" exclaimed the Nautonnier, clapping his hands in feigned delight.

Christian attempted to rise from his chair, realizing only then that he was completely paralyzed. He could move nothing but his head.

"And, yes, Christian," said the Nautonnier wickedly. "Your father knew very well of our little games, as did you your uncle Vladimir."

Christian was in tears of frustration. Through the Nautonnier's promptings he had now regained all the memories he had so thoroughly repressed. He could recall each and every cruelty perpetrated by those who were supposed to have loved him. The walls had broken, and all the subterfuges that Christian had created to hold onto himself were gone. There was nothing but the truth, and he refused to believe it. He refused it with all his will. He would never allow himself to accept this. Never.

As the Nautonnier came closer, something in Christian transformed. It arose from the depths of his soul, riding on a swelling wave of hatred and violence. It took form as a sudden surge of strength, and its power was intoxicating. Christian did nothing to repress it, choosing instead to observe the beast within him as a spectator might do. It felt primal and ancient, like something he had long ago once been, and since forgotten. In a fraction of a second Christian's dark inner self had taken full control.

Directly before him, Christian could see the Nautonnier's creased and wrinkled face. It was contorting with mock pity. He could smell the putrid breath, and the stench of it brought a pang of lucidity to his memories. Christian's childhood traumas were playing out before him. He was reliving every feeling, every sordid experience at the hands of this malevolent priest.

"You'll pay for what you did to me," he said in a low and trembling voice.

His rage was on the verge of explosion.

"Oh, he is upset with me," mocked the Nautonnier. "Is this a lover's spat?"

With one concerted effort, Christian broke from the spell that had held him paralyzed. He shot out a hand and took hold of the Nautonnier's wrinkled brittle throat. His strength seemed unreal.

I'm going to kill you, you son of a bitch.

To his surprise, Christian felt his fingernails perforating the cartilage of the trachea with a sickening crunch. Hot blood coursed from the Nautonnier's mouth in bubbling gouts, running down Christian's arm, and spattering his face and body.

Christian rose from his chair like an angry god, lifting the dying Nautonnier into the air as though he were a limp rag doll. He could see the old man's eyes bulging from the pressure, but there was still an icy smile on his bloodied lips, as though he were somehow encouraging his pupil to continue.

Christian was beside himself now. Running in his mind was a movie of all the torments he had suffered at the hands of this man. The humiliation. The sheer humiliation.

Christian reached down with his free hand and took hold of the serpentine dagger that lay on the table. Ever so slowly he sunk its blade into the Nautonnier's neck, sawing ineptly until he had at last severed the head. He dropped it onto the table along with the knife, and then watched the lifeless body crumple to the floor.

The Nautonnier's head had landed in the centre of the pentagram of burning candles. Its eyes were still blinking, and the stench of burning hair filled the room. Around the table the Zurvanites stood unmoving, flickering and shuddering in and out of existence.

Christian was in a kind of ecstasy. He felt sated and free, like one who had finally rid himself of a postulant wound, or pulled an infected thorn from his flesh. His hatred rang like a bell's note. He took a long, deep breath and looked up at the Zurvanites as they stood there before him, his eyes dark and reptilian.

"It is done," they said to him, bowing in reverence. *"The prophecy is fulfilled."*

Their voice was no longer a physical one. It came like a thought from somewhere deep in Christian's mind. A wave of fear and repulsion passed through him, for he knew in his heart that the Zurvanites were now inside him. He and they had somehow fused. He gagged and bent to vomit.

"Hail the new Nautonnier!" they hissed as he sank to the floor. *"All power to Ahreimanius, Lord of Darkness and Matter!"*

CHAPTER 33

Rome, Italy.

Natasha stood before the balcony in Gabriel's suite. The shutters were drawn aside, and eruptions of lightning could be seen painting the horizon, spreading sheets of light over the distant clouds. Framed as they were by the starry sky, they resembled mountains, dark and threatening. From them came an ominous rumbling that seemed to grow louder with every passing minute. An immense stormfront was drawing closer, and the busy streets of Rome seemed oblivious to its impending wrath.

Gabriel slept soundly in his bed behind Natasha. She knew that there was no reason to be frightened. She had only had a nightmare, but something in her seemed persistent in its warnings nevertheless. She passed her fingers through her hair.

"You're up," came Gabriel's groggy voice.

Natasha turned to find him propped on an elbow, his brow furrowing the moment he saw the expression on her face.

"What's wrong?"

She stood there without moving, looking helplessly back at him. Her eyes welled with tears.

"I'm so sorry for coming into your room like this, Gabriel."

He got up and went to her. He put a hand on her shoulder, not knowing what else to do.

"You're trembling."

"I had a dream," she said. "We were together in a horrible place. Then we became separated. Oh, Gabriel, I felt so lost…"

Natasha threw her arms around him and began to cry. Rolling thunder boomed outside.

"I can't understand," she sobbed. "Why is all this happening?"

"It was just a dream," Gabriel heard himself say. "Just a nightmare, that's all."

Natasha pulled her head back and looked into his eyes.

"Something unspeakable happened to us when we were babies…" she whispered, pushing aside his hair and tracing the tips of her fingers over the scar on his forehead.

An instinctive urge to deny what she was saying took hold of Gabriel, but he dismissed it. The idea that they could have spent the first fourteen months of their lives possessed by demons was extremely disturbing, but it had to be accepted. He reminded himself that it was only through this paranormal event that the bishop had found them. They were who they were today because of it.

Something unspeakable happened to us when we were babies…

He moved away from Natasha and stepped out onto the balcony. It was past midnight, but the streets of Rome were still bustling.

"I've had dreams too," he said slowly, facing out into the night. "All my life. I've always pretended that I didn't have them, but when they came, I always knew something was wrong."

"Then we're not alone in this anymore, Gabriel," came Natasha's voice, but this time there was a renewed strength in it. "That changes everything."

Gabriel turned to find that she had gone over to his bed. She was lying on her stomach, propped on her elbows and gazing into the glowing Cube.

Once again Gabriel was captivated. The Cube's blue light was washing over her face as though it were moonlight. He could see that she was no longer frightened, and her resilience surprised him, helping him to douse his own fears.

Gabriel shook his head in wonder. Just like the Cube, it seemed to him that deeper levels of Natasha were being revealed to him with every passing hour. This being said, it was getting easier for him to keep his distance from her. The more virtues he saw in her, the more unworthy he felt. She was intelligent, genuine, and compassionate, without ever coming off as prudish or self-satisfied, and he was, after all, a whore monger. He felt emptier than ever.

"Do you remember what Uncle Marcus said about the spiritual separation between us?" asked Natasha, her attention still fixed on the Cube.

Gabriel gathered himself before answering.

"He said there'd be dark forces attracted to you as long as we were not spiritually merged. Whatever that was supposed to mean."

Natasha looked over at him through dark, curling locks.

"Two days ago, I felt a supernatural presence in my workshop," she said, tucking her hair away behind an ear. "It was evil, Gabriel. That's why I went to stay with Uncle Marcus. It really frightened me. I thought I was going crazy."

"Two days ago," said Gabriel, letting himself fall into a chair next to the bed. "The same day I recovered the Cube."

"That would make sense," she said, sitting up and facing him. "Uncle Marcus said that dark forces were alerted to my presence when you retrieved the Cube without me being there."

Gabriel thought for a moment.

"Do you think the dark forces could be in tune with our separation, in the same way that the Cube is in tune with our togetherness?"

Natasha shrugged.

"Considering that all positive spirituality is based on unity, and that all negative spirituality is based on separation, it could be so."

"By negative spirituality, do you mean Satanism?"

"Among other things," she said. "There are two opposing belief systems. The right-hand path, and the left-hand path. Followers of the right look for integration with the godhead. They want to achieve divine creative power by achieving union with all. That's what *'All Is One'* means."

Gabriel nodded.

"And followers of the left?"

"They seek the glorification of the individual self, or the ego," said Natasha. "They want power over others, and fragmentation. That's what *'divide and conquer'* means. Throughout history the left hand has always been synonymous with evil because of these two different paths. As a matter of fact, in Latin, the word left means sinister."

"Dextra et sinistra," said Gabriel in Latin. "Right and left."

They both fell silent, caught up in their own thoughts. Natasha continued to examine the Cube.

"You know," she said at length, "I'm thinking we might find something if we could scan this with a BIRIS."

"What's a BIRIS?"

"It's a portable imagining scanner. I have one in my shop. It's on loan from the National Research Council of Canada. I'm using it to capture all the Vatican pieces I've been restoring."

"How does it work?"

"It uses three twin-aperture lasers to scan an object," she said. "Then it triangulates the data to generate a three-dimensional image. With translucent objects like this one, you can scan them inside too. A BIRIS is like an x-ray machine and an MRI, all in one."

Gabriel's face lit up.

"We've got to get that gizmo, Natasha," he said, a roll of thunder filling the room as he spoke. "It might give us a clue as to what makes this thing tick."

Gabriel's phone sounded just then, the name on the display filling their hearts with hope. Gabriel hit the speaker setting.

"Marcus?" they said in unison. "Is that you?"

"It certainly is!" came the familiar voice. "And I must say that I am delighted to be speaking with you both!"

"And Suora and Fra?" asked Natasha. "Are you all safe?"

"We are fine," came the humble voice of the old nun. "Our Father in heaven sent a noble giant to save us."

Gabriel and Natasha looked at each other.

"Bahadur?" asked Gabriel, following a hunch.

"That is correct!" said the old bishop. "He will be coming to Gibraltar to help us organize his family's rescue."

"I don't understand," said Gabriel. "I thought he was being held prisoner by Nasrallah."

"Bahadur was the leader of the men who invaded the rectory, my son. Nasrallah forced him to do his dirty work by threatening to kill his family. Bahadur has happily decided to join our side instead."

"You've got to tell him how sorry I am, Marcus," said Gabriel, frowning. "This is all my fault. I put his entire family in danger when I stole the Cube. I had no idea that would happen."

"It was not entirely your fault, Dr. Parker," came the deep voice of Bahadur. "Had I thought twice before giving you and Amir the information, all this might have been avoided. Nonetheless we will free them all. Everything will be fine. Of this I am certain."

"So what happens now?" asked Natasha.

"I have chartered a private plane to Gibraltar," continued the giant. "We will leave Rome immediately. There is a storm approaching. You must come quickly."

"Is there any way we can meet you in Gib?" asked Gabriel. "We need to pick up some equipment from Natasha's workshop in Florence first."

"That should not be a problem," said Bahadur. "I can arrange to have a plane waiting for you in Florence. How much time will you require?"

Gabriel looked at Natasha.

"Feel up to it?" he whispered, covering the microphone.

Natasha smiled and nodded eagerly.

"Let's see," said Gabriel into the phone. "It's about a three-hour drive from here to Florence, but in a fast car I could do it in less than two. We'll need an hour to gather the equipment. How about three hours from now? That would put us there at around three-thirty in the morning."

"Consider it done, my friend," said Bahadur. "I will text you the particulars."

"If you don't mind me asking," said Gabriel. "How can you be so sure you'll find a plane on such short notice?"

"My position has its advantages, Dr. Parker."

"Very well then," chimed in the old bishop. "Off you go! At the *Pillars of Hercules* shall we meet!"

The elevator doors opened, revealing the hotel's pompous lobby. They had not taken two steps forward before they were approached by the concierge.

"Dr. Parker," he said formally. "The car you have requested is waiting in the courtyard."

"Thanks," said Gabriel, stuffing a hundred Euro note into the man's chest pocket. "It mustn't have been easy to arrange at this hour."

"It was my pleasure, Doctor," he said cordially.

A peal of thunder shook the air as Natasha led the way outside. There was a black sportscar in the courtyard, its sleek curves reflecting the silent flashes of lightning that lit up the night sky.

"Wow," she said to Gabriel. "I'm impressed."

"We needed something fast," he said with a shrug.

Gabriel led Natasha to the passenger door and held it open long enough for her to fall in. A moment later she felt a dense thud as the door sealed itself shut, the vehicle's interior reminding her more of a fighter-jet cockpit than a car. In a moment Gabriel had entered as well, quickly firing the engine to life.

He slipped the car into gear and Natasha felt herself being pushed back into her seat as they sped out of the hotel and into traffic. Following Gabriel's example, she clicked her seatbelt home, delighting in the car's sexy interior.

"Here's where she really sings," said Gabriel, entering the autostrada's onramp and gunning it.

The car lurched instantly into dizzying acceleration, but just then heavy drops of rain began to strike the windshield, smacking into it with the force of small stones. They were headed directly into the storm.

Gabriel gripped the hand-stitched leather wheel and settled back into his seat.

"Good thing we've got all-wheel drive."

CHAPTER 34

Rome, Italy.

The rain was pummeling the tarmac, sending water shooting upwards in a myriad of splashing torrents. In all his years in Rome, the bishop had never seen a time when it had rained with such profuse density. It seemed an almost tropical storm; an anomaly in keeping with the strange and catastrophic weather conditions that had been battering the planet of late. On this night there was not a breath of wind to be had, only a slight breeze being stirred up by the rain itself.

"How can we possibly fly in this?" muttered the old bishop to no one in particular.

They were making their way out onto a runway that looked more like a fast-moving river. Up ahead, the bishop could vaguely discern the shape of a plane materializing through the downpour. It looked to be an old twin prop, its engines running.

"Please, come along!"

It was the deep boom of Bahadur that called to them. He was guiding them forward through the downpour, their umbrellas heavy under the falling water.

"We are almost there!"

Through a wall of rain, the bishop saw a staircase appear. He moved aside to allow Suora to pass first. Bahadur stepped up to help her, taking her umbrella and making sure she did not slip on the wet steel.

"Thank you, my son," she said as they made their way up. "God bless you."

Fra Bartolomeo followed, with the old bishop slogging his way up last.

The aircraft looked to be a relic of the early seventies; a silver cargo plane built like a tank. The interior was no different. Single rows of seats lined a wide cabin, leaving a broad cargo area running down the centre of the fuselage. It was hardly luxurious, but it offered a welcome shelter from the rain. The bishop took a seat behind Fra, strapping on his seatbelt and settling back into his chair.

Bahadur had just finished assisting Suora on the other side of the fuselage when the plane began to move. The bishop watched him swing his massive body into the seat behind her, strapping on his belt and turning to look out the window with bruised eyes.

The pounding rain, combined with the roaring engines, made for a very noisy takeoff, but in the space of a minute they were airborne. The plane rose sharply and banked to the right.

Outside the night was black under the dense rain, only to ignite into a flashing landscape of cloud when the lightning struck. The frequent claps of thunder were sending shuddering quakes through the fuselage, and crossing himself, the old bishop joined his friends in their well-earned slumber.

He had long ago given his life to God, and he feared death no more than one might fear a future dentist's appointment. That is to say, without looking forward to it, but accepting that the time would come when he would find himself sitting in that chair with a bib tied around his neck.

* * * * * *

Gibraltar

Amir hung up the phone and then picked it up again, dialing a new number. He had just arranged hotel accommodations for the bishop and brother, and had also, at the nun's request, called ahead to the convent to let them know to expect her. He was now in the process of phoning an old friend, one of Gibraltar's most infamous smugglers. He could hear ringing but there appeared to be no one home. He was about to hang up when someone answered.

"Yeah, yeah! All right for Christ's sake!"

The voice was gruff from too much smoking, and aggressive, its British accent rounded by its marriage with the Andalusian dialect.

"I'll get the bloody phone, darling. Don't you move a leg! Hello!"

"Scotty," said Amir in his steady tenor. "Sorry to be calling so late."

"Is that you, Amir?" came the reply. "Late? The night's just beginning, mate! Bloody hell! This witch of mine has had me locked up in here with her all day and it's bloody tiring! I'm bloody-well knackered from it!"

Amir smiled.

"Women tend to keep you out of trouble, old friend."

Robert's reply was being directed at someone other than Amir.

"Well, if she don't shut up, I'm gonna lock her fat ass in the closet again!"

And then in a friendly tone it added:

"What can I do for you, mate?"

Amir's dreadlocks shifted as he shook his head, smiling despite himself.

"I'm in a bit of a bind, Scotty. Could you help me out?"

"Of course, mate. What's the problem?"

"Nasrallah's putting the screws to Bahadur. He's taken our family hostage. He's even got granny."

"That bloody bastard..." said Roberts, genuinely shocked. "That's heavy shit, man. How can I help?"

"Bahadur's flying in from Rome tonight. He's thinking about taking Nasrallah down and busting our family out. They're being held in Nasrallah's digs."

"Bloody hell, mate," said Roberts, a little shaky. "That's a bloody fortress. I'd love to see it happen, but that's a bleeding war you're talking about."

"Listen, Scotty," said Amir, frowning with concern. "A few of us are getting together at Dickey's shop down in the docks, sometime around sunrise. I know it's early, but do you think you could make it?"

Amir could hear the smuggler screaming at his woman in the background, the rubbing sound of his hand on the phone's mouthpiece doing little to mute the dialogue.

"Shut up, you bloody whore!" he bellowed. "Can't you see I'm on the bleeding phone! …What's that? Well I don't give a bloody shit what you think, so you can shut your bloody mouth is what you can do!"

"Amir, my mate," said Roberts, returning to his good-natured self again. "For you, anything. I'll be there. And don't you worry. We'll find a way to get them out."

Amir nodded.

"Thanks, Scotty."

He heard the screaming continue for a few seconds before the line went dead, and then shook his head and smiled. Some people never changed.

CHAPTER 35

Los Picos de Europa, Northern Spain.

Isaac dragged the bloated corpse of his son onto the island's shore, the air entering and leaving his lungs in great gasps. His feet slipped in the soft clay, his bleeding toes curling into the earth to find traction. Over the course of the crossing, the cadaver had almost doubled in weight, the water having found its way in through the decomposing rib cage, leaving it waterlogged and wretched beyond belief.

Isaac strained to heave it up onto the rocks. Above him a thick tangle of trunks and boughs dissolved into the grainy depths of the island. Somewhere outside of that cursed mountain range the sun would be rising, but it was invisible to him. He was in a low valley, the sky above dimmed by a somber mass of cloud that churned and boiled forebodingly.

"To the Portal of Ahreimanius!" came the icy hiss yet again, but this time with an insistence that was almost crippling.

A muffled cry escaped Isaac's tightened lips. The demons within him were frenzied, and the corpse of his son had begun to lurch and contort again, its limbs thrashing violently in great spasms. The stench of it was outlandish. Clotted masses of maggots, excrement, and vitriol were being pumped from the broken carcass with every freakish contortion.

"To the Portal!" commanded the voice, and the fiendish words stabbed like needles into his brain.

With a desperate and frantic tug, Isaac dislodged the cadaver from the rocky depression where it lay and proceeded in haste to drag it to the place of its incestuous conception. The rocks were slippery with the blood that left his feet, the incline steep and treacherous. Nevertheless, Isaac did as he was compelled to do, so that after an agonizing ordeal, he arrived at last at the clearing.

The circle of standing stones was better lit than the tangled path he had followed. Whereas the dense trunks had blotted out almost all the predawn light, the clearing itself offered a dead glow of filtered illumination. It fell over the place like a pall, and the central monolith seemed to call out to him from it. It lay there heavy and massive, its weathered top flat, and ready to accept what had burdened him for so long.

With his last ounce of strength, Isaac heaved the corpse onto its surface, a chorus of icy whispers driving away the last remnants of sanity from his mind. Around him, spread out in a perfect circle, were the fourteen standing stones, as tall as men and disfigured as though they had been subjected to tremendous heat.

Isaac produced a shard of metal and proceeded to disrobe the jerking body. Black shadows had appeared on its skin, showing him where to cut. Without a word he began to butcher the undead flesh, all the while gagging and vomiting from the stench of it.

No sooner had the cadaver made contact with the central stone than it had begun to tremble. It was as if each piece of the grisly carnage were somehow alive; quivering and contracting as the crude blade divided it up, the fingers gripping, the toes curling and uncurling. The tortured voice of Isaac's soul cried out helplessly.

Dear Father in heaven! Deliver me from this evil!

With the corpse now divided, Isaac proceeded to take up the fourteen butchered sections, placing each one at the base of a different standing stone. Overhead, a mass of heavy black cloud rolled in under the boiling sky, and a great clap of thunder shook the island to its roots.

With the grisly sections at last distributed, Isaac stood motionlessly at the centre of the ring, looking down at the top of the stone where he had done his butchering. It was crawling with the maggots that had been left behind, and beneath them he could see the image of a labyrinth carved into its surface, with the crude figure of a man standing at its entrance.

"What horrors have you been forced to commit, Isaac," came a voice of such cunningness that he was instantly lured into its spell. *"Where is your loving god now? How could he have allowed this to befall you?"*

Isaac teetered as though on the edge of an abyss. He was suddenly back in the hospital room with the demonically possessed body of his son in the bed before him. To his right and left he could see the stiffened corpses of two priests hanging by their necks in the cold blue light.

"I am Ahreimanius," hissed his son from the bed suddenly, and Isaac looked down to find a pair of wicked eyes gazing up at him. *"Your blessed Father has deserted you, Isaac, but I can give you powers beyond your comprehension. Come with me, and I will make you more powerful than God."*

Isaac's soul groaned in agony. Ahreimanius was right. Throughout all his tribulations, he had never once felt the presence of God. On the contrary, he had felt as though God had abandoned him when he needed him the most.

A great temptation to accept the offer arose in Isaac, and as he considered it, a vision of himself on high appeared before him. No sooner had he contemplated these things, however, than a voice within him cried out against the insidious offer.

"Never!" he exclaimed with all his will, and just then he was back on the island, released from the demons who had forced him to butcher the body of his son.

"You and your stupid Cube!" hissed the voice of Ahreimanius in fury. *"Did you really think I would ever allow you to do anything but serve my purposes? You will never assist the Two in their endeavors! You will die here tonight, and your pathetic life will have served no purpose but mine!"*

Isaac staggered backwards, looking around in shock. He could suddenly think clearly again. He struggled to understand.

"What have I done?" he gasped, bringing his bleeding hands to his face. "Lord Jesus Christ, what treacherous sin have I committed?"

Like the world returning to one who has awoken from a long slumber, so was the unholy scene revealed to Isaac. Forgotten now by the demons that had possessed him, he found himself stumbling to the edge of the circle, cowering in the dense undergrowth but unable to look away from the centre of the clearing.

Whereas each of the standing stones had begun to sink into the ground, the central monolith appeared to be rising ever so slightly into the air, its bulking mass levitating until it hung there weightlessly. Countless worms and other lightless insects were scurrying around beneath it.

Quite suddenly, in the depression where the monolith had rested, there appeared a rapidly growing pit of fire and ice. The surrounding circle of stones were being sucked into it, along with their grisly charges. A great chorus of wicked cries was issuing forth now, and from the black pit there arose fourteen demons, like dense clouds of earth and dust. These were the Fourteen Emissaries of Ahreimanius, and their forms were horrendous.

One by one they rose, churning in the air like blackened masses of cinder smoke; one by one screaming in hatred before shooting upwards into the boiling sky.

Only then did the floating stone fall, its ancient bulk fracturing suddenly into countless shards before being swallowed by the gaping portal as well. Isaac was trembling with fear. Deafening claps of thunder were assaulting him from above now, and just then a violent barrage of lightning crackled down around him, setting the island alight. The demonic chorus was growing louder and louder as well, until it seemed to Isaac that the entire world would be consumed by it.

"What have I done?" he moaned, his hands covering his ears.

Before him he could see that a conflagration had begun, and that the twisted trunks around the clearing were fully ablaze. Stunned and exhausted, Isaac stumbled wearily through the thickets to the water's edge, throwing himself into the black lake so that his death might come by drowning, rather than by fire.

"Forgive me for what I have done, Father," he said, his somber face lit by the flames. "Save my soul."

CHAPTER 36

Florence, Italy.

The black sports car rolled slowly over the cobblestones, its headlights cutting through the downpour. Natasha was looking intently through her window, scanning the shadows as they proceeded. They were driving along a narrow alleyway in the city centre, and the heavy rain was falling like a curtain around them.

Given the weather, the drive from Rome to Florence had taken more than twice what it should have. It was almost sunrise now, and they were only just approaching Natasha's workshop. They had decided to take the back entrance in the off chance that Nasrallah had eyes on the place.

"So far so good," said Gabriel, easing the car forward along the constricting laneway.

He pushed a button and Natasha watched as the side view mirrors collapsed inwardly.

"It looks like there's an opening in the wall up ahead," said Gabriel.

Natasha peered into the curtain of rain.

"This is it," she said. "We're here."

Gabriel pulled the car up next to the opening so that Natasha could open her door into it, then he climbed over to her side and followed her out. They were soon making their way along a narrow passageway. It led to a gate that opened into an inner courtyard, partially sheltered from the rain.

Natasha produced an old iron key as they approached a timeworn set of doors.

"I hate this storeroom," she said, inserting it into the lock.

In a moment the smell of raw earth and ancient mildew was wafting out of the darkness to greet them. With the increased humidity, the musty air could almost be tasted on the tongue, and Gabriel breathed it in deeply, savouring the antiquity like a connoisseur.

"We left the torchlights back in the car," he said, squinting into the darkness.

Natasha produced her phone and used its flashlight app instead. The last time she had been in this storeroom a sinister presence had accosted her, and she could still feel its residue lurking in the many shadows and crevices the jumbled space had to offer. Even still, with Gabriel so near, and knowing what she now knew, its effect on her was nothing compared to what it had been that day.

Gabriel followed close behind, producing his phone to help light the way. They made their way through a maze of laden shelves and cluttered cabinets until they reached the front room at last. It was not as dark here, and the bluish light from the streetlamps outside filtered in through the watery panes, casting shifting patterns on the wooden floor.

"Make yourself at home," said Natasha, beginning to fill a field case with equipment.

Gabriel's phone rang just then, and he remained on it the entire time that Natasha packed the supplies. She could see that he was doing more listening than talking, but it was not until she had finished that it looked as though his conversation might end.

"All right then, Amir," he said. "If all goes well, we'll be seeing you this afternoon. Stay in touch."

He pocketed the phone, turning to Natasha.

"What is it?" she asked.

Gabriel's mouth formed a straight line.

"Our flight to Gib's been cancelled," he said, "We've got some driving to do."

* * * * * *

Gibraltar

The old bishop awoke to find the plane in a sharp bank. It was no longer raining, and looking out his window he could see the Rock of Gibraltar turning slowly below him, its city centre twinkling with a thousand lights. Stretching out into the distance, the shimmering waters of its bay and strait could also be seen, dotted with freighters and ships of all kinds.

To the starboard side towered Gibraltar's majestic peak, silhouetted against a predawn sky. It was a time-sculpted rock formation, topped with the famous single white cloud that had come to be known as *El Levante*, named after the easterly wind that was responsible for its formation.

In minutes they had circled the small peninsula, levelling off to make their landing approach on the short strip of runway that separated the British colony from the Spanish mainland. The bishop smiled in delight.

"Gibraltar!" he exclaimed. "One of the two great pillars of Hercules! The fortified bastion of the British Royal Navy, and home to the largest per capita density of pubs in all of Christendom! Aye, but a pint of stout would be nice. That and a breakfast of steak and kidney pie!"

CHAPTER 37

Amsterdam, The Netherlands.

It was just past six in the morning when prince Vladimir Rodchenko arrived at the Vanderhoff suite. The front desk had awoken him with orders from the Nautonnier to go there at once. Christian met him at the door and led him into the room, locking the door behind them.

The old prince gasped in horror. On a table at the back of the suite could be seen the severed head of the Nautonnier, propped in a pool of clotted blood. Christian had lifted the headless corpse into a facing chair, and it sat there stiff and macabre, like a gruesome figure in a wax museum.

"As you can see," said Christian, positioning himself behind his mortified uncle, "there has been a change in command. The Nautonnier has ceded his position to me."

The prince seemed only then to come out of his shock. He would have fled the room had Christian not placed a heavy hand on his shoulder.

"Do you remember when you used to drop me off and pick me up from school, Uncle?"

"Before and after every holiday," stammered the prince.

"Was it ever difficult for you?" asked Christian. "Knowing that you were taking an innocent boy to be buggered by the man who is now dead before you?"

The prince froze, unable to respond. The psychologists had assured them that Christian's memories would remain suppressed for the entirety of his life.

"I had nothing to do with it!" he stammered. "It was something between your father and the Nautonnier."

"You had everything to do with it! You knowingly allowed it to happen!"

"I will not be held accountable for your father's actions!" said the prince with rekindling authority. "I am leaving!"

He attempted to move but found that an invisible force was holding him fast. He struggled to free himself from it, his eyes bulging from the effort. Christian looked on. In the space of a few seconds, the prince's face had gone from a pasty, ashen white to a vivid purple.

"Sit down," snapped Christian with icy hatred. "I'm the Nautonnier now. You will leave when I am finished with you."

"Please, Christian," he said, giving up his struggle and sinking into a chair. "I am your family."

It was on hearing this reference to his family that yet another deep, childhood wound surfaced in Christian. Impossible as it might seem, it had been the cause of more pain than all the abuses suffered at the hands of Father Adrianus.

Christian had once had an older brother named Isaac. He had been the only source of love and support in his deprived life. It was not long after the birth of their sister, Alina, and the subsequent death of their mother, that Isaac had been sent off to study at Vatican City. From that point onward, everything in Christian's life had changed for the worse.

He had lost all contact with Isaac, and two years later had been shipped off to boarding school himself, returning home on his first holiday to find that his baby sister had also been displaced.

"What happened to my brother and sister?" said Christian, trembling with a strange combination of fear and rage. "Tell me about my brother and sister!"

The prince remained silent until he felt the force of a vicious slap to the back of his head.

"Your father sent Isaac to be manipulated by Father Adrianus," he stammered. "He was persuaded to disown himself from the Antov family. Your sister Alina was sent to be raised in another household."

The prince held up a hand to ward off another blow. Christian obviously wanted the full story. He proceeded with trepidation. He could well imagine the effect that the truth would have on Christian, and he feared for his life.

"Your father repeatedly raped your sister in Satanic rituals, Christian," he began. "He drove her to madness, and then disowned her at sixteen. She became a prostitute.

"Years later, in accordance with their plan, she was recovered and brought to Father Adrianus at the Vatican. She and Isaac were made to marry. Of course, they did not know that they were brother and sister, but through their union a hermaphrodite child was conceived. Alina died giving birth to it."

Christian looked down in silence, unable to comprehend what he was being told. It made no sense.

"The child was created to fulfill a Satanic prophecy," said the prince slowly. "Your father and the Nautonnier were obsessed with the occult. They used our science facility in Jerusalem to genetically mutate the child while it was still in Alina's womb. They used the genes in our bloodline to create a monster."

Christian broke from his stupor and turned to face the prince, his eyes smoldering with deadly intent.

"And you knew all this?" he said, coming slowly out of shock.

The prince shook his head from side to side as Christian bent down over him.

"No," he gasped, his eyes wide with fear. "You do not understand..."

Christian's face was contorting with the pain of betrayal now. This was his uncle. His family. How could he have allowed this to happen to innocent children? He reached out a hand, as if to caress the prince's face, but instead took him by the throat and began to shake him violently.

"You did nothing to stop it," he snarled. "You didn't give a shit!"

Christian was beside himself with fury now. How could such a thing be possible? It was too repugnant to even imagine. He released the prince in disgust and spat in his face.

In that moment, the same dark self that had possessed Christian when he had beheaded the Nautonnier, paid him another visit. All he could do was watch as it took control. In the blink of an eye the intensity of its presence had grown into such a murderous rage that it was impossible to contain.

"YOU'RE RESPONSIBLE!" exploded Christian in a thunderous roar.

His verbal assault was directed solely at the prince's face. It sent him recoiling into his chair, his head jerking backwards in terror. A second later the old man was clutching his chest, his other hand thrust outward, beseeching his nephew to desist.

Christian was suddenly calm and sated. He positioned himself directly over his uncle and smiled cruelly.

The prince's unfocused eyes were blinking erratically in the candlelight now, his facial features contracting with pain. Christian knew he was having a heart attack, and he cocked his head in curiosity. In the prince's cold eyes there could almost be seen a cry for mercy, but it seemed wooden and insincere.

Christian drew closer until his lips were brushing the old man's ear. He smiled coldly again, and his wickedness rang like an icy bell.

"Dear, Uncle Vladimir," he said with mock innocence, his words twisting into the prince's head. "Now you will... DIE!"

The volume and intensity of that final word caused the prince's pupils to contract in fear. A look of surprised desperation was contorting his features as he tried frantically to ward off the icy hand of death.

Christian moved away from him in disgust. He could see the life force slowly leaving the body and watched with great satisfaction as his uncle fell into a long, drawn-out death rattle.

When all was over, Christian spat on the corpse, and then bent immediately afterwards to tenderly kiss the forehead, a tendril of saliva stretching and breaking as his lips pulled away.

* * * * * *

The morning was still young when the chief inspector left the Vanderhoff suite with Christian at his side. Behind them, in a shaft of sunlight, the dead prince could be seen sitting opposite the decapitated corpse, the Nautonnier's waxy head still on the table.

"A tragic incident, Mr. Antov," said the inspector solemnly, closing his notebook. "It is clear that your uncle died of a heart attack after murdering Father Adrianus. No investigation will be needed."

"Very good, Inspector," said Christian darkly. "Thank you for your diligence, and please have this mess cleaned up. I will have my assistant make the funeral arrangements."

"Very good, Mr. Antov," he said. "And a peaceful day to you, sir. You have my most sincere condolences."

Christian watched the inspector leave.

The matters of the Permanent Secretary are above the law.

No sooner had Christian had this thought than he felt himself being pulled back into the room, as though by an invisible hand. He made his way to the Nautonnier's body, and acting on an impulse, removed a bejeweled ring from the corpse. He placed it on his finger, directly next to his father's ring, and moved to look at himself in the mirror. A chorus of whispers were sounding in his mind again, but his time with unprecedented intensity.

"Hail the new Nautonnier! All power to Ahreimanius, the Lord of Darkness and Matter!"

Christian shuddered as an icy chill rushed up his spine. In the mirror's reflection he could see the repugnant Zurvanites standing behind him now. They were positioned around the Nautonnier's severed head, their grainy forms jerking violently from side to side, untouched by the sunlight that streamed into the room. Christian spun around suddenly with boiling wrath.

"Get away from me!" he bellowed, but they had already vanished.

It was only then that Christian fully grasped the dark truth. He had indeed become the new Nautonnier, and he recalled what his wicked predecessor had told him of the Zurvanites only days before.

"They are the Four. Since ancient times they have served the Nautonnier and given him knowledge and power."

Like a floodgate opening, Christian was at that moment made privy to many strange and mysterious things, and he was certain that the Zurvanites had been the ones to impart this knowledge onto him.

As though through churning mists, there came to him strange and formless recollections, and in the blink of an eye he had been taken back through time; past the days of Herod, past the rule of the Zoroastrians, and further back still to when the world was watery, and men were like reptiles; murderous and cruel.

This was his ancestry, the lineage of all the Nautonniers who had gone before him. With it came a knowledge of the things that needed to be done at present, so that the dark plans of Lucifer might come to pass.

He picked up a handset from its place on a table below the mirror.

"This is Christian Antov," he said. "Get me Cynthia."

"Hello, Mr. Antov," came her silky voice. "How can I help you?"

"We will be checking out tonight."

"Of course, Mr. Antov," she said. "I'll arrange to have your things packed immediately. Will you be needing anything else?"

"Dr. Bennington will be getting here shortly. Call me the moment he arrives."

"Yes, sir," she said seductively. "Anything else?"

Christian turned to study his reflection in the mirror again and for a split second saw himself shift and transform as the Zurvanites had done. He bent closer to the glass. For that fraction of a moment, he could have sworn that his features had become reptilian.

Christian ran his hands over his face. He was beginning to understand.

"Connect me with the head secretary of our Jerusalem office."

Cynthia was silent for a moment, surprised by the odd request.

"Right away, Mr. Antov."

Christian waited impatiently.

"Yes, Mr. Antov," came the voice of a man, his accent Israeli. "How can I help you?"

"We will be moving all operations to the Jerusalem complex this afternoon. Coordinate with Cynthia. I want our pilots ready for takeoff at thirteen hundred hours, and I want everyone in the Steering Committee on that plane.

"I will accept no excuses. Set up a group meeting for tomorrow morning. Have my private jet fueled and ready for immediate takeoff. Is that clear?"

"Yes, sir, Mr. Antov. Immediately, sir."

CHAPTER 38

Gibraltar.

The old bishop watched the barriers on either side of the runway rise into the morning air. They had been lowered to stop the flow of pedestrians across the tarmac while their plane had made its landing. Now, as they taxied towards the small terminal, the traffic had begun to flow again, a milling crowd headed by a cavalry of electric scooters.

"Your Excellency will be glad to know that Amir has arranged accommodations for you and your friends."

It was the deep voice of Bahadur that spoke. He was out of his seat now, and on his way to open the hatch.

"Excellent!" exclaimed the old bishop happily. "You must thank him for us."

"You may do so yourself, your Excellency," said Bahadur, pulling open the hatch.

In an instant Amir was inside, embracing Bahadur heartily.

"Good cousin!" said Bahadur, rubbing Amir's back with his massive paws. "Have faith in Allah. We will get them out safely."

"I'm not worried," said Amir, his dreadlocks swaying. "We've got a small army to help us do it."

Amir shot a welcoming smile at the three seniors.

"You were lucky to make it to Gibraltar," he said. "They've shut down air traffic across Europe."

Bahadur's brow knotted into a frown.

"Why have they done this?"

"Terrorist attacks," said Amir, addressing each of them in turn. "All in the last hour. Bombings. One in Madrid, two in London, two in New York City, one in Atlanta, and only ten minutes ago a massive explosion in Rome. Thousands are dead. They've declared martial law in the U.S."

The bishop stood up in alarm, as did Suora and Fra.

"We must contact Gabriel and Natasha!"

"I only just got off the phone with them," he said respectfully. "They're fine. They're on their way here."

CHAPTER 39

The French Riviera.

The black sports car screamed through a curving tunnel west of Monaco, its tuned exhaust reverberating off the chiseled walls of the mountain pass. To the left, flickering through a series of gallery openings, the Mediterranean was shimmering under a rising sun.

At long last the rain had stopped, and they were finally getting a chance to make up for lost time. Gabriel looked down at the speedometer and shook his head in amazement.

Two hundred and forty kilometres an hour, and I'm barely pressing the accelerator.

With all air traffic having been suspended after the terrorist strikes, they had been forced to drive to Gibraltar. It was now seven in the morning, with very little traffic on the autoroute. If they could maintain an average speed of two hundred, they would be crossing into Gibraltar seven hours from now.

"Maybe we can look at this now," said Natasha, producing the envelope containing Professor Metrovich's journal.

"Do the honours," said Gabriel.

Natasha opened the envelope and removed the tattered book. It was thick and worn, and it smelled of old leather.

"Wow," she whispered, opening it carefully. "It's filled with illuminations..."

She held it up and Gabriel shot over a quick glance. In the second he had looked, he had seen intricate medieval illustrations, glowing gold leaf, and precise calligraphy.

"I had no idea," he said, shaking his head.

Many times, Gabriel had seen his father working in the journal, but he had never been permitted to know what was within. When he had asked, his father had always given the same response.

"When it is time, Gabriel, and only then."

The journal had always disappeared somehow, and as a boy, no matter how thoroughly he had searched for it, Gabriel had never once found it.

"So what's in it besides pretty pictures?"

Natasha was studying the book as she spoke.

"Eighth and ninth century texts," she said. "Perfect copies, Gabriel. Letters, scrolls, papyri, ancient maps. Some are in Greek, others in Coptic, Aramaic, Arabic… Here's a Latin manuscript. Guess who it's by."

Gabriel shrugged.

"Gutierrez de la Cruz," she said.

"That guy's everywhere."

Natasha turned another page. It was covered in gold leaf.

"This book's a masterpiece," she whispered. "I can't believe your father created this. It's even hand bound."

Gabriel only nodded. He missed the old man terribly.

"Listen to what he writes on the very first page," she said. "It's an excerpt from the Pistis Sophia.

"And the spirit of the Saviour was moved in him, and he cried, How long shall I suffer you? Do ye still not know? Do ye still not understand that ye are all Angels, and Archangels; all Lords, and Rulers? That ye are from all; of yourselves and in yourselves in turn; from one mass, and one matter, and one essence?

"It refers to humanity's divine nature," said Natasha, "and the high places we held before the Fall. The page next to it only contains a single line of text, but it looks really important by the way it's been illuminated."

Gabriel looked over at her.

"What does it say?"

Natasha read it aloud.

"To transcend the Cube is to see it in all things."

Gabriel raised an eyebrow but was soon lost in his thoughts. He was thinking of his father. Natasha continued to study the book.

"This journal's divided into sections," she said at length. "The first treats with a medieval author named Chrétien de Troyes, and his book *The Quest For The Holy Grail.*"

Gabriel paused to think.

"That was a fusion of Celtic folklore and Orthodox Christianity, wasn't it?"

Natasha nodded.

"Yes, and Jewish mystical symbolism too. It can be interpreted on many different levels. Some say it's an allegory of the secret teachings of the Alchemists."

"The ones who could turn lead into gold," said Gabriel.

Natasha nodded again.

"The Alchemists were Gnostic priests," she said. "The Church burned them all and destroyed their knowledge. It was called *gnosis*, and your father was obsessed with finding out what it was."

Gabriel smiled and shook his head.

"That sounds like Dad."

Natasha pulled an iPad from her backpack, her eyes wide with excitement.

"What are you doing now?" asked Gabriel.

"Researching," she said, tapping at the screen.

Gabriel gave a nod and let her surf the internet in silence. Several minutes later she had found what she was looking for.

"According to this," she said, glancing over at Gabriel, "the person who possesses gnosis becomes an immortal creator of heavenly worlds. His every desire is fulfilled, and life takes on a perpetual state of excitement and bliss."

Gabriel raised his eyebrows.

"Sounds like Las Vegas."

Natasha shot him a sidelong glance.

"The only problem is that there are practically no traces of gnosis left. The little that remains is veiled in legend and myth."

"So basically, it's a lost knowledge."

Natasha continued scanning the document she had found.

"Acquiring gnosis was an initiatory path," she said. "Pieces of the knowledge were given to the student as he or she advanced. The alchemists believed that gaining gnosis was the meaning of life. It was about remembering to be something that we once were, and still are, instead of trying to become something we're not."

"So what are we?" asked Gabriel.

Natasha looked over at him as he drove.

"It says we're all God."

"Gnosticism," said Gabriel, thinking. "The ultimate heresy. Christianity as myth."

Natasha nodded.

"The alchemists combined Judeo-Christian mythology with other ancient mythologies. To them, the story of the Garden of Eden wasn't so much the cause of the Fall, but rather the result of it. In their version, the serpent isn't even the devil. She's the benevolent Mother, and the knowledge contained in the apple is the gnosis that reminds Adam and Eve of the Virtue they lost as a result of the Fall."

Gabriel scanned the road ahead.

"Like in the myth that Marcus told us about."

Natasha put away the tablet and returned her attention to the journal, reading silently for a while longer before looking up at Gabriel. Her eyes were wide with the wonder that only a theologian can feel about such things.

"The next section's about Gutierrez de la Cruz," she said. "According to this, he wasn't just the one who found the lost

Cube. He was also a member of an organization called the *Council of Six*."

"What's that?"

Natasha scanned the page.

"It was comprised of representatives from each of the six world religions. All summoned by the Moorish Caliph of Toledo in 866 to translate the proto writings inscribed on the Cube."

Gabriel recalled the parchments that had previously covered the artifact. They had been written in six different languages. He had only skimmed over them at the time, but it now occurred to him what they must have spoken of.

"Of course," he said. "That's what's written on each of the six parchments: Discourses on the translations they made. But why? Why gather scribes from the four corners of the earth to translate crude symbols that could have meant absolutely anything? Could there really be some kind of secret knowledge locked up in the Cube?"

Natasha shrugged.

"Your father suspected that everything would be explained in The Book of Khalifah."

"That's why he was so obsessed with finding it," said Gabriel. "That book must be pretty damn special."

Natasha looked over at him.

"We need to find it, Gabriel."

"I agree," he said, his eyes glued to the road. "Keep reading. I want to know everything my old man knew."

CHAPTER 40

Los Picos de Europa, Northern Spain.

Isaac woke to find a brown hunting dog licking his face. The sun was up now, and the terrible storm had passed. His mind worked to remember where he was, and how he had arrived there.

Where did this dog come from? What is happening?

He saw that he was on the shore of a small mountain lake. At its centre he could see a little island burning steadily. His memory returned a moment later. He reached up and patted the dog's head.

"It is thanks to you that I am alive."

Isaac shuddered as he recalled the horrific events that had transpired, and how he had waded out into the waters to escape the hellfire. He had been certain he would drown, and was on the verge of letting the lake take him, when a dog had swum up to him unexpectedly. He had lost consciousness shortly after.

As Isaac lay there, his mind went over all that had happened since the plane had gone down, and he was perplexed by his clarity of mind. It was as though he had regained his judgment, something his doctor had told him would never happen. He looked at the dog, puzzled by the deep intelligence in its amber eyes.

"Where did you come from, my friend?" he asked. "There can be no explanation for your appearance other than divine intervention."

The dog gave a round nod and barked. He put a paw on Isaac's chest as he lay there, and it seemed to Isaac that the animal was trying to communicate something to him. He examined the dog's collar. It was made of rough twine and passed through a crude hole in what looked to be the lid of an olive jar. Isaac saw that there was a name written on its underside.

"Sir Shackleton," he read, smiling. "A fitting title."

Groaning with pain, he sat up and took a deep breath of the fresh mountain air.

"I cannot recall when my head was ever this clear," he said to Shackleton. "Perhaps it was when I was a boy. Everything's so vibrant… So beautiful…"

Isaac looked around in wonderment, only then remembering his medication. He had not taken it for many days now. He searched his pockets, a panic beginning to take him. In over forty years he had never once missed a dose.

"I must find my pills…"

Just then he felt Shackleton's muzzle poke him in the side, and he turned to see that the dog's eyes were focused intently on him. There could be no mistake as to what the dog was trying to tell him. His failure to take his medication was the reason for his recovery. He looked at the dog, his brow furrowed with confusion.

"But Father Adrianus always insisted that I never miss a dose," he muttered. "He said that my sanity depended on it."

Shackleton gave him another poke.

"Very well," he said, frowning. "I will get up."

Isaac rose unsteadily to his feet, noticing only then that Shackleton had returned him to the very place where he had first embarked onto the lake. Not a few paces away was the makeshift sled he had used to drag the corpse from the crash site, as well as his shoes, and the pack of supplies he had taken from the dead Father Franco. Isaac looked down at the dog.

"Who are you, my friend?"

Shackleton let out a resounding bark in response. He trotted over to Father Franco's pack, picking it up in his maw and dragging it to Isaac's feet. Within, Isaac found cured sausages and biscuits. It was not long before he had sat himself down and was sharing a meal with his new friend.

"Something of great importance has happened, Shackleton," he said, looking out over the water. "I must try to understand."

The flames on the island were beginning to subside now, replaced by a thick plume of rising smoke. Even though the sight of it served to affirm the reality of the demonic horrors he had experienced, the smoke was also strengthening his faith in God. That such a powerful evil could exist only confirmed the existence of an even greater force of good.

As he looked out over the lake, it seemed to Isaac that all the events of his life had led him to the place he now found himself. He took a deep breath and rose to his feet, scanning the mountainous peaks that encased them.

"I do not understand, Father," he prayed quietly. "Lucifer used me and discarded me. He left me for dead. I am an abomination. I dismembered the corpse of my own son. I released an unspeakable evil onto the world. Why do you spare my life? Why do you send this noble animal to help me? Should I not be despised and cursed by you?"

Isaac returned his gaze to the island, his eyes filling with tears.

"My life is yours, Father," he whispered. "Help me and guide me so that I might put right the terrible wrongs I have done."

CHAPTER 41

Gibraltar.

Bahadur was standing on the edge of a rusty dock in the shadows of the lower port. Around him loomed the clutter of Gibraltar's industrial marina, the smell of stale diesel fuel and brine filling the air. A dusty sun had just risen behind the rocky peak, but the sky in the west was still holding on to a few scattered stars. The dawn had come up blood red, and there would be hard weather today.

"A good day to storm a castle," said Amir, emerging from a dilapidated workshop.

He struck a match and stoked his chillum until they were engulfed in its fragrant smoke. He took a deep haul and offered the pipe to Bahadur, but the giant shook his head absently and turned to look out to sea. His broad face was a mask of consternation.

"They'll be fine, cousin," said Amir, noting his dread. "Nasrallah knows you. He'd never hurt them. He's a coward."

Bahadur glanced over at Amir.

"Where is Gabriel?"

"He's on his way. He says to expect him at around two or three."

"Your friend knows how to drive."

Amir released a billowing cloud of smoke.

"He's been averaging two-twenty all the way from Florence."

Bahadur nodded and then looked off to sea again, frowning.

"I am concerned about the men," he said in his deep basso.

"They'll all be here soon."

The brown giant shook his head darkly.

"It is not our men I am concerned for, cousin. It is Nasrallah's men I am thinking of. They are good men. They have wives and children. They work hard. They do not deserve to die."

"They know Nasrallah," said Amir, poking aside a wayward dreadlock. "If they choose to work for a murderer, they—"

"They do not choose!" said Bahadur, turning to grasp Amir's shoulder before proceeding more gently. "They have families to feed. It is that simple."

"Cousin," said Amir in earnest. "Maybe there's another way. Once Nasrallah's been taken out, our new coalition will be in control. There will be work for everyone. If we could somehow let Nasrallah's men know about our plan. They'd rather work for you."

"We cannot take that risk," said Bahadur gloomily. "It could easily go the other way. Men take what is real. They do not risk their lives on promises. Nasrallah pays them at the end of every month. That is all they are concerned with, and I cannot blame them for it."

"Then men will die," said Amir, spitting into the oily water. "Men will die."

CHAPTER 42

Costa Brava, Spain.

The rocky cliffs were racing past in a blur, and Gabriel was enjoying the drive tremendously. The purring sports car was finding no difficulty in maintaining a cruising speed of two hundred and forty kilometres an hour. It felt like the car was on rails. Natasha looked up from the journal.

"There's an Arabic document here your father transcribed," she said, bending closer to the book. "It's dated 661 CE and addressed to the Umayyad Caliph of Cordoba. It's from one of his clerics."

"What does it say?"

Natasha scanned it for a moment before answering. She wanted to make sure she was translating it correctly.

"It says that Arab forces found the Urn of Theophilus after taking Alexandria."

"I've heard of that artifact before," said Gabriel, scratching his head, "Theophilus found the Urn in the Great Library of Alexandria, just before he ordered it burnt to the ground."

"Theophilus the bishop of Alexandria."

Gabriel nodded.

"He led a Catholic movement at the end of the fourth century. Their orders were to destroy anything that was heretical. Sacred temples, priceless art, ancient writings."

He paused to remember.

"Legend has it there were some pretty old tablets in that urn. They were supposedly written by the first Mesopotamian kings."

Natasha was shaking her head in amazement.

"According to this letter, those tablets spoke of a Cube of Knowledge, Gabriel. It's there where the Arabs first learned of the artifact. Listen to this. I'll do my best to translate it.

Know, oh Prince of the Faithful, that at the time of the emperor Theodosius, the bishop Theophilus issued forth an order for the demolition of the great heathen library of Alexandria. From therein he was brought a golden urn of such beauty and richness that he could not bring himself to destroy it, but instead took it secretly as his own.

Within this urn were ancient tablets belonging to Alulim, who was the First King of Sumer, and who reigned for 28,800 years in the kingdom of Eridu, in Mesopotamia. The tablets spoke of a Cube of Knowledge, and of the Nephilim, who took the Cube from its resting place at the entrance of a great labyrinth and gave it to Alulim, to whom they taught many wondrous things.

At the End of The World this Cube is said to reside, oh prince, in the land of the warrior-priests. It was recovered by the Kristos of Judea and laid within the tomb of his brother who guards it until the day of reckoning.

"Kristos is Greek for Christ, right?" said Gabriel.

Natasha was still studying the text.

"It comes from the word *Krishna* in Sanskrit."

Gabriel thought for a moment.

"If the tomb belongs to the brother of Jesus, it means that this document is referring to the same tomb that Gutierrez found. Do you think there's a connection between the labyrinth it mentions and the one in the Egyptian myth that Marcus told us about?"

"I do," said Natasha, tucking her hair behind an ear.

"That would mean that the entrance to this labyrinth is on the same island where Gutierrez found the tomb..." said Gabriel, turning to look at her.

Natasha looked back at him and nodded excitedly.

"You said the markings on the Cube were Basque, right?"

"Proto-Basque," said Gabriel, squinting into the distance as he drove.

"Aren't the Basques and the Celts of Ireland related?"

Gabriel shrugged.

"That's what the DNA suggests..."

"Gabriel," said Natasha. "There's hard evidence that Christian evangelists landed in Ireland just four years after Jesus was crucified. They were led there by James the Just, and they succeeded in converting the Druids to Christianity."

Gabriel frowned.

"The Vatican deemed the Celtic Church heretical," he said. "They called it Insular Christianity. How could it be heretical if it was created by Jesus' own brother?"

He scratched the back of his head, his frown deepening.

"I see what you're getting at though," he continued. "The Druids must have known about the labyrinth. That's why the runes on the Cube are Proto-Basque, and that's why Jesus delivered the Cube back to them. The Druids must have been its original keepers."

"Of course it's just speculation," said Natasha, looking down at the journal, "but your father seemed to think the same. He was convinced that the end of the world was not so much a time, but a place; a Celtic place..."

"Finisterre, right?" asked Gabriel.

"Yes," said Natasha, looking up from the book in surprise. "How did you know?"

"Because it's not far from Santiago de Compostela. It's a small village on the west coast of Galicia, but it's also been called *The End of The World* since the time of the Druids."

Gabriel sped past a grouping of trucks.

"So, the labyrinth is in Finisterre…"

"Not exactly," said Natasha, "but your father believed that it was somewhere close. According to him, that whole area was considered to be the end of the world."

Natasha turned to a different part of the journal.

"This section's dedicated to the labyrinth. Your father refers to it as *The Great Labyrinth of Sarras.*"

Gabriel raised his eyebrows.

"Sarras was the heavenly city in *The Quest for The Holy Grail.*"

Natasha looked up from the book and nodded.

"The place where Galahad saw the Grail and healed the Fisher King."

"Thus, satisfying the legend, and restoring life to the kingdom…"

Natasha nodded again.

"Some historians believe that the original Grail romances were written by members of *Rex Angelus*, and that they carried secret messages that contradicted the Church's doctrine."

"Rex Angelus?"

Natasha chewed her lip.

"A society that claimed to be the direct descendants of Jesus Christ, and the keepers of his original teachings."

"A bloodline of Christ…" repeated Gabriel, rolling his eyes.

"It's a well-known hypothesis," said Natasha with a shrug. "Gutierrez de la Cruz claimed to be Rex Angelus himself. Your father believed that he only became a priest to infiltrate the Church."

Gabriel had to break hard and wait for a car to get out of the passing lane.

Natasha read one of the professor's annotations aloud.

"To all Rex Angelus, the Holy Grail is a symbol of the original gnosis. It is the receptacle of the wisdom that Jesus himself taught, before it was distorted by the Vatican in order to control the masses.

In the story, when the Christ-like Galahad is pure enough to behold the Grail, he restores the Fisher King to full health, and in this way the wasted kingdom is restored.

If we follow the allegory, this is another way of saying that when humanity is ready, the true teachings of Jesus Christ will triumph over the greed and hypocrisy of the Vatican and result in a kind of heaven on earth."

Gabriel shook his head in astonishment.

"So, it's exactly as Marcus was saying back in the catacombs. The Cube and the Holy Grail are the same thing."

"It seems so, Gabriel," said Natasha, her eyes alight with excitement. "Your father makes the point that throughout history, the Grail has not only been described as a cup, or a chalice, but also as *A Stone Within A Cup."*

She read from the journal again.

"A stone which fell from heaven and symbolizes the wisdom that is imbibed when one drinks from the metaphorical cup of the Kristos."

Natasha looked up from the book.

"According to Rex Angelus, there's only one primordial source of wisdom. It's a doctrine that became fragmented over the ages, with different parts being adopted by each of the six world religions.

"It would appear that the ancient Druids were the guardians of that original knowledge. They were the warrior-priests that the letter spoke of. The Keepers of the Cube.

"Your father believed that if the fragmented parts could be unified again, then there would be harmony between all the religions, and humanity would at last have access to the entire truth, instead of just small fragments of it."

"What exactly have we stumbled onto here?"

"Your father's life work," said Natasha in awe.

Gabriel rubbed his eyes to stave off the sleepiness. There was so much to consider, but his faculties were losing their edge. He needed to shut his eyes for a while. Natasha continued to carefully turn the pages.

"What are you reading now?" he asked at length.

"You're not going to believe me."

Gabriel looked over to see her flipping back to earlier sections of the journal, her head shaking from side to side.

"This is impossible," she muttered, "but you can see it everywhere in the diary."

"Try me."

She glanced over at Gabriel through a lock of chestnut hair.

"Your father claims that Gutierrez speaks of you and I in his writings. He refers to us as *The Two,* but that there's an ambiguity in the translation."

"What kind of ambiguity?"

"In certain Coptic dialects, The Two, also means *The Primal King and Queen.* Your father wasn't sure why this particular word would have been used, when a more specific numerical terminology existed."

"But how could Gutierrez know of us?"

"Uncle Marcus said we were a part of all this, Gabriel. Remember?"

"It's just a product of my father's overactive imagination. He was making assumptions, Natasha. Nothing more."

"Gutierrez refers to you as *Gabriel, Hero of God,* and to me as *Natalia, The day of the Saviour's Birth.* Your father writes that you and I are spoken of in the ancient prophecies as well. The same ones that speak of our heroic mission."

"Our mission?" asked Gabriel, turning to face her. "What mission?"

Natasha held up the journal to show Gabriel an illumination when a loose page fell into her lap.

"What's that?" asked Gabriel.

She fell silent as she read it.

"Well?" asked Gabriel again. "What is it?"

Natasha was shaking her head in disbelief.

"It's a reminder that your father wrote to himself, Gabriel. It's about us. It's so strange that it should have fallen out of the journal at this particular moment..."

"What does it say?"

Natasha read it aloud.

A Matter of Grave Importance

When the Cube is retrieved, Gabriel and Natasha must go immediately to the Bodega del Pi in Toledo to see Yuri. Any delay could have serious repercussions on their mission. I must inform Father Franco of this development.

Natasha lurched forward against her seatbelt, surprised by the sudden deceleration. Gabriel was braking hard.

"What are you doing?"

"We're taking this exit to Toledo," he said. "If we cut through the middle of Spain this *Bodega del Pi* won't even be out of our way. Besides, it's your turn to drive. I can hardly keep my eyes open anymore."

CHAPTER 43

Somewhere over the Mediterranean Sea.

"This is Galaxy Network News, the most trusted news network in the world. Spain is reeling this morning after a string of seventeen car bombs ravage Bilbao, Barcelona, Madrid, and Zaragoza. Hundreds are dead, and many more injured. As well, violent riots spreading throughout the Muslim communities of the United States and Europe. Is the war spreading into our homes? Stay tuned for a special GNN report: *The Fist of Islam. Christendom is Burning.*"

Dr. Bennington's attention was fixed on the monitor mounted to the cabin wall. He was in a private jet enroute to Israel, being taken there against his will.

He was an older man; lean, clean-shaven, and almost entirely bald. He wore rimless spectacles and a light beige suit with a golden cravat. His demeanor was exceedingly gentle and consistently calm, even in his current situation.

Three hours earlier he had arrived at Christian's hotel only to be stuffed into a limousine and driven to a private airfield. Under the care of three armed security guards, Bennington had then been escorted onto Christian's jet and made to wait there for over an hour. After arriving, Christian had disappeared into the cockpit, leaving Bennington alone in the luxurious cabin as the plane took off. The gentle doctor could not believe what he was seeing on television.

"Well, Steve," said the expert being interviewed, "this kind of fighting is nothing new. Taking shelter in populated urban sectors allows the terrorists to use civilians as shields. For the most part, these Muslim communities are made up of great people, but they've got some bad apples in the bunch, and it's these guys who have banded together to fight this war."

"This war you are referring to, Mr. Peterson. Who exactly are the fundamentalists waging it against?"

"Against whoever opposes them, Steve."

"Now isn't that the loveliest circus you've ever seen, Doctor?" said Christian, returning from the cockpit.

He muted the monitor and threw himself onto a leather sofa across from where Bennington sat. Much to Christian's relief, his father's whispers had subsided after the last appearance of the Zurvanites, and he was enjoying the reprieve tremendously. He reached lazily for his glass of wine.

"There's nothing lovely about war and chaos, Christian," said Dr. Bennington.

"They are a means to an end," said Christian offhand. "The lovely thing I was referring to is the instability."

"I don't understand."

"Can't you see that we're all in great danger?" asked Christian sarcastically. "The terrorists are very terrifying, and the population needs the government to protect them. *The Enforcer of Laws* has become our new hero. He will protect us, but we must do exactly what he tells us to do. This is war after all."

"And what will we be told to do, Christian?"

"We'll be told to comply, Doctor. The masses will soon surrender the majority of their civil rights."

Christian lit a cigarette and returned his attention to the television. They were showing footage of a Muslim uprising taking place in Washington D.C.

"It's all just propaganda of course," said Christian, yawning. "It's nowhere near as big as it looks. The Muslims are as docile as lambs."

"And how can you be so sure this is just propaganda?"

Christian gave a dry chuckle.

"Because my organization is producing these stories. We own the mainstream media, Doctor. We decide how people perceive things."

"How can you possibly expect me to believe that?"

Christian rolled his eyes.

"I hope you're not one of those people who refuses to believe in conspiracy theories."

Bennington held his gaze but remained silent.

"Well, it's time you revisited your opinions and considered the validity of at least one of them."

"And which one might that be?" asked the doctor.

"Do you know the one about the group of cigar smoking men in the dark boardroom who are secretly running the world?"

"Yes," said Bennington. "That theory is familiar to me."

"Well, it's true, Doctor, with the exception that all those men answer to only one man, and I don't smoke cigars, I smoke cigarettes."

Christian took a long draw from his cigarette and smiled with self-satisfaction. Bennington shifted in his leather seat, crossing his legs. He had garnered very little from Christian up to this point, and he wanted nothing more than to keep his patient talking.

Christian was showing every sign of megalomania, and Bennington's professional instincts could sense tremendous turmoil behind the confident facade.

"Christian, you must forgive me if I find it difficult to believe that you're the leader of a shadow government directing every nation in the world."

"I direct most of them, Doctor, but not all of them. Not yet. With regards to your doubt, consider that we're the only civilians flying over European airspace right now."

"I'm aware that there have been restrictions made on flights," said the doctor. "But I'm also aware that given your new position, you must have certain privileges."

"Yes, Doctor, I do," said Christian, gesturing towards the window. "Perhaps these privileges would explain our military escort."

Bennington rose from his seat, sliding the blind up as he bent forward. There, not fifty feet from their plane and staggered in perfect formation were three RAF fighter jets.

"Are you beginning to understand, Doctor?" said Christian, enjoying his new companion tremendously. "There are another three on our starboard side as well."

"Understanding would imply knowing, Christian," said Bennington, returning to his seat, "and I'm sure I know very little."

"Not to worry, Doctor, because I'm going to tell you everything. I feel like I have found a very good friend in you."

"Friends don't force their friends to accompany them to Israel by taking their wife hostage."

Christian sat up suddenly, an anger alighting in him.

"Your wife is staying in a three thousand-euro-a-night suite in the Paris Ritz. You would think that would be good enough for anyone. Perhaps you might show some gratitude, Doctor. I am your patient. I am in need of your help."

"You threatened to kill her, Christian."

"No one's going to kill anyone if you do your job."

"And what might that be?" asked Bennington. "Altering your doses to prevent hallucinations? That will not be sufficient to treat what ails you, Christian. You must talk to me. You must tell me what is wrong."

Christian rose from the sofa and walked to the bar to refill his glass. He lit a cigarette and focused his eyes on the doctor.

"Strange things have been happening... Unnatural things."

"Perhaps you could be more specific?"

Christian continued to stare intently at Bennington.

"I was tricked into making a pact with the devil," he said. "I savagely murdered the man responsible. I also murdered my uncle. After I did all this, four demons appeared to me and told me that I was the son of Lucifer, destined to rule the world, but that's not the worst of it."

Bennington nodded slowly. It was important that Christian did not feel judged.

"What is the worst of it, then?"

Christian took a heavy draw from his cigarette and then placed it carefully in the ashtray. He took a sip of wine.

"The worst of it, Doctor, is that I believe them."

CHAPTER 44

Toledo, Spain.

An ancient hand emerged from the shadows, unlatching the heavy gate and pushing it outwards towards them.

"This is the place," whispered Natasha into Gabriel's ear. She pointed to the battered sign that hung above them.

La Bodega Del Pi

Gabriel studied the pale hand and saw that it belonged to an old woman.

"Buenos dias, Señora," he said. "I'm Gabriel, Agardi Metrovich's son."

"Indeed, you are," came the old woman's voice. "And an angel of hope you are too. Enter, my child. I have been expecting you."

Gabriel shot a puzzled glance at Natasha and went in first. Everything was draped in shadow, but the darkness was soon vanquished when a shutter squeaked open. In the dusty light of the window, he could see an ancient woman dressed as a gypsy. Her silver hair was covered in a crimson shawl, and her eyes were big and green, shimmering with mystical power.

"Come in, come in," she said in her thick accent. "You too, Natasha. Come in. You are even more beautiful than I imagined."

Natasha smiled politely and entered timidly, looking around her as she did so. They were in a small tavern, its walls and ceiling comprised of ancient stone masonry.

Centred under a massive arch was a dark wooden bar, behind which sat dozens of open wine bottles, lined up on oaken shelves with their corks stopped into their necks. There was a large roast on the bar, covered in a glass dome. The old woman took up a knife that was lying next to it and used it to point out two stools. Gabriel and Natasha obeyed her silent order and sat down.

"You have driven a great distance," divined the old gypsy woman, turning to face an antique espresso machine, "and at great speeds, I might add."

She worked the machine, the smell of coffee filling the room.

"There is confusion in your minds, and your bellies are empty. This combination is not conducive to learning. I will make you breakfast."

The old woman sliced some of the peppery pork roast and stuffed the meat into crusty rolls, pressing them in what looked to be a fifty-year-old panini grill. She watched in silence as Gabriel and Natasha ate, speaking only when Gabriel had finished the last dram of his caffè latte.

He nodded to her in thanks as he put down the glass.

"I sense that your father has crossed over," said the gypsy woman soberly.

"Yes, he has," said Gabriel, looking down into his empty glass and turning it pensively. "He died earlier this month in a plane crash."

"Only his body is dead, my child," said the woman tenderly. "Now if you please. Come with me."

They followed her to a wrought iron staircase in the corner. It spiraled up into the stone ceiling and down into the wooden floor. As the old woman approached it, she came to a stop, her ancient hand clasping and unclasping the handrail as she thought.

"My husband's body is also dead," she said, studying the stone wall before her. "His name was Yuri Blavatsky. He was a procurer of ancient texts and writings. For fifty-nine years he assisted your father in his research, Gabriel. Many were the secrets they unearthed together; secrets of wisdom and power."

Gabriel looked over at Natasha, feeling the same curiosity he saw in her eyes. What secrets was the old gypsy referring to? Why had the professor seemed so urgent in his note? Why had he never told Gabriel about Yuri Blavatsky?

The air became cold and damp as they descended, and they soon arrived at an old wine cellar. Rack upon rack of vintage bottles surrounded them, and each was blanketed in thick cobwebs and caked in dust.

"Toledo is an old woman," said their guide over her shoulder, lighting a battered lantern as she spoke. "But as you will soon see, her womb still bears fruit."

They had descended well into the depths of the cellar when they came upon a heavy, time-blackened rack, laden with bottles. It was built against a wall of living stone.

The old woman hung her lantern on a nearby hook and reached slowly into one of the racks, pulling on a lever hidden within. In an instant the sound of scrapping stone gave way to a mechanical rumble of gears and counterweights. The massive rack slid aside.

"For reasons of secrecy," she said, retrieving the lantern from where she had hung it, "no electricity has ever been installed in this room. Follow me."

She led them through a low tunnel that opened into a circular chamber, about thirty feet in diameter. In the darkness they could make out a few cluttered shapes, but it was not until the old woman had lit a large candelabra that they could truly see the wonders the space had to offer.

Circling the entire chamber was an unbroken line of shoulder-high shelves; oaken, and crammed with ancient books, codices, scrolls of papyrus, vellum, and treasures of every kind. Covering its stone floor were luxurious Persian rugs on which could be seen several leather wingchairs, and sturdy desks laden with still more books and scrolls.

The room looked to be a library of sorts, but it was the stone ceiling that gave the chamber its unique character. Masterfully built, it formed a perfect semi-spherical dome above them.

"This is *The Chamber of the Sphere*," said the old gypsy. "It was built by Toledo's first Caliph. Here we have stored our greatest treasures."

Natasha swallowed slowly and followed Gabriel into the space, her eyes wide.

"What's that?" she whispered, pointing to a strange spherical apparatus that lay glimmering at the centre of the room.

Gabriel turned to look and saw that the device was mounted on a low wooden pedestal. Its diameter was about the size of a beach ball.

"From here it looks like some kind of optical instrument," he said, squinting through the dim light. "I've never seen anything like it before..."

He made his way slowly forward, his eyes never leaving the strange machine. Even in the half-light, it shone in all the spectral colours of a prism, reflecting and magnifying the rays from the old woman's candelabra into a million sparkling points of refracted light. He drew up to the sphere and circled it.

"It's beautiful," whispered Natasha, approaching from behind. "Look how it shimmers..."

"Hand ground salt crystal lenses," said Gabriel, amazed. "Hundreds of them. And just look at the work in this brass armature. By the construction of these linkages, I'd guess that the position of each lens could be calibrated to within a thousandth of an inch."

He looked over at Natasha and then back to the sphere, his eyes straining to take in as much information as possible.

"We're looking at a technological wonder of Islam," he said. "The likes of which few have ever seen. They were masters in optics and mathematics, but I had no idea they were capable of building an astrolabe this precise."

Natasha moved to Gabriel's side, looking deeply into the crystalline sphere.

"This is an astrolabe?"

Gabriel nodded; his eyes still fixed on the contraption.

"An ancient astronomical instrument," he said, still in awe. "They had many uses, including locating and predicting the positions of celestial bodies, navigation, astrology, surveying, timekeeping, and let's not forget *Qibla*."

"Finding the direction of Mecca," said Natasha. "That was the main reason why the Muslim astronomers built them. People needed to know which direction to pray in. But this doesn't look like an astrolabe to me, Gabriel."

"I know," he agreed. "Astrolabes were normally flat instruments, but the more advanced ones became spherical in shape. I've never seen one like this before. It would appear to be an optical astrolabe. I had no idea they even existed."

"That astrolabe was built by Al-Sufi," said the old gypsy from where she stood at the chamber's entrance.

"*Abd al-Rahman al Sufi?*" asked Gabriel, turning to face her, "The famous Persian astronomer?"

The old woman nodded slowly.

"If anyone knew astrolabes," continued Gabriel, looking at Natasha, "it was that guy. He outlined more than a thousand uses for them back in the tenth century."

"He built it for the Caliph of Toledo," said the woman, approaching. "Following instructions found on a Babylonian tablet dated to 5000 BCE."

Both Gabriel and Natasha turned to face the old woman.

"But I thought Hipparchus was the first to invent the astrolabe in 200 BCE," said Gabriel, already doubting himself.

He was rapidly learning not to believe everything the history books had taught him.

The old gypsy woman said nothing in return, but came directly towards them with the candelabra, her timeworn features shifting in the flickering candlelight.

Reaching over she depressed a linkage in the astrolabe's armature, and they watched as a section of the contraption swung aside to reveal a cubical orifice located directly at its centre. It too was lined with crystal lenses.

"I believe you are in possession of an artifact that will fit within this space?"

Gabriel looked over to find Natasha staring at him, her eyes wide with wonder. The niche looked to be precisely the same size as the Cube. Without a moment's delay, Gabriel produced the artifact from his pack, holding it aloft before him so that the old woman could see.

"The Compostela Cube," she whispered in awe, her voice trembling. "If only my husband were here to see it..."

"And my father along with him," said Gabriel solemnly, handing the old woman the glowing artifact. "Please, do the honours, Señora. Do it for both of them."

The old woman handed Natasha the candelabra.

"Your lungs are stronger than mine, child."

Natasha blew out the candles and the Cube's blue light took centre stage.

"It casts a wonderful hue, to be sure," said the old woman, taking hold of it. "I have never seen its like..."

With a remarkably steady hand she inserted the Cube into its slot, carefully closing the armature door over it. The effect was instantaneous.

With the Cube now installed in the centre of the astrolabe, its dim light had magnified itself tenfold, creating a spectacular cloud of glowing light that surrounded the contraption like an atmosphere around a planet.

"It's beautiful," whispered Natasha. "It's as though I could touch it."

"It looks like some kind of hologram," said Gabriel. "But what's the purpose of it?"

"The Cube's light is not sufficiently bright," said the old gypsy. "This is not the effect that the ancient scribes spoke of."

"I think we can make it brighter, Señora," said Natasha, smiling naughtily.

Gabriel turned to her with a questioning glance, only to see her rise up on her tiptoes and kiss him fully on the lips. The nature of the kiss took them both completely off guard. It was indescribably thrilling; a chemical reaction so encompassing that it was only the gypsy's cry of surprise that broke them from its spell.

When they opened their eyes, they saw what their kiss had done to the Cube.

Hair-lined streams of blazing blue light were shooting through the artifact like tendrils of plasma now. They were pulsing and building in intensity with every passing second, magnified and refracted by the astrolabe's innumerable lenses. An instant later their light reached a critical point, exploding through the crystalline instrument in a blinding detonation that caused them all to cry out in surprise.

A glittering atmosphere of shimmering light was being emitted from the sphere now, reflecting off what looked to be tiny, polished stones concealed in the dome's structure. The result of the optical interaction was a brilliant hologram that filled the entire space. It surrounded the three awestruck observers in such a way that it appeared that they themselves were a part of the projection.

"Is it a galaxy?" whispered Natasha, moving her hands through the illusion.

"It's *our* galaxy by the looks of it," said Gabriel, his eyes wide with wonder.

The projection was a perfectly scaled replica; an exact shimmering recreation of the Milky Way in all its entirety. What was more, it appeared to be in motion, its bright core and many arms orbiting a fist-sized, black sphere at its centre. It was being projected directly above the astrolabe itself. Natasha was the first to notice it.

"What's that?" she asked, pointing to it.

"It's what astronomers would call a super-massive black hole," said Gabriel, pushing back his messy hair as he studied the thing. "It sits at the centre of our galaxy and has the density of about a trillion stars."

The old gypsy woman stared into the black hole.

"The ancient astronomers of Sumer knew more of this black hole than all our scientists combined," she said. "Watch and see all their fears confirmed."

"What do you mean, Senora?" asked Natasha. "What fears?"

In answer to her question, the old woman pointed to an arm of the galaxy. There was a magnified section there, glowing within its own shimmering sphere.

"That is our solar system," she said. "Draw closer to it so that you can better see its precarious position."

Gabriel and Natasha did as they were told, wading past countless stars and nebulas to arrive at an inconspicuous location within one of the galaxy's many arms.

"I see nothing unusual about its position," said Gabriel. "Are you sure you've got your information right?"

"You must lower your line of vision until it aligns with the galactic plane," said the gypsy.

"Galactic plane?" asked Natasha.

Gabriel looked back at the old woman before answering Natasha's question.

"The galactic plane lies along the galaxy's equator," he explained. "As a result of their overwhelming mass, super-massive black holes spin at unbelievably high rates. Because of this, their projected gravitational field isn't spherical anymore. Instead, it gets flattened out and forms a massive spinning disc; kind of like a pancake. Ours is a hundred thousand light years in diameter, but only a few centimeters thick."

Gabriel bent his knees until his line of vision had aligned with the galaxy's equator. Natasha followed his example. To their utter surprise, the hologram's light vanished completely as their eyes passed through the thin disc of the galactic plane, only to return to its original splendor as their line of vision emerged from its underside.

"Why's this happening?" asked Natasha, lowering and raising her line of vision above and below the galactic plane.

"The gravitational field is just like the black hole," said Gabriel, doing the same. "It sucks up all the light that comes into contact with it."

"To the ancients it was known as the *Dark Rift*," said the old gypsy. "Our solar system will soon pass into it."

Gabriel and Natasha could see that the old woman was not mistaken. In the holographic projection, the magnified section that contained the earth's solar system was clearly moving closer and closer to the galactic plane.

"But what does this mean?" asked Natasha, looking at the old woman.

"It means the end of an age, my child," she said, walking towards them.

"You said that the ancients feared this," asked Natasha, "Why?"

Gabriel was the first to answer.

"Because every time our solar system passes through the galactic plane, the sun and the planets are exposed to massive magnetic and gravitational fields. Getting close to it would be devastating. Crossing it would be catastrophic."

Natasha considered the implications.

"So, all the strange weather we've been experiencing for the last decade, all the earthquakes and tsunamis and tornados and hurricanes, they're all being caused by our proximity to this gravitational field?"

"That's what it looks like," said Gabriel with a shrug. "Provided this hologram is accurate... According to astronomers, our solar system travels in a kind of wave pattern as it moves along its orbit. It dips up and down through the galactic plane every fifty million years or so. Every time this happens, our north and south poles shift in position."

"And how do they know this?"

"Core samples, mostly," said Gabriel. "They take them in Antarctica and use them to study the magnetic alignment of the molecules frozen into the ice. Every fifty million years they see massive and sudden changes recorded there. But that's not the only evidence. They also know that many of the places that are now arctic were once tropical, and vice versa. The earth hasn't always spun on the poles it spins on now."

"The end of each age is marked by a great cataclysm," said the old woman, nodding in acceptance.

"But why all the destruction?" asked Natasha in horror. "What causes it?"

Gabriel stroked his chin pensively.

"The earth isn't a hard ball of rock like everyone thinks," he said. "It's a ball of liquefied magma covered in a thin crust of stone. It's so malleable that when it spins, it actually bulges at the equator. Shift the locations of the poles and it'll bulge in different places."

"And the oceans and tectonic plates will shift to fill in the gaps," whispered Natasha.

"A natural occurrence for the planet," said Gabriel, "but one that's pretty devastating for all us insects living on its surface."

Gabriel and Natasha watched as the old gypsy removed the Cube from the astrolabe. The hologram vanished as suddenly as it had appeared.

"We pass through the Dark Rift on the twenty-first day of this month," she said, relighting the candelabra with a flaring match. "The cataclysm is unavoidable, but its catastrophic effects on both the earth and humanity can be mitigated, if you fulfill your purpose."

"What purpose do we have to fulfill?" asked Gabriel, drawing closer to the old woman.

"You must awaken humanity to a true knowledge of itself."

"And how exactly are we supposed to do that?" snapped Gabriel, frustrated.

The gypsy woman scowled back at him.

"You must return the Cube to the *Great Labyrinth of Sarras*."

Gabriel moved to say something, but the old gypsy silenced him with an upraised hand.

"You must pass through the *Seven Portals* and open the *Seven Seals of Gnosis* to the world. In doing these things, you will save us from perpetual darkness."

Gabriel exchanged a look with Natasha. If it were not for what they had just seen, they would have thought this old woman a lunatic, but given the oddity of everything that was coming to pass around them, her words seemed impossibly valid.

"But how can you expect us to accomplish any of this?" asked Gabriel. "The labyrinth could be anywhere in those mountains, and besides, what possible difference could our efforts make? This is a geological phenomenon. It's unstoppable."

"The passing of our planet through the Dark Rift will affect changes on both physical and metaphysical levels. It will affect matter, but it will also affect consciousness."

"How so?" asked Gabriel.

"Every mind will be cast into darkness and confusion," said the gypsy with a frown. "Humanity's collective consciousness will come under great duress. We are in dire circumstances, my children. Over countless millennia we have unwittingly allowed the forces of darkness to penetrate our souls. These forces have twisted and distorted the truth about life and death. They have isolated us from one another, and more importantly, from our true selves."

The old gypsy woman looked into the flames of the candelabra.

"This coming age will mark the passing of yet another galactic year. It will be the first anniversary of the complete annihilation of our distant ancestors. If you fail in your mission, humanity will follow in their footsteps. Our souls will be drawn into the lower spheres of Hades and reside there for aeons to come."

"Wait a minute," said Gabriel, turning to face the old woman. "It takes two hundred and fifty million years to complete a galactic year. Are you suggesting that there were people on the earth back then?"

"The beings that existed then were not like us," she said, "but their society was as fully developed as our own."

"And what happened to them?" asked Natasha.

"They passed through the rift in a state of spiritual darkness, and the Great Cataclysm ensued."

Natasha looked at Gabriel to find that he was shaking his head incredulously.

"What's wrong?" she asked. "What are you thinking?"

"Only that two hundred and fifty million years ago was when the Permian–Triassic extinction event occurred. It's also referred to by geologists as P-Tr, or *The Great Dying*."

Gabriel began to pace back and forth.

"P-Tr was the mother of all extinction events," he continued. "It makes the one that wiped out the dinosaurs sixty-five million years ago look like a terrestrial hiccup. When P-Tr occurred, ninety-six percent of all marine life was completely decimated, along with eighty percent of all the terrestrial vertebrate species. Even most of the insects were wiped out, and that never happens..."

Gabriel scratched his head.

"It never occurred to me before, but P-Tr happened around the time of our galaxy's nineteenth birthday."

Natasha frowned and bit her lip.

"And this galactic year we turn twenty?"

Gabriel was still coming to grips with the realization.

"Astrophysicists would say, yes," he said. "Give or take a few thousand years... But if what Señora Blavatsky is saying is true, we'll be turning twenty when we pass through the galactic plane five days from now."

"This is our last chance to turn the direction of the spiritual spheres," said the old gypsy. "The Great Cataclysm is once again upon us. Succeed in returning the Cube to its original resting place before the crossing is made, and humanity will be preserved.

"Pass through the *Seals of Gnosis* and the knowledge held within them will be released unto mankind. Only then will the balance of our universe be tipped in favour of the Light. Our collective mind will then manifest itself in a new world of peace and societal evolution. If you fail, all will be lost."

"Release the gnosis from the seals?" asked Gabriel, perplexed. "How are we supposed to do that? You must forgive us, Señora, but we don't know anything about this artifact."

"And even if we did know," said Natasha, "how could it be done? The world can't change in less than a week."

The gypsy sat down in one of the leather wingchairs.

"To transcend the Cube is to see it in all things..."

Gabriel and Natasha looked down at her, their eyes filled with confusion.

"You must be in truth," she continued, nodding slowly, "but you must also be in love. Once you have fully merged, the exact location of the lost Book of Khalifah will be revealed to you. It is imperative that you find this codex. Within it are the six translations needed to unlock the Cube's mysteries."

"You said *fully merged*, Señora," said Gabriel, looking over at Natasha. "What does that mean?"

"You were both demonically possessed when you were infants. Did you know this?"

Gabriel and Natasha nodded slowly.

"And do you know the origin of your scars?"

"We do," said Gabriel uncomfortably.

The gypsy woman smiled darkly and continued.

"Before they were exorcised, the fourteen emissaries infected both of you with demonic parasites," she said. "These entities infect you still. They work to keep you apart. Find them! Bring them into the light of awareness! They will dissolve like smoke in the wind. Only then will you merge."

"How do we find them?" asked Natasha, her eyes glassy with concern.

"You must look within, my child," she said with a smile. "They will be hiding where you least want to look. They will be shrouded in your fear."

The gypsy rose to her feet.

"You must begin your search for the Book of Khalifah at once. You must find the Labyrinth and complete your mission."

Natasha sat down in a chair next to where the old woman had been sitting. Gabriel remained standing. He had packed away the Cube and was examining the astrolabe again.

"We will do this," he said solemnly. "But not before I fix the damage I've done."

"What are you saying, child?" said the old woman, turning to face him. "Of what damage do you speak?"

"Because of my efforts to retrieve the Cube, innocent people are being held prisoner by a very bad man. Their lives are in danger. I'm not doing anything until they're safe."

The old gypsy came up to him, a sense of urgency filling her.

"Gabriel Parker," she said firmly. "You will leave all else aside and fulfill your destiny! You know very well there is not enough time!"

Gabriel turned to look at the old woman only to feel her grasp his wrist. Her green eyes seemed to him just then like churning waters, and he was instantly drawn into their emerald depths. The room around him was suddenly transforming, a cataclysmic wasteland of oblivion and destruction materializing before his eyes.

Stumbling amongst the devastation could be seen throngs of twisted corpse-like figures. Their eyes were lifeless, their mutilated bodies riddled with festering wounds. By some unknown power the gypsy woman had filled Gabriel's mind with a vision of the despair that would befall humanity, should he and Natasha fail. He tried desperately to break from the enchantment. He had somehow been carried into the depths of hell.

"There will be time for everything, Señora," came Natasha's voice, and Gabriel was immediately released from the vision, opening his eyes to see Natasha smiling at him.

She had gently taken hold of the old woman's hands.

"But the Dark Rift approaches..." pleaded the gypsy, only to grow suddenly calm.

She took a deep breath and smiled, seating herself next to Natasha.

"Of course, my child," she said, patting her hand. "Your wisdom is true."

Gabriel looked gratefully at Natasha. She had pulled him from a horrible place, but it had nonetheless left its mark on him. The gypsy's dark future would need to be avoided at all costs, and an almost desperate sense of urgency filled him now.

Perhaps there would be time for everything, but they certainly had no time to waste. Gibraltar was still hours away, and they had yet to make their way to Nasrallah's castle and free the prisoners.

"Come on," he said to Natasha, shouldering his pack. "We're leaving right now."

CHAPTER 45

Somewhere over the Mediterranean Sea.

Christian opened his eyes to find the doctor looking down at him. He was lying on the sofa, the luxurious interior of the jet's passenger compartment reminding him of where he was.

"What happened?" he asked.

"I had you in a hypnotic trance, Christian," said Dr. Bennington, his gentle smile doing nothing to mask the concern in his eyes.

Christian's memory came flooding back to him. He rubbed his face and sat up.

"What did you learn about the Cube?"

Bennington sat down opposite Christian and scribbled some notes onto a pad of paper. Before the induction, Christian had told him everything that had transpired up to that point, beginning with the death of his father and culminating with the murder of the Nautonnier and his uncle.

Bennington had asked many questions, and Christian had answered them all, insisting finally that he be put under a hypnotic trance. He had wanted to uncover the meaning behind his father's incessant whispers, and to clarify his own role in the events that were transpiring. He had warned Bennington to conceal nothing, reminding him that the entire induction would be recorded on the jet's security system.

"Well?" asked Christian.

Bennington looked up from his notepad.

"It's important that we deal with this calmly and methodically," he said. "You're a very troubled individual."

Christian rose to his feet, snatching the notebook from the doctor's hands.

"I'd say that's pretty obvious, Doctor. Why don't you tell me something I don't know?"

Christian flipped through the pages, trying to decipher Bennington's illegible script.

"What did you learn about the Cube?" he demanded, flinging the book back at him.

"You told me many things, Christian, but we must be careful. You're not ready to know everything."

Christian's face grew dark and menacing.

"What did you learn?"

Bennington sat back in his chair, thinking of his wife. There was nothing he could do but comply. He would have to tell Christian all he had learned. He could not afford to take any chances.

"You repeatedly referred to an ongoing battle between good and evil, Christian. You spoke of Jesus Christ and Lucifer as being the personifications of the two opposing sides."

"And I'm on Lucifer's side."

"Yes," said Bennington. "Your task, as you described it to me, is to lay waste to the world. When this is done, you are to rebuild it in a way that removes all civil liberties and spiritual pursuits. In essence, you believe that your purpose here is to make the earth as much like hell as possible."

"And why am I supposed to do this?"

Bennington paused before answering.

"You believe that Lucifer demands it of you, Christian; that you are to do whatever is needed to prevent humanity from rising to its next level of societal evolution."

"Why?"

"You claim that it is the only way that our souls can be stopped from escaping into the higher realms."

Christian frowned in confusion.

"And why doesn't Lucifer just let the souls go? What does he care?"

"If he lets them go, he loses power," said Bennington. "An overlord is only as powerful as those he holds beneath him. Take away his subjects, and a tyrant becomes nothing. This, you said, is why kings and emperors live in constant fear. Lucifer is no exception."

Christian's eyes seemed to light up with understanding.

"I see," he said, crossing his arms. "Please, continue."

Bennington swallowed hard. He knew that what he would say next would give Christian a direction of intent that would be detrimental to his sanity. All his instincts told him to keep this information from his patient, but he knew it was futile. Christian's words would have been recorded by the plane's microphones regardless, and he had the safety of his wife to consider.

"You told me that many souls had already ascended since Jesus Christ opened the way two thousand years ago," he began. "Despite Lucifer's continuous attempts to stop them from doing so. You said these ascended souls no longer require to be incarnated again and again; that they have used Earth for the purpose it was created and have purified themselves enough that they can now live in the higher spheres. From there, you said they will assist other souls incarnating on earth and help them to ascend as well."

"Is that so?" said Christian quietly.

A deep understanding was penetrating him now, and it seemed to him that it came from those same churning mists that the Zurvanites had shown to him the previous day.

Bennington studied his patient's face with concern. It was as though a hollow darkness had come over it. Something in Christian was transforming before his eyes.

"You claimed that humanity is still very much bound to Lucifer," he continued reluctantly, "but that there is something that threatens to change this relationship."

Christian looked intently at the doctor.

"Yes," he said. "What is it?"

"A mysterious, cube-shaped artifact," said Bennington, holding Christian's gaze.

"Finally!" he exclaimed, beginning to pace excitedly. "The Cube! What is it? Who made it?"

"By some it is called the *Cube of Knowledge*," said the doctor. "By others, the *Compostela Cube*. You said it's an artifact that is ancient beyond reckoning. You asserted that humanity only requires a consolidated push in order to move up to the next level of societal evolution, and that this Cube is capable of giving us this push."

"I don't understand," said Christian, looking intently at the doctor. "How can an artifact do that?"

Bennington held his gaze.

"You were not sure, Christian," he said. "You claimed that it is not so much a question of what the Cube does, but what humanity does with it. You explained that the Cube is a tool of sorts; a key, or a map, if you will. You admitted that you know very little about this artifact."

Bennington stood up and put a hand on Christian's shoulder.

"Do not lose sight of the metaphorical meanings behind your delusions, Christian. The Cube would appear to be a container of knowledge, and knowledge is always symbolic of freedom."

"I see," said Christian, nodding. "And this is why the Cube must be destroyed."

"The Cube does not exist, Christian," said Bennington. "It is a creation of your unconscious mind. What is important to note is that you have endowed your creation with the capacity to dissolve all fear, and to liberate humanity. This is a very positive construct."

"First of all, Doctor," said Christian, turning away, "the Cube *does* exist. It's very real, and so are the stories I've told you. Secondly, I have no interest in dissolving fear. Fear is what we use to control people; to make them do what we want them to do. I have no interest in liberating the masses. That would be pointless and stupid. How could any wealth be generated without the masses to do the work?"

A blank expression filled Christian's face.

"All power is based in fear," he uttered by rote. "If fear in the masses were ever lost, everything we have worked so hard to build would be destroyed. Fear must be maintained at all costs."

"But can you not see that those are not your own words, Christian?" pleaded the doctor. "Can you not see that you were programmed to say them? I know that this all seems very real to you, but you must believe me when I tell you that it is all in your mind. It is myth. If you make the effort to understand the stories, you will be able to make sense of them, and find peace."

"What else did you learn, Doctor," said Christian, turning to face Bennington. "You will tell me everything."

Bennington let himself fall into his armchair, defeated.

"You told me that your brother and sister conceived a hermaphrodite child so that an ancient prophecy might be fulfilled. You said that this child was born so that a portal to hell might be opened, and a great host of demons be unleashed onto the world.

"You told me that your brother would accomplish this by returning the corpse of his son to the place of its conception, where he would divide it into fourteen pieces, just as the Egyptian god Set had done to his brother Horus."

"I see," said Christian, squinting ever so slightly. "I remember now. There's a tremendous symbolic meaning behind this division, Doctor."

He looked down at Bennington, his arms hanging limply at his sides.

"Fragmentation is Lucifer's way…"

As Christian spoke these words, a dark roll of thunder sounded ominously outside the plane. With this last piece of information, it was as if a curtain had been drawn aside for Christian, and all the knowledge of which he had only previously glimpsed, was at last made fully available to him.

The jet banked and began its descent into Jerusalem.

"What are you going to do, Christian?" asked Bennington, his voice fearful and unsteady. "Surely you will not act on these mythical constructs."

"I will do what I was born to do, Doctor," said Christian, already becoming lost in his thoughts. "I feel I am finally ready to begin."

Here ends **Book One – The Dark Rift.**
The Last Artifact Trilogy *continues with:*
Book Two – The Lost Labyrinth

www.ingramcontent.com/pod-product-compliance
Lightning Source LLC
Chambersburg PA
CBHW060611030726
47498CB00005B/1632